SILVER FANGS

CARL BOWEN

author:	carl bowen
cover artist:	steve prescott
series editors:	eric griffin
	john h. steele
	stewart wieck
editor:	philippe r. boulle
copyeditor:	jeanée ledoux
graphic designer:	aaron voss
art director:	richard thomas

More information and previews available at
white–wolf.com/clannovels

ISBN 1-58846-813-5
First Edition: August 2002
Printed in Canada.

White Wolf Publishing
1554 Litton Drive
Stone Mountain, GA 30083
www.white-wolf.com/fiction

No one who goes visiting far-off lands is more welcome than a strong and noble warrior.

—Beowulf (Burton Raffel translation)

saw a maiden that he wanted for wife, he spoke of it to his parents or grandparents. Then his people went to see the girl's people. If it was agreeable to the elders, and if the girl agreed, the young man simply came to her home to live with her, becoming one of the household. Hawaiians preferred girl children because the girl remained with her people while a boy went to his wife's parents' household. An old saying puts it: *He malama makua hunowai ke keikikane.* "A boy supports his parents-in-law."

Sometimes a girl's parents would take the initiative in making a proposal to the parents of a good looking, industrious boy. This might be at the girl's behest, or on their own initiative. No girl would "propose" to a young man herself— she would be too shy. But she had her ways of attracting him. Neither girl nor boy was forced to marry contrary to heart's desire, except perhaps in certain rare instances when compulsion was necessary.

Their words and expressions relating to mating and marriage are capable of telling in brief more about the habits and points of view of Hawaiians past and present, for persons who at all comprehend Polynesian mentality, than many pages of "learned" dissertation. Below are some of the more common of these words. To those who do not comprehend that even modern Hawaiians are, like their ancestors and all Polynesians, people to whom natural functions are "natural," hence nothing to be ashamed of, and who may be shocked by some of the terms or implied *mores*, it may be necessary to say that it is not just to judge these people by standards of morality other than their own. The collapse of standards due to the sudden abolition of the *kapu* in 1819 preceded the first teaching of Christian principles. Yet responsible Hawaiians, both before and since Christianization, have had and still have a code of right and wrong of their own as definite and as honestly adhered to as that of any other civilized people. In fact, the suffering to be expected from neglect or wilful disobedience to this code affecting sexual relations and responsibility to 'ohana was more drastic and immediate than anything in Christian ethics or modern common law. The 'aumakua (family guardians) did not postpone to an indefinite and vague "future life" punishments for broken *kapu* or shameless behaviour, neglect or irresponsibility. Present behaviour determined the future state, but it also induced immediate effects, good or bad. "Sin" (*hewa, hala*) will be discussed in our next chapter.

The following are post-discovery terms.

In old Hawai'i there was no such thing as an illegitimate child. After the coming of the missionaries and the introduction of the Christian marriage, such terms as these became generally used:—

Wahine mare. A wife whom one has married.
Kane mare. A husband whom one has married.
Wahine manu-ahi. A mistress; a woman who is not legally a wife.
Wahine kapae. (A woman set to one side.) A mistress.

The word *manu-ahi* (fire-bird) was originally the name of a Hawaiian who used to work in a store in Honolulu. He would often give a little extra as a gift to a customer; so, many went to buy *manu-ahi.* Soon *manu-ahi* became synonymous with free: something freely given.

Thus a *kane manu-ahi* or *wahine manu-ahi* became a mate free of the ties of marriage, and a *keiki manu-ahi* (illegitimate child) was the result of a free union.

Noho kapae (living to one side) is another way of saying, an affair without wedlock.
Keiki kameha'i (mystery child) is one term for an illegitimate child, and the *keiki po'o-'ole* (headless child) is another—because he has no sire or "head of the family." (How my mother hated this term, and often said that every baby has a head, including those born out of wedlock!)
Inoa 'ole (no name) is also used to indicate an illegitimate baby.

The following are all old terms relating to mating and marriage.

Noi wahine is the old word for a proposal. *Ua hele mai lakou e noi wahine.* (They came to ask for a wife.) Today, it is *noi mare,* or marriage request.

Ua 'ae ia ka noi means "The proposal is accepted," and *Ua ho'ole ia ka noi* means that it is rejected.

As a *ho'opalau* or betrothal was very binding in the olden days, I have never heard of any term or expression meaning a broken engagement. To break an engagement today is to *uhaki* or *ho'opau i ka ho'opalau* (break or end the engagement).

Nohu pu—"Just to live together," as man and wife.

Ho'omau keiki—A mating of a high chief and chiefess for the purpose of obtaining a child of high rank.

The marriage between young *ali'i* who were brother and sister (or with half-brother or half-sister), which was permitted only at the level of the highest *ali'i* for reasons of genealogical status and what is termed today "line breeding" in biology, was referred to as *pi'o* (arching) and a child born of such a union was a *ni'aupi'o* (coconut frond arched back upon itself).

Marriage within the family circle was called a *ho'i* or returning. "*Ho'i i ka makuahine a puka o mea.*" (He returned to his aunt and so and so was born).

TRIBE NOVEL:

Silver Fangs

CARL BOWEN

Prologue

No one challenged Gashwrack or Bile-Claw as they walked from the toxically noisome pit around which this hive had grown, toward Arastha's chamber. They passed the smoke-dimmed Bane forge, which produced prized fetishes and other weapons of war. They passed the hive's fertility chamber and changed course one corridor shy of the spawning pit. Gashwrack could just make out a chorus of his brothers and sisters doing their biological duty for Father Wyrm and enjoying themselves at it. Not that any of the homid cubs born of this effort would be mature and ready soon enough for the Final Battle, of course, but there was no harm in going through the motions.

Gashwrack approached the last corner leading to Arastha's chamber with Bile-Claw following behind in his jet-black Lupus form. When Gashwrack turned that corner, however, he was surprised to see a cocky cub sauntering from the direction of Arastha's room, wearing only a pair of leather pants. The cub glanced up at Gashwrack, recognized him and planted his feet in the middle of the hallway.

"Where do you think you're going?" the cub asked with arms crossed. "You're not even due back here yet."

Gashwrack's stride faltered in surprise and he glared at the cub. Bile-Claw kept walking behind him. "Who are you? What are you doing here?"

"Lady Arastha sent for me while you were gone," the cub said with a lascivious smirk as Gashwrack came toward him. "She always does when you're not here, Gashwrack. She says she prefers her hive's strong, young warriors to you old men."

The cub must be new here, Gashwrack thought, if he expected this sort of thing to get under his skin.

Everyone in the hive knew about Arastha's appetites, and any healthy male in the hive could expect to take a trip to her chamber at least once. Only the really young and stupid ones convinced themselves that that made them special. A stupid upstart's challenge was still a challenge, though.

Without missing another step, Gashwrack shot an open hand forward and caught the cub in the chest. The blow knocked the younger man flat on his back, bouncing his head on the stone floor with a wet crack.

"You're not even sweating, pup," Gashwrack said over his shoulder with a derisive sniff. "Arastha didn't even know you were inside her."

"So true," came a silky, sensual voice. Gashwrack could see his lady's familiar silhouette through the bone-lattice door into her chamber. She was dressed in an outfit of dedicated leather and iron buckles, which did much more for her figure than age and giving birth to multiple litters ever had. "He is too young and overeager. Not like you. Your timing, dutiful Gashwrack, is always impeccable. I was just coming for you. Join me inside."

Arastha slid the bone lattice aside, and Gashwrack did as he was told. Bile-Claw followed, not even slowing to glance at the idiot on the floor. When everyone was inside, Arastha slid the door back in place.

"I'm glad you've returned at last," Arastha purred as she led the two visitors into her chamber. "I was growing lonely."

"I saw," Gashwrack growled. "Who was that?"

"I don't know his name," Arastha said with a coy smile. "He never gave me reason to say it aloud."

"You've sent for him while I was away," Gashwrack said, unable to fight down the irrational jealous urge that he had just disdained in the cub outside.

Arastha's smile turned from coy to mocking. "He's just a boy, jealous Gashwrack," she teased. "A cub. He might even be one of mine for all I know."

"Fine," Gashwrack snapped, walking past her. "I didn't come for games. We came to report on what we've found."

He stomped the rest of the way across the room and stood looking at Arastha with his back to the bone mosaic of G'louogh, the Defiler Wyrm, and Mahsstrac, the Urge of Power, that decorated her wall. Bile-Claw stood up into his Homid form. In this shape, he was a tall, thin man dressed in jet-black hooded robes. His face was hidden in shadow, but his bright amber eyes reflected the flickering torchlight in the room.

"Alas," Arastha murmured sardonically, stroking Gashwrack with her fingertips as she walked away from him. "Then report. What have you and my loyal Theurge scout discovered?"

Gashwrack shuddered at Arastha's touch, but he restrained himself from grabbing her. It had been so long since he'd had her in his arms. The last time had been just after his return from the Tisza River Hellhole where Splinterbone and Shrike's Thorn—his former packmates—had died. They had been there performing a ritual to reveal the nature of the enormous spirit-ward that imprisoned an ancient Wyrm-spirit called the Forgotten Son. The ritual had been successful, but the others had paid for their victory with their lives. Yet Arastha had considered the mission a success. She had spent the next three days congratulating and rewarding Gashwrack before pairing him with Bile-Claw and sending the two of them back out to follow up the old mission with one of scouting and reconnaissance. Gashwrack hadn't been with Arastha at all since, and it was all he could do not to just pin her down and take her.

Instead, he only watched hungrily while she crossed the chamber to an obsidian table that dominated the center of that half of the room. On it, Bile-Claw laid out a map of southeastern Europe that he'd been carrying under his robe. He'd been adding more to this map nightly during his and Gashwrack's sojourn, and it had grown extremely detailed. Aside from the physical contours of the land, he had marked the map with the boundaries of werewolf protectorates and dotted it with the locations of both Wyrm pits and Gaian caerns, as well as human cities and political boundaries. Some of the glyph marks denoted caerns that Gashwrack had never seen or heard of, and others were ones that had long since been abandoned and grown dormant. And covering a large portion of this map as a result of their scouting was a matrix of dotted lines representing pattern chains like the one that had crossed the Tisza.

"As you ordered, Lady Arastha," Gashwrack began, "Bile-Claw and I have been scouring the countryside looking for more pattern chains like the one Shrike's Thorn's ritual revealed at the Tisza River Hellhole. We have been from Hungary to Romania to Bulgaria to Macedonia to Albania to Serbia, and we've found at least seventeen different chains throughout the region."

"Yes," Bile-Claw said. "As we suspected from the beginning, the late Shrike's Thorn's ritual was designed to reveal the bonds of the Forgotten Son's prison by making them resonate throughout the spirit world. Unfortunately, as you know, that resonance aggravated the poisoned spirit of the Tisza, which gnawed the chain in half before anyone understood what was going on."

"Yes," Arastha breathed, squirming in such a way that Gashwrack took an involuntary step closer. "I wish I could have seen that."

Bile-Claw ignored Arastha's interjection and kept right on talking. "When the chain snapped, it generated a spiritual backlash strong enough to stir up the storms that now plague much of the local Penumbra. Luckily, although that incident altered the frequency at which the other chains were resonating, it did not damp out that resonance altogether. Gashwrack and I have been able to detect it through its effect on the Umbral storm, and thus extrapolate the locations of many of the chains in question."

"I see that," Arastha cooed, leaning over the map to get a better look at it. She stroked Bile-Claw's back idly with her right hand as he pointed out where he'd marked the locations of the chains. Gashwrack's eyes narrowed.

"Tracing these chains as we plotted them here," Bile-Claw went on, not reacting at all to Arastha's touch, "we discovered that they all extend toward the caerns indicated here."

"Each of those caerns has since gone dormant or been captured for the Father," Gashwrack said, coming closer to the table to distract Arastha from Bile-Claw. The Theurge had been serving Arastha and the hive much longer than Gashwrack had, which meant that Gashwrack had to try that much harder to win Arastha's attention. "Some are so old that no one else remembers they're there. Bile-Claw only found them by meditating at Owl's Rest."

Still stroking Bile-Claw's back and bending over the map, Arastha looked at Gashwrack over her shoulder—all but presenting herself. "I see, helpful Gashwrack." She patted the table with her left hand and added, "Won't you join us?"

Gashwrack did just that, standing as close to Arastha as he dared without actually touching her.

"Yes," Bile-Claw said, seeming not to notice. "We were able to trace these chains to these caerns, many of which we have yet to exploit. But in the other direction, the chains all lead into this region." As he said that, he held out a gloved hand over the lower-right portion of the map where, indeed, the lines all seemed to go. "To men, this place is between Kosovo and Serbia. In what they call the 'buffer zone.'"

"But to us," Gashwrack cut in, "this territory is ripe for conquest in the Father's name. The squalor and fear and misery there have been feeding Banes and curdling the Penumbra for years. Bile-Claw and I have seen it firsthand."

"It is fertile ground, eager Gashwrack," Arastha agreed, brushing his thigh with her hand as if by accident as she turned to look at him. "But where exactly is the Forgotten Son? None of these lines converge on any single point. Shouldn't they if this is a prison ward?"

"Not necessarily," Bile-Claw said. "That type of ward, you see, would rely on the integrity of each chain component, so that if even one broke, the entire ward would dissolve. No, according to our survey data and my calculations, this ward is laid out roughly thus." Withdrawing a black iron folding compass and another bone stylus from a pocket of his robe and using the lines he'd already marked as a reference, Bile-Claw began to sketch out the long-hidden ward over the Forgotten Son's prison, creating many of the lines from scratch based on mathematical extrapolation. Not being a child of the crescent moon himself, Gashwrack had to assume that Bile-Claw knew what he was doing.

"In the end," the Theurge said, "each individual strand doesn't have to be as strong as the ones in a center-point ward would. These all reinforce one another so that losing one or several does not compromise the ward. It's an ingenious design for the primitives who must have constructed it."

"Quite," Arastha said, putting a hand on Bile-Claw's shoulder and squeezing it gently. Fuming, Gashwrack tried to see if that shoulder was more muscular than his.

Bile-Claw continued, pointing to different parts of the map as he spoke, "The energy of this ward travels from its anchor caerns through these nexus and balances here at the center. Somewhere within this part of the 'buffer zone.' I wish I could be more precise, but without an exact survey of every single pattern chain that comprises this ward, I cannot. But somewhere, hidden among these mountains, is an ancient, lost caern that is the center of the Forgotten Son's prison ward."

"It's good enough to begin a search," Arastha said, exulting in the news. She stood up straight and put a hand on Bile-Claw's left biceps and Gashwrack's right. Gashwrack flexed that muscle just a little bit. "Now we must begin immediately. Bile-Claw, make copies of this map and take them to the Gatekeeper's chamber. I want every hive on that map informed about what you've found, and I want warriors and hunters from each sent here to assist us. When they arrive, gather everyone to the pit at once, where we will choose our own finest warriors and sharpest hunters to join in the search. The Forgotten Son's time has come, and it is we who will set him free. Go now."

With only a nod, Bile-Claw rolled up his map and headed for the door. As soon as he'd cleared the threshold, he dropped down into Lupus form again and disappeared down the hallway to do as he had been bidden. When he was gone, Arastha crossed the room and closed the door behind him. She then walked back toward Gashwrack with coal-fire lust smoldering in her eyes. Gashwrack couldn't tell how genuine it was, but he didn't especially care.

"And you, sweet Gashwrack," she purred, walking right up to him and pushing him back against the obsidian table with her hands on his chest. "Did you think I'd forgotten you?"

"I'm not so easy to forget," he blustered, grabbing Arastha's shoulders at long last.

Arastha shivered exquisitely at being manhandled thus, but a cruel, icy smile lit up her eyes. "You aren't," she murmured, gently fending off Gashwrack's attempts to press their mouths together. "How could I forget my sweet, loyal Gashwrack? You've done so much for me since you left your—"

"Let's not talk about that," Gashwrack said, pulling Arastha closer. "Let's talk about my reward."

"Such presumption, Gashwrack," Arastha replied, leaning the upper half of her body away from him yet rubbing her hips against his.

Gashwrack growled, trying even harder to pull Arastha to him. He hated these games he had to play with her to get what he wanted. Were all Galliard females so coy? "I know what I deserve."

"Oh?" Arastha sneered. "And what is that, Eric?"

Gashwrack froze as if Arastha had thrown a glass of cold water in his face. "Don't call me that," he snapped.

"It's who you are, isn't it?" Arastha said, her merciless gaze boring into him. "Eric Fire-Stealer. Shadow Lord Ahroun. Guardian of the Owl's Rest Caern."

"No more!" Gashwrack shouted, slapping Arastha as hard as he could across the mouth. She was his queen, but he couldn't stop himself. "That isn't who I am now! I told you, only call me Gashwrack!"

All lingering lust-warmth evaporated from Arastha's eyes. She boiled into her hulking, Neanderthal-like Glabro form and easily broke Gashwrack's rough grip on her. One of her hands flew to his throat, and the other clamped onto his crotch like a bear trap. The sudden transformation knocked Gashwrack back in surprise, and he wound up bent awkwardly backward over the obsidian table with Arastha on top of him. She stood over him, half straddling him, and held her feral face just inches above his.

"I am the leader of this hive," she barked, spraying spit in his eyes. "You will not speak to me like that! Do you understand?"

"Yes," he breathed. His throat and his genitals hurt so much that he couldn't see anything but white. He knew it would be suicide to try to change into a more powerful form, though. Arastha was stronger than she looked—she'd crack his spine over the corner of the table. Yet, against his will, his agonized body was responding to the warmth and the weight of her.

"Good," she snarled. She let up the pressure on his neck a little, but that was it. If anything, her other hand squeezed harder, stirring Gashwrack's member to life between her fingers. "Now understand something," she continued. "Regardless of how much glory you win, you are nothing but what I made you. I spared you when we overran your caern, and I brought you back here with me. I showed you the truth about the Father, and I made it so that you could share in the glory of helping to set the Forgotten Son free. You are nothing without me. You are an exile and a traitor besides."

At that, she lifted Gashwrack and threw him down flat on the table. He came to rest with his arms above his head. The air he breathed tasted like blood and burned his throat. Every heartbeat throbbed like an

Silver Fangs

explosion in his crotch, but even still, he was now fully erect. Arastha jumped onto the table, straddling his hips and pinning his wrists above his head with her left hand. Trying not to panic, Gashwrack squirmed again, trying to get free.

"And when you come making *demands* of me," Arastha said, grinning maniacally and holding Gashwrack down as if he were a child, "I wonder why I made you anything at all. With one howl, I can undo everything and name you Eric Fire-Stealer again—Gaian spy and prisoner of war from the Owl's Rest Caern."

Gashwrack's eyes flashed, and he writhed more vigorously, trying to get free. Arastha bucked with him, then grew up into her enormous Crinos form, crushing him down.

"Don't make me regret you, Gashwrack," she snarled in the werewolf tongue, gnashing her long fangs right in front of his eyes. "You are mine."

"I won't," Gashwrack choked out. "Lady Arastha. I am yours. Please."

"Yes," Arastha snapped. "Mine."

So saying, she shifted her weight and lifted one of her legs. With one extremely careful kick, she tore his belt and the front of his pants into strips and pulled them down over his hips. She then sat back down on him, pushing him as deeply into herself as she could between their two mismatched forms.

"Mine," she growled again, starting to rock back and forth. "Gashwrack is mine."

Gashwrack whined in shame and submission and lay perfectly still.

"But if you ever forget," she snarled, "Eric Fire-Stealer will wish I'd left him to die at Owl's Rest. Do you understand?"

"Yes, my lady," Gashwrack whined. "I understand."

Chapter One

Jonas Albrecht stood on one side of the bed in the cramped room, fighting back the snarl that made his lip twitch. He alternated between stuffing his large hands into the deep pockets of his tattered trench coat and idly fingering the hilt of Solemn Lord, the grand klaive that hung from his belt. When his palms got too sweaty, he wiped them absently on the front of his faded blue jeans. There wasn't even enough room in here to pace around, which made him feel like he'd locked himself in a cage.

"I'm not sure if she knows you're here," the kid across from Albrecht said, "but you're making *me* edgy. Maybe you ought to sit down or something."

"Wouldn't help," Albrecht said through clenched teeth. "Besides, I'm not staying that long."

"Then you probably ought to say something before you get going," the kid said. "In case she can hear you."

Albrecht looked down at the bed between him and the kid. A woman lay on it—a woman Albrecht cared about more than anybody else in the world, except maybe the kid. She was short, olive skinned and wiry. Mostly Hispanic, with a little Greek mixed in, too. Most of the time, she was a tough broad who took no shit from anybody, but now, she was weak, pale and emaciated. Her eyes hadn't opened in weeks, and her body lay limp, seemingly weighed down by the thin sheet over her. She was lying on a mound of feather pillows on top of a padded bedpan like an invalid, and she couldn't even roll herself over. The dusty sunlight slanting in through the window shone on her face, only making it more obvious how miserable she was.

"God damn it, Mari," Albrecht growled at the woman. "I told you not to go. Why couldn't you just listen to me for once?"

"I know how you feel," the kid said, "but she's going to be okay. I know she is."

Albrecht looked up at the kid and almost—almost—took his word for it. The kid, Evan, had grown up a lot since he and Albrecht had met. Back then, Evan had been just another scrawny runaway with trouble in his shadow. Now, he was proud and strong and sure of himself. Evan reminded Albrecht of himself as he used to be a lifetime ago. He knew who he was and what he was supposed to do with his life. Evan was at that point where he was one tragic reality check away from truly becoming a man. Albrecht hoped this wasn't about to be it, losing Mari like this when there was nothing either one of them could do to help her.

"Of course she's going to be okay," Albrecht said for Evan's benefit. "She's seen worse, right?"

"We all have," Evan said. "You certainly have, and she's way tougher than you are."

Albrecht grinned, but the gesture was a lifeless imitation of the real thing.

"So what's our plan now?" the kid asked.

Albrecht turned around and looked out the window toward the setting sun. His shadow fell over Mari's gaunt face, relieving some of the hard edges there. "You," he said, "are going to stay right by her side and be the first thing she sees when she wakes up. She needs her packmates right now. She needs you standing guard and being with her, and she needs me to make sure this sort of thing never happens again."

"Of course," Evan said. "Should I even bother asking what you're planning to do?"

"You know good and well," Albrecht said, still squinting in the sunlight. "I'm going over there. I'm going to find the thing that did this to Mari, and I'm going to kill it. Then I'm going to find Arkady and kill him, too, for being involved. And if Konietzko or any of those European pricks gives me any shit about it, I'm going to kick their asses."

"I figured," Evan sighed. "Are you sure you at least don't want me to come with you? There's something to be said for diplomacy in these times of crisis, you know."

Albrecht shook his head without turning back around. The sun out the window behind him reflected off the unadorned crown he wore and lit up his shoulder-length, silver-blond hair.

"No way," he said. "Diplomacy's what they're all about over there, and look where it gets them. Look where it got Mari."

"I know," Evan said. "But—"

"No buts, kid," Albrecht said. "I need you here with her while I'm off taking care of this."

Evan crossed his arms and leaned back against the wall next to the door. "You know, this Arkady thing does have to be dealt with, and whatever this thing is that's growing in Europe has got to be stopped, too. But you can't do this alone. Mari tried that, and, like you said, look where it got her."

"I know," Albrecht said. "But what choice do I have? I made this mess in the first place. I let Arkady go when I should have killed him. Then these Euros put him on trial, and I let Mari traipse off to go watch and testify. Next thing we know, Mari's in trouble, there's a literal shit-storm going through the Umbra, and Arkady is popping up blathering about silver spirals before vanishing to Gaia-only-knows-where. None of this—" he waved down at Mari's withered, unconscious body, "—would have happened if I hadn't just killed Arkady when I had the chance. Go ahead, Evan. Try to deny it."

"You did the right thing," Evan said. "I mean, it's not like you let Arkady escape. You *banished him*. He consorted with the Wyrm, he got your grandfather killed, he tried to steal your birthright from you in a duel—"

"A *rigged* duel," Albrecht muttered.

"—he tried to swipe the Silver Crown from you, and he almost tortured you to death. In all that, he even nearly let a caern be defiled. And even then, you held back."

"Yeah, what an Ahroun I am," Albrecht growled. "King Shitty the First. That's me."

"Damn," Evan said, "I guess that did sound pretty bad. Sorry. But that isn't what I meant. The point is that in spite of everything he did to you, you didn't just go berserk and hack Arkady into fertilizer. You punished him justly."

Albrecht huffed and crossed his arms over his barrel chest.

"People talk about the way a king treats his enemies, Albrecht," Evan pressed on. "If he's savage and merciless, they tiptoe around him, doing their best not to piss him off. But if he's honorable and just, they feel like they can trust him."

"You read that in a New-Age business manual, didn't you?" Albrecht said over his left shoulder with a smirk.

"I've seen it, Albrecht," Evan said. He knelt down on the floor beside the bed and put his hand over Mari's. "Mari and I were both there that day you banished Arkady. We saw it with our own eyes. You made us proud, and you haven't let us down yet."

"Oh, yeah?" Albrecht said, turning around. He glared down into Evan's eyes. "You think Mari'd back you up on that, kid? Look at her! Sure, I showed Arkady mercy, but now it's all coming back to bite me on the ass. It's kicked hers, and if you'd gone with her—or instead of her—you might even be dead right now. All because I let that filthy scumbag live."

"Jonas, don't act so damn naïve," Evan snapped, coming to his feet and refusing to back down from Albrecht's gaze. "That's just self-pitying bullshit."

Albrecht had to blink a couple of times before he was able to speak. He was glad the sun was behind him right then. Hopefully, that way Evan wouldn't be able to see the look of utter astonishment on his face.

"What did you say?"

"You heard me," Evan said. His voice had a tone to it that Albrecht knew pretty well. With his back straight and his arms crossed, he stood stately and dignified like an old tree. "We both know the score from back then. You knew what kind of hell Arkady had to go through to get here to the States from Russia, and the first thing you did when you had Arkady at your mercy was you sent him right back there. You *commanded* him to go."

"I sent him to his room without supper," Albrecht muttered.

"No, he was almost the king then, Albrecht, remember?" Evan said. "People didn't know he was a traitor yet. You exposed him and you exiled him. You sentenced him to go back where he came from without any help from anybody. You ordered him to march alone straight back through the gates of hell. You knew it, and he knew it, too. It was a temporary stay of execution."

Albrecht didn't say anything.

"But," Evan concluded, "you allowed him the chance to die on his way back home, fighting the spawn of the Wyrm. After everything Arkady did to you, you still gave him back just that much dignity."

Albrecht stood still for a few moments, trying to think of something to say rather than just blinking like a dumbstruck idiot. Evan had that effect on him sometimes. Pretty much whenever the kid was right about something important and Albrecht was being bull headed.

"Well?" Evan said after a few more seconds of silence. He put his hands back by his sides and stuffed them into his pockets. Standing completely in Albrecht's shadow, he cocked his head slightly. Albrecht lifted the back of his hand to his good eye and sniffled quietly.

Evan leaned forward a little uncertainly now that he was done preaching. He was his usual, considerate self once more. "Albrecht, I... What is it?"

"It's just..." Albrecht began. "Listen to you." His voice trembled, and he sniffled again. "My little man... You're all grown up." He wiped the back of his hand across his eye with a flourish then smirked.

Evan sighed and rolled his eyes. "Asshole."

"Sucker."

Albrecht looked down at Mari then glanced to his left at the door out of the room. His proud, noble profile stood out in sharp relief against the sunlit world out the window behind him.

"But you're right," he sighed, not turning to look at Evan. "I guess what's happened isn't *all* my fault."

"It'd be arrogant to think so," Evan said.

Albrecht glanced at the young man and smirked again. "Yeah, I guess. Sounds like you're getting pretty wise there in your old age, kid."

Evan shrugged. "Part of the job."

Albrecht nodded and looked down at Mari one more time. A moment later, he looked toward the door and said, "Someone's coming."

As if on cue, that someone opened the door without knocking. It was Nadya Zenobia, the eldest Black Fury Theurge in the Finger Lakes Sept. She had been taking care of Mari all this time. She was a hard, thin African American woman who had survived the Garou lifestyle on into a healthy middle age. She was carrying a basket of clean bed linens and fresh clothes like the ones Mari was wearing and a large wooden bowl full of warm water perched serenely on top of her entire load.

"Out," she said, not looking either Evan or Albrecht in the eye. She knew just as Evan and Albrecht did that she was treading a fine line by taking care of Mari while Mari was wounded like this. The letter of Garou law commanded healthy werewolves not to tend the sickness of the weak and wounded.

"I think we'll just—" Evan started to protest.

"Yes, ma'am," Albrecht cut in instead. He crossed the room and put a hand on Evan's shoulder. "C'mon, kid. Mari's been lying there a long time, you know. This lady's got to clean her up and whatnot. You know, change her sheets and—" he glanced toward the bedpan under Mari's hips "—stuff."

Evan put up a little resistance, forcing the Black Fury to shove past him and Albrecht in order to get to Mari's bedside. "But we're her packmates. Shouldn't we be helping or something?"

"Being by Mari's side is one thing, kid," Albrecht said, propelling Evan gently but inexorably toward the door. Nadya set her bundle on a low stool at the foot of the bed and lit a stick of pungent incense on the bureau against the far wall. "This is different. You think Mari'd want us to see somebody else having to clean her up? You think she wants us to see how completely helpless she is? No way. She'd be too ashamed to even bitch at us."

"Oh, yeah," Evan said. He stopped to pick up the fetish spear he'd propped by the door when he'd come in, and he looked back at Nadya. She was wiping down Mari's forehead with a soaked cotton rag and murmuring softly in Mari's ear. "We won't be far," he told her, "and I'll be back in a few minutes. Take good care of her."

"I will," the woman said. She didn't even look up. "As His Highness wishes."

Albrecht pulled Evan outside and shut the door behind them. He took a huge breath of clean air then glanced over at the window as the Theurge closed the shutters. There was nothing he could do and he knew it, so he started walking. Evan trotted up on his right and fell into step beside him.

"What did that mean?" Evan asked when they were out of earshot of the cabin. "'As His Highness wishes'?"

"It means what you think," Albrecht grumbled, staring straight ahead. "I told her to stay with Mari. Even after Antonine left and she told me there wasn't anything more she could do, I told her to stay and keep trying."

"Basically to tend Mari's sickness, you mean."

"Yeah."

"And she didn't challenge you or anything?"

"No. She just grumbles and acts like she's got PMS all the time."

"I'd take that as gratitude, then," Evan said. "Nadya likes Mari, and she doesn't want to have to watch her waste away any more than we do. You did her a favor, I'd say."

The two of them walked on in silence then, each thinking his own thoughts and trying to enjoy each other's company for as long as they still could. At last, it was Albrecht who broke the silence.

"You know what's most unfair about all this Arkady business?" he said before the two of them had gotten anywhere in particular.

"What's that?"

"Commie bastard didn't even have the good grace to get himself killed. He actually made it back home in one piece. Can you believe that shit?"

"I tell you," Evan grunted, looking straight ahead. "Silver Fangs are so inconsiderate."

Albrecht glanced at his young friend and packmate and bumped him hard, shoulder to shoulder. "Watch it, smart guy," Albrecht said with a grin as Evan stumbled a few steps sideways. "I hear they're touchy about their heritage, too."

"Yeah," Evan muttered. "They would be."

He was grinning as he trotted back to Albrecht's side, as was Albrecht himself, but neither expression was genuine. Although both men seemed happy on the outside, their worry and doubt about Mari's condition were chasing each other's tails in their minds.

They walked on quietly to a spot near the heart of the caern to find the Gatekeeper sitting under a tree in Lupus form, scratching his shoulder with his hind leg. He glanced up as Evan and Albrecht approached, but he made no move to stand or approach them.

Evan spoke first. "So you're going tonight, then?"

"Tomorrow," Albrecht corrected him. "Enough time to rest up, pack and make sure the moon bridge from North Country to Night Sky is set up."

"Don't you think you'd better gather some support first?" Evan asked. "Maybe some warriors to help fight this Jo'cllath'mattric thing."

"All the warriors I need are already there and waiting."

"Don't you think you'll look a little… aggressive if you go over there and just start giving orders?"

"I don't care how I look," Albrecht said. "I just want this thing dead, and I want the ones who're responsible for that part of the world to take care of it."

"So why are you even going at all?"

"Those people don't have their acts together. I've got to go over there to make sure they do the job right."

"Then why not take a war party of people you trust with you?"

"Because people have been shitting on my tribe over there for years. If I go over there leading a bunch of warriors, it's going to look like some hotheaded Silver Fang quartering troops and trying to rekindle old glory."

"I thought you didn't care how things looked."

"That only goes for how *I* look. I'm not going to make my whole tribe look bad with something this important on the line. But if nobody over there is going to take responsibility and get some results, then I have to. I'm the king. It's my job."

"Fine," Evan said. "There's just one more thing I can think to say, then."

"What's that?"

"Be careful, okay? I don't want to lose you, too."

Albrecht didn't say anything for a few seconds. He hadn't thought about what it would be like for the kid if he were to die before Mari got better. He'd be left with nobody, just like he had been before Albrecht had met him.

"You mean you don't want to tell me to go jump off a cliff or something?" he said.

Evan actually smiled at that and shook his head. "Not yet. I think I'll save that for when you show back up later saying, 'I told you so.'"

"And I will, too," Albrecht said. "You can count on that."

"I always do," Evan said. "Even when I suspect you're being a stubborn idiot, I still have faith in you. Mari and I both do. After all, you're the king, aren't you?"

"You're damn right I am."

With that, he signaled the Gatekeeper, who stood, stretched out his back legs and started walking toward them. The wolf looked in expectation at Albrecht, cocking his ears and tilting his head. The tip of his tail rose slightly, making no secret of his annoyance at having to wait by the sidelines for so long.

"I need a bridge back to the North Country Caern," Albrecht said. "I'll be expected." He nodded toward Evan without looking away from the wolf at his feet. "He's staying."

The Gatekeeper lowered his tail in acknowledgement and turned away. He paced a few yards away into an immaculate clearing that centered around a still pool of clear water, where he began a low, melodious howl. He turned his body this way and that as he sang, looking into the spirit world and invoking the guidance of those who dwelled there. The spirit halves of Evan and Albrecht's bodies oriented themselves toward the heart of the caern like iron filings around a magnet. The air above the pool began to shimmer and grow opaque as a circular portal opened there.

"Looks like my cue," Albrecht said to Evan. "Remember what I said, kid. Stick by Mari's side. You got me?"

"I got you," Evan said.

"Good." And with that, Albrecht stepped through the portal and headed home.

Chapter Two

Gashwrack crouched in Homid form on a rocky ridge in the southwestern mountains of what had once been Yugoslavia, holding a pair of fetish binoculars to his eyes. They showed him the spirit world on the other side of the Gauntlet, where a storm was blowing, mirroring his excitement. Throughout the tumult, fell shapes swooped and flocked almost playfully. Many of them looked like long black eels, as thick as a man's arm, and with enormous gaping mouths full of inward-curved teeth. They dodged through the storm on wide, membranous wings and slashed at each other with slender, tapered tails.

No one in the physical world could see or hear this spirit-storm, but it affected the physical world nonetheless. No living thing had given birth to live offspring since the storm started, and the rain that frequented this place naturally now tasted flat and metallic and smelled faintly of coal smoke. At night, every domestic animal within twenty miles howled and cried in terror, although their human masters could find no reason why. Of course, Gashwrack could see the reason clearly. The effects of the spirit-storm were bleeding over into the physical world. It made him smile, as he hadn't since Arastha's lesson about dominance several weeks ago. He put down the binoculars, squinted in the physical world's bright sunlight and turned to Bile-Claw, who was behind him in wolf form. The Theurge's bright amber eyes peered at Gashwrack, reminding him of the superior yet inquisitive way Shrike's Thorn—one of his two dead packmates—had looked at him.

What do you see? Bile-Claw asked in the growl and posture of wolfspeak.

"We're close," Gashwrack answered. "I can feel it. The storm's responding very strongly to the vibrations the chains are putting off here."

Yes. The caern is nearby. Maybe within a mile.

"A mile," Gashwrack repeated in wonder. "We'll have found it by the end of the week. Maybe even the end of the day if we can summon enough of the others."

Yes, Bile-Claw said. *I will bring them. But first she must know we are close.*

"Yes," Gashwrack agreed, feeling his excitement turn hollow and shrivel up inside him. "Arastha will want to be the first to set foot in the caern. I'll return to the hive for her. Have everyone meet us back at this spot."

Yes, Bile-Claw said. And with that, he turned and dashed back the way they had come. When he was gone, Gashwrack hung his head and tried to steel himself for the return trip. Arastha would be pleased by the news he brought. Thrilled. She'd want to reward him. Gashwrack shuddered. He hadn't even seen Arastha since she'd sent him back out. It hadn't been long enough.

Chapter Three

Night had just fallen as Albrecht stepped off the moon bridge at the North Country Caern. He smacked his lips and took a deep breath. He hated to leave Evan and Mari behind, but it was still good to be home. He nodded once to Eliphas Standish, his Gatekeeper, and heard the portal to the moon bridge close behind him. He peeled off his weather-beaten trench coat and draped it over his shoulders.

It was here, in this place tucked away in the Green Mountains of southern Vermont, that Albrecht had spent his childhood. He'd played with the other Silver Fang Kinfolk children here. He'd chopped this forest's fallen trees into firewood with only a hand ax to build up his strength. At the feet of the Grand Oak, he'd learned all about Gaia and the duty of the werewolves to protect Her land. On the enormous lawn behind the royal manor, he and the other children had drilled in armed and unarmed combat. In the manor's library, he'd spent hour upon boring hour learning Garou history, politics, war craft and the genealogy of the most prominent Silver Fangs of that generation.

He'd showed no greater or lesser aptitude in any of the subjects he was forced to study back then, except for swordplay, at which he trounced all the other kids without half trying. He'd showed only passable skill at everything else, though, so he'd seemed doomed to fade into obscurity just like his father and mother had both done. Yet, he'd captured everyone's attention one late-August afternoon in his thirteenth year when he'd freaked out during a sparring match and exploded into the full glory of his Crinos form for the first time. The odds against him experiencing a First Change had been astronomical since both his parents were only Kinfolk themselves, but the gleam of his frost-white pelt had testified to the purity of his Garou blood.

After that day, Albrecht had become the favorite of Jacob Morningkill, then king of the protectorate. Son of the infamous "cowboy werewolf," Isaiah Morningkill, Jacob was as old and strong a king as Albrecht could possibly imagine. He got his way by being smarter and stronger than anyone who questioned him. He'd ruled with an iron fist but recognized honor and glory where he saw it. The old man had loved Albrecht like a father loves his son, even though he was actually Albrecht's great-grandfather. He had devoted every spare moment after Albrecht's First Change to teaching his descendant what it meant to be a man and what it was to be a king.

Therefore, it had broken Albrecht's heart to see King Morningkill grow deeply senile as the years passed. Where once the old man had ruled with wisdom and honor, he later relied on petty bullying. Where he'd once commanded loyalty and respect from the nobles of his court, his burgeoning paranoia alienated them, until the only ones who stayed by his side were those too scared or just too damn decent to turn their backs. And where once he'd groomed Albrecht to rule in his place someday, Morningkill had become jealous of the youngster's growing skill and fame and exiled him. For a long time, Albrecht had crawled into a bottle and learned to hate the old king for treating him like that. He'd spent many nights sprawled on a couch in a cheap apartment with only the cheap television and a bottle of cheap scotch for company, grumbling that he'd never be such a horrible monster if he were king.

But he'd had to lay all that bitterness to rest just a few years ago when a treacherous surprise attack on this very caern had left the old king mortally wounded and demanding that Albrecht be returned to take his place on the throne. Albrecht had returned grudgingly, nearly lost his birthright anyway to the usurper Arkady, whom the old king had once trusted, and only managed to reassert his rightful claim to power by questing deep into the Umbra for the legendary Silver Crown that he now wore. That made this manor and the surrounding lands his home and the North Country protectorate *his* protectorate. It made him the king of his entire tribe, and by extension, the king of all werewolves the world over.

Sure, most werewolves would never see it that way, but many did. Many of the elders recognized the significance of the fact that Albrecht could even *wear* the crown. Many younger werewolves followed their elders' lead. Even those who didn't care for symbols could still see that he was an able leader who didn't act like people expected a Silver Fang to act. Those who bothered to give him the benefit of the doubt saw a powerful man who led his followers with a renewed faith in himself and in the Garou Nation. They saw a reflection of a younger, saner Jacob Morningkill.

Trying not to dwell on the implications of that comparison, Albrecht headed out of the woods toward the Grand Oak, which towered over the royal manor. Among the gnarled and impressive roots of that tree stood the massive oaken throne that was rapidly becoming the center of all Silver Fang authority in North America. His throne.

As Albrecht approached the tree, he could see a jet-black wolf with a white chin crouched on the wooden dais, partially hidden among the roots, but unafraid of being noticed. Albrecht acknowledged the wolf with a wave and changed course to approach her directly. When he was within the circle of the Grand

Oak's roots, the wolf stood and padded over to him. The wolf was Regina, Albrecht's Warder, the eldest warrior in the sept, and she guarded the place while Albrecht was gone.

"Ho there," Albrecht said as Regina rolled on her back once to show deference toward her king. "All's been quiet, I take it."

Regina shook herself once then stood up into her Homid form. She was a woman of diluted Huron descent that still tried hard to show through a mostly Anglo-European mask. Battle scars decorated her exposed flesh like symbols on a map, and her eyes were grim and distant.

"Quiet outside, yes," she said. "No attacks today. No one even died."

"Good. Any messages from Night Sky?"

"Yes," the Warder frowned. "The house-dog of that place said he would be waiting to meet you when you arrived."

"House-dog?" Albrecht asked. "The steward?"

Regina snorted in contempt. "Yes. As he called himself."

"So all the arrangements have been made, then?"

"Yes. The moon bridge will be opened as you requested. They await you most anxiously, to hear the house-dog tell it."

"Well, that's good to know," Albrecht said. "Anything else I should know about?"

"You have a visitor," Regina said. "A stranger came while you were visiting Mari. He said he would not leave without speaking to you."

Albrecht looked over toward the manor and saw that the light was on in one of the downstairs common rooms that never saw much use except during moots or family gatherings. "What's he want?"

"I don't know."

Albrecht frowned. "So who is he?"

"I don't know," Regina said again. "I haven't spoken with him or consulted with any who have. I only watched as he was led inside to await your return. He is Garou. Likely American, though not local. He travels alone rather than with a pack. That was all I could tell."

"I see," Albrecht said. "Is he friendly at least, or was he strutting around like he owned the place?"

"He has behaved," the Warder said. "And Eliphas let him in without incident. They seemed to enjoy each other's company."

"So he got here by moon bridge," Albrecht deduced. "I guess he came from a long way. Or in a big hurry."

"Or both," Regina said with a shrug. "Now that you're back, I'll go bring him out to you. If you'll have him. Otherwise, the Guardians and I will harry him to the edge of the bawn and send him away."

"Nah," Albrecht said, after thinking about it for a few seconds. "Just send him out here to the tree, then go get some rest. You've been up and on patrol since sunup, and I'm pretty sure you didn't take any breaks while I was gone."

"No breaks," the Warder agreed. "Especially not while you were away."

"Then you deserve one," Albrecht said. "Send out my mystery date, check on your Guardians, then hit the sack."

The woman nodded and headed for the house without question. Albrecht watched her go, then turned to face the throne before him. He stepped up to it and put a hand on one of its high, strong arms. It was immovable and ancient, like a second strong tree growing right up through the roots of the first. It was a symbol of all the strength and dignity that Silver Fangs all over the world were heir to. It embodied the Fangs' divine right to rule over all of the Garou Nation.

Albrecht shrugged his trench coat off his shoulders and tossed it over the back of the throne like the thing was nothing more than a common dining-room chair. The frayed end of the jacket hung right down to the looping glyph that had been carved into the center of the chair's back by the claws of the craftsman who had made the throne.

That's better, Albrecht thought. *The thing looks a little lived-in now and a whole lot more comfortable.*

Feeling a little more relaxed, Albrecht stood tall on one of the roots of the Grand Oak and put his booted left foot on the seat of his throne. Then, propping his left hand on his knee and stuffing his right halfway into his jeans pocket, he turned toward the house and waited for his guest to come to him.

A moment later, a hard and weary warrior emerged from the house. He wore a long gray duster jacket over a gray tank top and faded, split-knee blue jeans. His black hair was shoulder length and shaggy, kept in check by a band at the base of his neck. He had a scruffy-looking black goatee that was shot through with white, and he looked like he hadn't slept in several days. Incongruously, though, he wore a wide golden necklace that lay flat on his neck, and golden bands on his wrists peeked out from the threadbare cuffs of his sleeves. Even the tall walking stick he carried, planting it before him like Moses as he walked, was topped in a carved cobra head that if not solid gold was probably gold plated. Albrecht had met the man at the Finger Lakes Caern not too long ago. He had brought Mari back there after she'd been attacked and debilitated in Europe. Because of him, Mari was still alive and in the care of people Albrecht trusted.

"Mephi Faster-than-Death," Albrecht said. "I didn't expect to see you again so soon."

Mephi stopped in front of Albrecht and the throne and actually bowed. "King Albrecht," he said. "I apologize for coming uninvited."

Albrecht waved the apology away. "Shit, don't worry about it. Everybody treating you okay here?"

"As if I'd come home," Mephi said. Albrecht smiled at that and stepped forward to shake Mephi's hand and clap him on the shoulder.

"Not to sound rude, but what are you doing here? When we last talked, you lit out in a hurry. You said you had places to go."

"I did," Mephi said, retrieving his hand and standing back a bit. "I had to take a message to the Painted Coyote Caern out in New Mexico."

"I know that place," Albrecht said. "The Screaming Trailblazers were from there. That was why you went, right? To tell their friends and family they were dead."

"Yes," Mephi said. "Them and one other person I didn't tell you about. She was an old and dear friend of mine from there who died with the last of the Trailblazers over in Hungary. Since I was there when it happened, I owed it to her memory to take the news back home for her."

"I'm sure the ones she left behind appreciated it."

"I hope so."

"And now you're back," Albrecht said. "You know, if you'd come tomorrow, you'd have missed me."

"So I figured," Mephi answered. "When we spoke at the Finger Lakes Caern, I could tell you were already getting restless. I could see you were itching to get involved in what's happening."

"That's right," Albrecht said.

"That's why I hurried to get back here. I thought I might go with you."

"You did, huh?" Albrecht said.

"If you'll have me, that is," Mephi said. "Your Gatekeeper told me you were going alone, but I think I can really help you."

"Eliphas talks too much," Albrecht mumbled. Then, to Mephi he said, "Don't you think that's a little presumptuous on your part?"

"Maybe," Mephi said. "But I also think you don't care very much if it is. I have skills you need and don't have. I also think you'd welcome the company in that strange land, what with both of your packmates staying behind."

"You think you know me pretty well, don't you?"

"I know *about* you," Mephi said. "I told you when we met that *The Saga of the Silver Crown* is my most popular tale. I tell it all the time. It paints a pretty clear picture of the kind of person you are. I know, for instance, that you're smart enough not to refuse help when you know you need it."

"So how is it you'd help me?" Albrecht asked.

"First, I've actually been over there in that part of the world. I know how bad it's getting. Plus, I've been to Night Sky, which is where I figure we ought to go first. That's where the seat of power is, and where you're likely to find the most willing warriors. On top of that, I'm a better than average linguist, and I'm a skilled warrior myself who'd be proud to follow you into battle."

Albrecht sighed, but he had to admit that Mephi had a point. He could use some firsthand experience in the area where they were going, and having someone there on his side who spoke the local language would speed things up immeasurably. Plus, some of the firebrands at Night Sky might be more willing to listen to someone they themselves already considered a hero rather than some Silver Fang they'd only heard stories about.

"All right," he said. "You've got a point. I will need some help over there, and you've already proven you've got the skills, bringing Mari back safely through all that mess like you did. But you know what the clincher is?"

"What's that?"

"You haven't once brought Mari up like you were trying to call in a debt I owe you," Albrecht said.

"There's no debt," Mephi said. "I was just doing what I had to do."

"I know," Albrecht said. "And because of that, I'd be glad to have you by my side for this trip."

"I'm honored, King Albrecht," Mephi said with another bow. "I won't let you down."

The two men stood silent for a moment, contemplating what lay before them. Albrecht didn't know Mephi very well, and he'd only recently started hearing stories about him from other septs, but they all made him out to be a stand-up guy and a trustworthy ally. Albrecht certainly could have wound up with worse partners on this quest. Of course, now that Albrecht was no longer going it alone, Evan was going to be pissed that he couldn't come, too. Well, the kid would just have to get over it. Mari still needed him here.

"All right then," Albrecht said into the silence, looking vaguely east across the lawns. "You've seen what it's like over there."

"Yeah," Mephi said. "It's pretty bad."

"So how do you like the odds of you and me convincing Konietzko to even let us in on his plans to take this Joe Killa Matrix thing on?"

"Long odds," Mephi said, "but anything's possible. The fact that you wound up with that crown in the first place proves that."

"I guess it does," Albrecht said. "Good point. Now go on inside and get some rest. I'll see you tomorrow. We'll leave at moonrise."

Mephi nodded and started to walk off toward the manor.

"Hey, Mephi," Albrecht said before the Strider had gone very far. "One more thing." Mephi stopped and looked back.

"Yeah?"

"Thanks in advance for your help. I get the feeling I'm going to need it."

Mephi lowered his gaze, shrugged and smiled sadly. "No problem. Besides, it's not like I have pressing matters to attend to at home."

And with that, he turned back the way he was going and started walking again. When Mephi finally disappeared inside, Albrecht turned and flopped backward onto his throne. He dangled his hands over the arms of the chair and laid his head back against his coat where it still hung behind him. He gazed up into the sky, trying to get straight in his head what he'd just committed himself to. He was about to walk across the ocean into a den of seasoned politicians and grizzled veteran warriors and demand that the better part of them take up with him on a quest to find and destroy an ages-old spirit that nobody had even heard of until recently. And only his reputation and the notoriety of the Silver Crown were supposed to convince them.

"Damn," he said quietly, smiling up into the sky. "I wish Evan and Mari could see me try that."

Silver Fangs

Chapter Four

"It's beautiful, isn't it?" Arastha crooned, pulling Gashwrack along behind her. "Come. Look."

Gashwrack stumbled forward. He, she and Bile-Claw were standing in a semicircular antechamber that connected to an even larger underground dome across the way from the branching tunnel they'd followed to get here. Sourceless blue light pervaded the chamber, leaving no shadows anywhere.

Gashwrack followed Arastha into the next room obediently, and Bile-Claw came, too, rising into his Homid form. None of the others had made it this far into the tunnels yet. They were still setting up camp in a chamber closer to the surface and digging out defensive positions in the valleys and canyons that led to the entrance of this system of caverns.

The chamber into which the three walked was a smooth-walled dome with a large pillar in the middle, which seemed to rise up from a black hole in the floor. There was a matching antechamber on the other side of the pillar, and pictograms of all shapes and sizes had been carved all around the room in tangled patterns that the eye would go blind trying to follow. They covered the dome's interior from the edge of the floor, up to the apex of the ceiling, then down the room's central pillar. Gashwrack saw symbols that appeared to be Garou glyphs, Nordic runes, ancient cuneiform, angelic script, Egyptian hieroglyphics and even older and stranger markings, but he could make no sense of them.

In the center of the chamber, a wide, dark hole took up much of the floor. From three equidistant points around its edge, three stone beams stretched across the void to meet in a circular stone platform over its center. And from the ceiling, the room's central pillar pierced the platform and ran down into the darkness beyond. The words and images and symbols all over it marched straight down its sides into the inky blackness of oblivion. Looking down, Gashwrack's eyes couldn't find the end of it or the bottom of the hole. It emptied into the Abyss for all he knew.

"It is impressive," Bile-Claw said, looking around in what Gashwrack assumed was wonder. "It is so old and long lost, yet it is still not entirely dormant. There is still earth-power here."

"Is *he* here?" Arastha asked, turning away from Gashwrack to take Bile-Claw by the hands. Gashwrack breathed a quiet sigh of relief and backed away from Arastha to the edge of the pit. "Can you feel the Forgotten Son?"

"Yes," Bile-Claw replied. "But he is buried deep and well bound."

"Can he feel us?" Arastha asked.

"He only knows that he wants to be free," Bile-Claw said, shaking his head.

"So how do we free him?" Gashwrack asked.

"He is not yet ready to be free," Bile-Claw answered. "Shrike's Thorn's ritual at the Tisza awoke him, but it did not clear his mind of hunger and rage. Besides, he is too weak. He's had only a trickle of sustenance all these eons."

"What does he need?" Gashwrack asked. When he did, Arastha smiled at him knowingly but deferred to Bile-Claw.

"Thought-essence," the Theurge said. "Which his spirit servitors take from their victims."

"You mean those Banes in the storms?" Gashwrack asked.

"Yes," Arastha piped up. "The same ones you saw being born at Tisza."

"They gather memories for their master that he may devour them," Bile-Claw said. "And in so doing, he grows strong."

"The Forgotten Son eats memories?" Gashwrack asked. "What kind of spirit is he?"

"He is a servitor of Eater-of-Souls," Bile-Claw said, "who preceded Lethargg, the Urge of Apathy, in the Dawn Times, before the Weaver-bitch ruined everything. He was created when our Father was free to help us forget the things He destroyed when their time had come. But when He was taken from us, the Forgotten Son no longer knew which memories to take and which to leave alone."

"So instead, he tried to take them all," Arastha lilted. "He ate any memory his servitors could bring him. And for this simple crime of not knowing any better how to fulfill his purpose, he was beaten, tortured and imprisoned here deep within the earth. Lost for eons, soaking up only what memories those in the world above threw away."

"If he's been lost so long, how did you find out about him?"

"Because part of the Forgotten Son's prison touches the Dream Zone," Bile-Claw said, "and from time to time, his dreams have touched others through it. In the past, he has been too weak to make contact thus, but he has grown more powerful as mankind has grown more willing to ignore and forget its problems rather than face them. Especially in such places as here, where racism, genocide and cruelty have been second nature for centuries. People all over the world know about the evils that happen here, but they simply choose not to think about it. The acts themselves, and the suffering they cause, feed the Banes that swarm over this area, but the willful ignorance others direct toward those acts, and the suffering *that* causes, feeds the Forgotten Son. It is not enough to give him the strength to break free, but it has been enough to finally make contact with those who could help him. I am such a one. Your packmate Shrike's Thorn was as well."

"He never told me any of this," Gashwrack said.

"Good," Arastha said. "I commanded him not to tell anyone until we were certain we'd found the prison, lest word of our efforts reach our enemies and inspire them to action."

"But now here we are," Bile-Claw said. "So close to setting him free once again. We have only but to feed him and give him strength."

"Then I have plenty of memories to sacrifice," Gashwrack said. "If he'll take them."

"Oh no, indeed, my bitter Gashwrack," Arastha said. She crossed to him and guided him away from the pit's edge. He stiffened at her light touch on his shoulder. "I need you still. You and Eric Fire-Stealer both."

Gashwrack cut his eyes toward her petulantly but said nothing.

"You must see to the defense of our newfound treasure," Arastha continued. "I leave it to you to post sentries and fortify the terrain surrounding these caverns. Until you have used it to assure these caverns' security, you must not sacrifice any of your former life's experience."

"Yes, Lady Arastha," Gashwrack murmured, hope fading in his eyes.

"Good. Now, Bile-Claw, tell me of defiling caerns."

"Our tunnels are already working for us, Lady Arastha," Bile-Claw said, "but we can accelerate the process with moon bridges. Follow me." He led her across the cavern to the small chamber opposite the one from which they'd entered. In it was a short stone basin full of clear water with a flat, white pebble in the bottom.

"This is the caern's pathstone," he said. "I can still feel its energy. We can use it to open bridges to our most powerful pits in the region. As the energy of our Father's essence converges, it will taint this place by degrees and help revive the Forgotten Son further. I also know of a ritual that will allow me to direct that energy against the bonds of the Forgotten Son's prison. I can break select chains with it, allowing the Forgotten Son's servitors to reach him. When he has regained his full strength, I can then cut him free."

Arastha's eyes flashed in orgasmic delight. "Then I'll return home at once and organize the other hives. What do you need here to make this wonderful dream come true?"

"More Theurges to summon the Forgotten Son's servitors," Bile-Claw said. "And to help me with my ritual."

"I can use them, too," Gashwrack said. "There are enough Banes crawling through the Penumbra to provide for our defense, if they can be harnessed properly. Of course, another contingent of warriors born under the Full Moon wouldn't hurt."

"Then it will be done," Arastha said. "And when our work is finished, the rewards will be sweet. The Father's, the Forgotten Son's and my own."

Gashwrack only nodded. He wanted nothing more from Arastha than the chance to make his sacrifice to the Forgotten Son.

Chapter Five

Albrecht and Mephi left the North Country Caern alone at moonrise the next night after a long day spent making preparations for the king's absence. First thing after Albrecht woke up and ate breakfast, the Warder, the Gatekeeper, the Keeper of the Land and the Wyrm Foe all had to be given orders and assigned specific duties to handle in his stead. Finding the right balance of authority among them was a little touchy, but he delineated their extra responsibilities by age and told them to stuff it if they didn't like it.

After that, Albrecht spent the afternoon explaining to everybody at the manor and in the sept where he was going and why. He told them a little more about what had happened to Mari, but he assured them that Evan was away watching out for her. He then introduced Mephi, told everyone that the Strider was going to accompany him and made sure that everyone knew that it was Mephi who'd saved Mari from sure death at the Sept of the Anvil-Klaiven.

When that was all over—*finally*—he'd eaten a huge late lunch and gone to get his gear ready. He gathered a couple of extra changes of dedicated clothes, a whetstone for Solemn Lord, an all-weather crimson cape, his fur-insulated forearm bracers, a fur-insulated sword belt and a fetish necklace King Jacob Morningkill had given him after his First Change. Finally, he'd thrown on a long, shiny leather jacket that Evan and Mari had chipped in and bought him last year at Christmas. He preferred his old, trusted trench coat, and he hardly ever wore this leather one, but this occasion seemed to merit some degree of class. Sure, he was still wearing long combat boots, heavy blue jeans and a white turtleneck sweater with quilted pads at the shoulders and elbows under the jacket, but it wasn't like he was getting married or anything. Besides, since Evan and Mari couldn't come with him, it was good to bring something that reminded him of them both.

At nightfall, Albrecht had stuffed all of his gear into a single large rucksack, slung it onto his back and headed for the heart of the caern. Eliphas Standish and Mephi met him shortly thereafter, as the moon broke the horizon. Eliphas had then opened the bridge to Night Sky, and off Mephi and Albrecht had gone. They stopped only once about halfway there to rest and eat once more, then continued on. Now, at the Night Sky Caern in Hungary, they stepped off the moon bridge sometime in the late afternoon. They were met not only by the caern's Gatekeeper, but by a dour little man with a big nose and bushy black hair. That man strode up to Albrecht, held up his hand and started rattling on in a language that was coming out of his mouth so fast that Albrecht couldn't even identify it. Whatever he was saying, though, he didn't sound very happy about it. Mephi started prattling back with an open hand raised in front of him, but Albrecht stopped him.

"What the hell's he saying?" He looked the black-haired man in the eye and said, "You savvy English?"

"I do," the man said, peering at Albrecht with narrowed eyes. "I have a passing facility with it." He then looked back at Mephi and started going on again in his own language.

"That's good enough," Albrecht said, raising his voice over the chatter. "Let's stick to it."

Mephi stiffened at that, but the small man did as Albrecht said. "I was saying," he began, "that I am Korda Laszlo, the steward of this fortress." He gestured down at the brown wolf at his side. "This is Fire-Shadow, the

Keeper of the Spirit Gate." Fire-Shadow tilted his head slightly and looked back and forth between Albrecht and Mephi.

"Great," Albrecht said. "Nice to meet you both. Now—"

"I am sent by the margrave," Laszlo cut in. "To welcome you and ask you to state your business. You bring a stranger here, bearing no sign of invitation from the margrave. So explain yourself. No spies or would-be usurpers go any farther into the Night Sky Caern."

Albrecht looked sideways at Mephi and murmured, "You believe this guy?"

"It's just a formality," Mephi said out of the side of his mouth. "It's because he didn't expect anyone else to be showing up with you."

"Whatever," Albrecht said. Then, turning back to Laszlo, he said, "Knock off the games and listen up, you two. You damn well better remember Mephi Faster-than-Death, because it hasn't been that long since he was here last. He's here now at my request because he's had actual experience dealing with these problems Jo'cllath'mattric's caused you all."

Laszlo flinched and Fire-Shadow's hackles rose at the mention of the Wyrm-spirit.

"The two of us are here," Albrecht went on, "because that damned monster's been making a mess of things. We're not here to usurp or spy. I'm here to help."

Fire-Shadow huffed skeptically.

"And in return?" Laszlo asked.

Albrecht faltered at that, so Mephi spoke up. "In return, Lord Albrecht asks that Margrave Konietzko rally his noble warriors to join him in battle against this ancient foe. All for the glory of Gaia."

"What he said," Albrecht added.

Fire-Shadow relaxed his tail to show he was satisfied with that answer, and Laszlo relaxed as well. He bowed slightly and inclined his head in an attitude of deference. "I believe you, King, and I bid you and your comrade welcome. You may leave your traveling equipment here, and Fire-Shadow will have a page take them to the room I've had made ready for you within the fortress."

Albrecht and Mephi shucked off their satchels, and Laszlo gestured for them to follow him. While he walked, Laszlo talked in his native tongue again. Mephi nodded and answered in more of the same.

"It seems like Konietzko's been in consultation with some other sept leaders for most of the day already," the Strider said to Albrecht sotto voce. "He's mentioned Black Furies, Red Talons, Children of Gaia and a couple of others."

"Good," Albrecht said. "I didn't hear you mention any Silver Fangs, though."

"He didn't, either," Mephi said. "I guess you're the only one. I'm probably the only one from my tribe, too."

"Well," Albrecht grunted, "at least we'll have the respect those tribes usually give ours working for us." Which was precious little, of course.

The rest of the short tour passed in silence, and Albrecht quietly took in the grandeur of the place. The heart of the protectorate was a looming, misty mountain in the center of a craggy, forbidding range. The road from where the moon bridge had ended was a broad, winding track, paved and cobbled like a Roman road. It led through a rocky pass that would have been a great spot for an ambush had some enemy force tried to break through it to the caern. Although he couldn't see them, Albrecht knew that camouflaged Guardians in concealed spots all along the way were watching them with weapons trained on them. He wondered how many of them knew who he was or recognized the crown on his brow.

The path wound through a high-walled switchback and ended at the foot of the mountain itself. A huge archway had been carved into the base of the edifice, and Albrecht knew that they'd reached the entrance to Margrave Konietzko's fortress. The arch was three times as tall as a man, and it had been carefully refined and touched up over the long years that Garou had defended this place. On the lintel were etched a row of glyphs representing a caern, the moon and stars, thunder and lightning and the tribe of the Shadow Lords. Individually, they were not especially descriptive, but read together, they made sense on an instinctive level, much in the same way scent and body language conveyed meaning. *This is the Night Sky Caern*, the message read. *By the grace of Grandfather Thunder, we Shadow Lords honor and protect this place.*

More guards stood on either side of the entrance, but Laszlo didn't even pause to acknowledge them. He led the guests into the fortress's grand foyer, through a wide meeting hall beyond it, then into the main hallway. The floors and walls of the place were meticulously polished like the dwelling places of man. Benches, tables, chairs and stools dominated the common rooms, and thick rugs covered the cold stone floors. Tapestries and paintings hung on the walls, depicting heroic battles that had taken place here, as well as scenes from stories in the Silver Record in which Shadow Lords had figured prominently. Every dozen feet or so along the hall, an alcove had been carved into the wall, in which statues of famous heroes stood or plaster re-creations of ancient weapons and fetishes had been mounted on display stands in glass cases. A mixture of torches and hidden electric lights illuminated the inside of the place, making it feel more like the inside of a freestanding building than the belly of a mountain.

Several rooms and hallways later, Laszlo led Mephi and Albrecht toward a T-intersection that framed a large marble statue of a proud and strong warrior. The figure stood dressed for battle and held a wicked-looking sword in his right hand. His head was held high, and a light mounted above gave the effect that the man was staring boldly toward the sun, ready for adventure. Looking at the statue and the legend under it that read "Boris Thunderstrike," Albrecht snorted and rolled his eyes.

"It is not much farther," Laszlo said, slowing down in front of Albrecht and turning backward to face his guests as he walked. He pointed down the hall to his right. "If you go to your left past four doors, the fifth on the right is available and at your disposal. Had I been informed that you were bringing guests, I would have made more space ready."

"That's okay," Mephi said.

"In any event," Laszlo went on, still walking backward, "you may rest there after meeting with the council if you so choose. If it is not to your liking, arrangements—"

"Thanks," Albrecht said, glancing down the way Laszlo indicated. "I'm sure it'll be fine."

Laszlo bowed once more, then turned smoothly on his heel to head in the opposite direction. Mephi and Albrecht maintained course past the statue, took the first left and headed down another long hallway in silence, enduring the curious stares of the locals who passed them by. At last, Albrecht spoke up behind Laszlo.

"So who all's expecting us at this council the margrave's holding?"

Laszlo slowed and thought for a moment. "Prominent regional sept leaders," he said. "Helena Slow-to-Anger of the Black Furies tribe. Swift-As-the-River from the Red Talons. Guy Houndstooth from the Sept of Mountain Springs. Sergiy Dawntreader from the Sept of the Dawn. Supporting warriors from their representative protectorates. Queen Tamara Tvarivich from the Sept of the Crescent Moon has come as well, although she has proven somewhat... problematic."

"You don't say," Albrecht said. From what he'd heard of Tvarivich, she was a unifier and a brilliant tactician at her home caern in Russia. She'd probably come seeking a joint command with Konietzko and been rebuffed. "I've heard of her. And some of the others you mentioned, too."

"We expected even more visitors," Laszlo said, "but not everyone was available. Local warriors are hard pressed to find spare time for travel. Times are changing very quickly in this hemisphere."

"Well, things are about to start changing for the better," Albrecht said. "That's what we're here for."

Making no acknowledgement of that, Laszlo led the two guests to a set of wooden double doors, where he stopped. He pushed the doors open with both hands then stepped gracefully out of the way, ushering Albrecht and Mephi into the room. All conversation inside stopped as more than a dozen pairs of eyes turned to regard the newcomers.

Albrecht had just enough time to take in the general atmosphere in the room before Laszlo was at his side again, leading him toward the middle of the room. Dour, grim faces of men and women surrounded him, and Albrecht figured their unhappy expressions weren't just because of the interruption. The air was thick with tension and frustration already, and the arrival of new people was just one more complication no one really seemed to need.

The room certainly didn't lend itself to pleasant discourse or relaxation, either. It was cramped and ill lit, considering how many people were trying to use it. A large oval table stood in the middle of it, and most of the room's occupants were crowded around with little elbowroom. There were no chairs or even stools around the table, which allowed more people to squeeze in around it. In fact, the only stools in the room were the four or five that had been pushed back against the walls and taken by people who were obviously not important enough to merit an immediate place in whatever discussion had been going on. Those unfortunates sat or stood in front of colorful, gruesome wall tapestries of old Shadow Lord heroes ripping ancient villains to bits.

Albrecht took all of this in and stepped forward with Laszlo. A space opened up at the foot of the table as two men fell back respectfully, and Albrecht took it. He noticed that the table was strewn with scrolls, musty books, maps and all sorts of writing utensils, but he didn't have time for more than a cursory glance. Now that he was here, he could feel all eyes on him, including those of the old man opposite him at the table's head.

"Margrave Konietzko," Laszlo said, "honored guests, allow me to introduce Lord Jonas Albrecht, king of the American North Country Protectorate, scion of House Wyrmfoe of the Silver Fangs tribe."

Albrecht glanced around the room as translators related the introduction to those few who didn't speak English. He wasn't expecting an outburst of applause or anything, but even still, nobody seemed particularly impressed. Mostly, everyone just kept right on staring at him grimly. Maybe it was the idea of using "king" and "American" in the same introduction that put them off. After a short, awkward silence, Margrave Konietzko himself raised a hand in greeting and spoke.

"Welcome, King Albrecht, to the Sept of the Night Sky," he said in heavily accented English. "Your fame precedes you, even so far from home. You were not invited to this council, I admit, but no slight was intended. Join us now and tell us why you have come."

Albrecht stared at the old man as he spoke, looking for signs of sarcasm or disdain. None was evident, but that might have just been because Konietzko was an impassive, stony-faced son of a bitch. He stood proud and utterly relaxed, with the dim lighting casting his eyes in shadow. His gray hair was long and straight, and not a single strand of fur on his cloak was out of place. The sword at his hip was as large as Solemn Lord, and his fingertips brushed its leather scabbard. He exuded the total ease of a wolf in his den. In a lot of ways, he reminded Albrecht of the way King Morningkill had looked sitting in his throne under the Grand Oak. He seemed every bit the strong, self-possessed warrior, worthy of his subjects' trust, admiration and respect. Above all, their respect.

"I'm here," Albrecht answered, "because of the shit that's been going on that nobody around here's been doing anything about." Respect wasn't the same as deference. "I know all about how the Wyrm's been trying to use the Tisza River's defiled spirit to set something called Jo'cllath'mattric free, and I know what Jo'cllath'mattric is capable of. It's time something was done about him, and I'm just the man to see it gets done."

A big fellow in the middle of the table sputtered something in what Albrecht thought was German after another round of translation. Albrecht didn't understand the words, but the disdain was clear.

Albrecht looked over behind him at Mephi and noted idly that Laszlo was nowhere to be seen. "What'd he say?" he asked the Strider. "And who the hell is he?"

"That's Guy Houndstooth," Mephi whispered. "The head of the Sept of Mountain Springs. He's asking just who you think you are."

"I see," Albrecht said. "Thanks. Stay put and keep translating for me." Then, turning back to Houndstooth, he said, "To be honest, it doesn't much matter to me who you guys are. I know you're all Garou and you're all warriors. And I know you need me."

Outrage bubbled up at that all around the room, but only one person replied directly to Albrecht. He was a gigantic man wearing a bearskin over his back, who was standing only two places away from Konietzko. His voice was as strong and loud as a hammer blow. As the man spoke, Mephi translated for Albrecht, but not before telling him that this was Sergiy Dawntreader, from the Sept of the Dawn.

"That means little to us coming from a Silver Fang, I'm afraid," the huge man said. "Or an American."

"This isn't about tribes or countries," Albrecht said, biting down a hot, counterproductive retort. That was Evan's influence rubbing off on him. "This is about a problem that needs a solution."

"Your solution?" a black-haired, olive-skinned woman standing near Albrecht asked. "Did this council's incompetence call out to you across the ocean?"

"No, it didn't," Albrecht answered. He didn't even need Mephi to tell him who the woman was. She reminded him enough of Mari for him to figure she was probably the Black Fury Laszlo had mentioned. "I wouldn't be here if I thought you were incompetent, but you do need to get your act together."

Mephi winced.

Carl Bowen

53

A scruffy, dirty man with tangled hair and an unkempt beard, who was wearing nothing more than a buckskin vest and tattered drawstring pants, was the first to reply. He puffed into his even more hirsute Glabro form and slammed his hands down on the table.

"How dare you?" the man shouted in the Garou tongue, which erased the language barrier. "We don't need you or want you here!"

Albrecht boiled up into his Glabro form as well, refusing to back down from the man's rage. "You're Swift-As-the-River, right—the Red Talon?" he answered back in the Garou tongue. "Well, tell me this, two-legs, how's your tribe faring over here lately? The way I hear it, you can't keep your rivers clean, and you can't defend your caerns from attack. So your tribe's been killing humans instead of fighting the real problem. Don't tell me you don't need something better. That's horse shit!

"And you," Albrecht snapped, turning toward Houndstooth. "Isn't the Sept of Mountain Springs in Switzerland? You're a long way from home if you don't need some kind of help." He turned then toward Helena Slow-to-Anger. "And *you* can stuff your sarcasm. You don't want to even get me started on what your tribe's let happen." Finally, he turned to Dawntreader. "And you, being a Child of Gaia, ought to know better than to make judgments based on where I'm from or who my ancestors were. The lot of you ought to be ashamed of yourselves. It's no wonder you've got a million-year-old Wyrm-spirit digging its way up through your backyards!"

Everyone who'd spoken to Albrecht thus far stood seething, yet it was the margrave who spoke first again, cutting through the tension with cool, measured words.

"Tempers," he said softly, looking first at Albrecht then scanning the others around the table. "All of you.

This council has been an exercise in frustration since it began." All eyes slowly turned to the margrave, and several of his guests relaxed.

"I believe that Lord Albrecht is right, after a fashion," Konietzko continued with a nod down the table. "We have been trying in vain to fix the location of Jo'cllath'mattric for quite some time. Two packs of brave warriors have died trying since our concolation at the Sept of the Anvil-Klaiven, and despite forestalling Jo'cllath'mattric's escape, the prophesied Silver River Pack has yielded us precious little we can use against our new enemy as of yet.

"Perhaps, then, what we need is a fresh perspective. Let Lord Albrecht stand with us and share with us what he knows. Let him combine his warriors' skill with ours that we might all be made stronger." Then, to Albrecht, he said, "Your warriors are camped outside at the mountain's base with the others who've come to join me?"

A light heat of embarrassment rose behind Albrecht's ears, but his gaze didn't waver. "No," he said.

The margrave cocked his head. "Surely you have not quartered them here, inside this fortress? This place has not been a home for Silver Fang warriors since the elder Heart-of-Fury was judged too weak to protect it."

Albrecht blinked once and said, "No." He could feel the heat growing. Maybe Evan had been right about more than Albrecht had wanted to admit. "I didn't bring any of my warriors with me."

"A coalition of allied soldiers, then," the margrave said. "That sounds more typically American."

The heat inside Albrecht blazed, and now there was more than embarrassment in it. "No coalition," he growled. "Just the two of us and the skills we bring to the table."

"Only two?" Konietzko said, knitting his eyebrows in a frown. "Could it be that Jo'cllath'mattric is not as formidable as we all thought? Or do you simply think that a Silver Fang's leadership is all we need to win the day? You would not be the first to think so."

When the margrave said that, Dawntreader gave a lopsided grin, Helena Slow-to-Anger smirked, Swift-as-the-River snorted in amusement and Albrecht almost lost it. He almost jumped up on the table in his Crinos form and started letting everybody in front of him know what he really thought of them and their centuries-old traditions of being world-class pricks. He would have done it, too, had it not been for Mephi sighing and lowering his head. The Strider's reaction told Albrecht that if he pressed on now, he was only going to look like more of a barking cub than he already did. So he put the cork back on his anger and sank back into his Homid form.

"It isn't like that," he said in response to the margrave's gibe. "I'm not here to take over. But something *is* wrong, and I can't just stand by without doing what I can to help. And if that's typically American, I can think of worse ways to be."

"Then tell me," Konietzko said, "just how do you intend to help? I know you are a warrior of great renown, but how deep is your understanding of the spirit world? Do you have a Theurge's intuitive understanding of sacred geometry and astral metaphysics that will be necessary to help us locate Jo'cllath'mattric's prison?"

"Well…"

"And how well versed are you in our local lore?" Konietzko continued. "Can you call to mind ancient tales from this region that might offer important clues in our search?"

"No, I can't," Albrecht admitted. "But in the past—"

Konietzko shook his head. "You are a brave warrior, Lord Albrecht," he said, "and by legend, you are a good king at home. But a good king must recognize when he is out of his league and know when to delegate responsibility to the experts. This is one of those times."

Any other Silver Fang—especially one from this region originally—would have gone ballistic hearing a Shadow Lord talk to him like this. In fact, Konietzko had probably seen it plenty of times since he'd taken control of this sept. Albrecht knew better, though. Fifteen years ago, King Morningkill had said almost exactly the same thing about delegating responsibility. Now he could practically hear his old great-grandfather's voice coming out of Konietzko's mouth and see the same weary experience in Konietzko's eyes. Now, as then, Albrecht choked down his indignation and controlled his temper.

What made it all worse was the fact that the Shadow Lord was right. Werewolves ran in packs and had different auspice duties in the first place for this very reason. He'd learned that lesson back when King Morningkill had taught it, and he shouldn't even have made an issue of it now. He was going to have to backtrack and recover some of the ground he'd lost.

"You're right," he said at last. "Coming all this way with no supporting warriors and with no direct information to help solve the puzzle in front of you was a little reckless. I can see that." All around him, the leaders from the other septs smirked and nodded to one another. This was the sort of talk they liked to hear from Silver Fangs in Konietzko's presence. "But even still, that doesn't change my mind. I'm here now, and I'm not going anywhere until I've done everything I can to send Jo'cllath'mattric back to the hell he came from once and for all."

Shock at his audacity widened eyes and loosened jaws all around Albrecht, but Konietzko kept his cool. In fact, the old man's eyes narrowed, and he peered at Albrecht with an expression of bright, lupine cunning. None of the others said a word.

"Then there may be, I think, a way that you can do your part after all, Lord Albrecht," the margrave said. "If you are as eager as you say."

"I am. What is it?"

"Do you know Queen Tamara Tvarivich from your tribe? She comes from the Sept of the Crescent Moon in the Ural Mountains."

"I've never met her," Albrecht said, "but I know of her. Your steward said she was here somewhere."

"That is true," Konietzko said with a tiny, wry smile. "She has come at my invitation, and she has even brought with her a contingent of warriors to aid in our campaign. Yet, she categorically refuses to work with us. She will not even accept my hospitality and stay in the room my steward prepared for her in the fortress. She and her warriors sequester themselves on the outskirts of my bawn, demanding that we come to them."

"What?" Albrecht asked. "That doesn't make any sense." It sounded to him like something a petty, senile old Silver Fang might do just to make his Shadow Lord host come crawling to him, but Queen Tvarivich supposedly knew better. In Russia, she was one of the most influential unifiers the Silver Fangs had. As far as Albrecht knew, all of her major victories were the results of successful intertribal cooperation.

"True," Konietzko said, "yet still she refuses. Her reason, you see, is personal, and perhaps you will find it so as well. It's because of the Silver Fang warrior named Arkady, of the Firebird Sept."

Albrecht's blood burned just to hear that name, but he suppressed any visible reaction except a tightening muscle in his jaw. "What about him?"

Konietzko breathed deeply in what was almost a sigh and said, "Queen Tvarivich still has a great deal of faith in that once-hero of your tribe. She refuses to abide by the judgment that Sergiy Dawntreader, Swift-As-the-River and I helped pass on him in council among the Sept of the Anvil-Klaiven."

"Which means what, exactly?"

"Upon her arrival here," the margrave answered, "Queen Tvarivich told us that Arkady spoke to her some time ago of a threat growing unknown in this region, whose name was Jo'cllath'mattric. She claims that he revealed something of great importance to her, yet asked her to keep it secret while investigated further."

"I knew he was wound up tighter in this than anybody had told me," Albrecht hissed. "So what was the secret?"

"That is the source of the problem," Konietzko said. "For you see, she will not tell us. In fact, she says that she will not share with us anything Arkady told her until I call another concolation and hold new hearings against him. Ones in which Silver Fangs can sit in judgment and Arkady can speak on his own behalf. At such a time, she assures us, Arkady's innocence will reveal itself, and he can recoup his 'stolen' honor by leading us into battle against Jo'cllath'mattric himself."

"Say *what?*" Albrecht barked. "You've got to be kidding me."

"That is the ultimatum she gave us," Konietzko said. "The queen is young and proud, and she refuses to discuss the matter further. But she might still be willing to talk to you."

"Oh, I get it now," Albrecht said with a heartless smirk. "She'll talk to me because she's pretty much got to, right? Because I'm wearing this crown."

"We cannot summarily erase our judgment about Arkady," Konietzko said, "but perhaps you can show your Tvarivich the truth as you know it and convince her to tell you what the traitor revealed to her. It may be all misdirection and lies, but even lies can reveal a kernel of truth. If you would relate the queen's information to us, we would consider it a worthwhile contribution to our efforts."

Albrecht nodded, ashamed of this queen whose pride had the potential to do as much damage as Arkady's treachery. "All right," he said. "If that's what you need, I'll talk to her."

"Excellent," the margrave said. He then addressed his other guests once again. "Then we will adjourn until tomorrow. Lord Albrecht, I encourage you to rest after your long journey, and I invite you to our feast hall when you are hungry. I look forward to your success getting through to Queen Tvarivich, and when you do, assure her that we bear her no ill will. We understand that zealous loyalty can sometimes turn out to be misplaced."

"Me, too," Albrecht said quietly, feeling more like Konietzko was patting him on the head like a puppy than he was expressing confidence.

"I rest assured that you won't let us down," Konietzko said. "We're counting on you."

And with that, he dismissed the leaders and soldiers for the rest of the day. By turns glaring at or ignoring Albrecht, the others filed out of the room, likely heading for the feast hall themselves. Mephi backed up a step as well, standing behind Albrecht uncomfortably and waiting for his chance to leave. As the margrave himself moved to leave the room, Albrecht noticed behind him a large, floor-to-ceiling tapestry on the wall that looked familiar, even though he'd never seen it before. The reason it did, he realized, was that the main character depicted on it was the same one who'd been immortalized in stone in the main hallway, Boris Thunderstrike. In the tapestry, he was holding a stylized depiction of a pathstone with the glyphs that meant Night Sky on it. At the bottom of the picture, Thunderstrike was stepping on the neck of one of his fellow Garou. The victim wore a pitiful expression, and his limbs were weak and stick thin. On his armor was the looping glyph of the Silver Fang tribe as well as a set of glyphs that read "Heart-of-Fury." The poor bastard didn't look especially furious, though. He looked impotent and ridiculous. And as Albrecht filed out of the audience chamber at last, he could almost sympathize.

Chapter Six

After a quick stop to stow their weapons in their room, Albrecht and Mephi ended up in the fortress's gloomy feast hall, looking for a meal. They saw Slow-to-Anger and Swift-As-the-River sitting together in their respective breed forms, surrounded by a handful of warriors each from their own septs. Near them but facing away was Sergiy Dawntreader, entertaining everyone at the table in a great booming voice. Guy Houndstooth and his knot of warriors sat sullen and brooding in a corner of the hall, and Konietzko's warriors and staff took up most of the rest of the space. The only free table was one near the back corner by the door. Trying not to draw attention to himself, Albrecht led Mephi that way, and they sat down together.

"He played me in there," Albrecht said as a Kinfolk servant put two glasses of water down between them and disappeared. "And I let him."

"Beg pardon?"

"King Morningkill used to do that to people all the time," Albrecht said. "I've even done it myself. It's what you do when some clown comes barking into your court and making an ass of himself. You play the high-and-mighty and do everything you can to make him feel useless. Then, when he's just about to crawl away, you come up with some shit job you don't want to do and make it sound like something only this guy can possibly handle. I set myself right up for it like a damn cliath, and Tvarivich's idiocy sure didn't help. That was a damn disaster."

"I suppose it could have gone better," Mephi agreed.

Albrecht growled in irritation and thumped his elbows up onto the table to lean forward in thought. Not for the first time, he wished he could have brought

Silver Fangs

Evan. The kid was a diplomatic whiz who knew how to get people to take him seriously. He'd be able to say what Albrecht meant to say a hell of a lot better than Albrecht himself could say it. Mari'd be a big help, too. She knew how to make sense of Konietzko's "sacred geometry" and "astral metaphysics." If she and Evan had been there, everyone would still be gathered around that table in that cramped little room going over all those old maps and Umbral charts one more time, trying to ferret out Jo'cllath'mattric, Tvarivich be damned. It was just this kind of situation where he needed his packmates most, but it was because of it that neither of them could be here with him. And, of course, he had no one to blame for that in the end but himself.

Before self-recrimination got the better of him, though, a long, mellifluous howl from the other end of the room distracted him. It came from a tall, lithe werewolf of indeterminate tribal heritage who was walking up the center aisle of the feast hall from a table near the opposite end. The guy was in Crinos form, begging the attention of all who would listen, and all eyes in the room turned his way.

"Gryffyth SeaFoam," Mephi whispered. "The sept's new self-appointed Talesinger." The tone in Mephi's voice told Albrecht not to expect too much from SeaFoam's work, but that might just have been job-related cattiness.

When SeaFoam had garnered enough attention from everybody, he introduced himself and launched into some song he'd written about what a great guy Margrave Konietzko was. He walked up and down the aisle with a big, stupid lupine grin on his face, exhorting his audience through song and howl to join him in praising Konietzko's "grim determination," "unerring intellect" and other such shit. Some listeners warbled out a few bars at SeaFoam's urging, and even Dawntreader thundered out a couple of lines from the refrain, much to SeaFoam's delight. The tune was catchy in its way, and it seemed pretty popular among the locals.

Albrecht could only take so much, though. He was in no mood to hear any more about how great Konietzko was. The cult of personality that seemed to have arisen around the margrave couldn't help but remind Albrecht of the flock of sycophants and naïve fools that had surrounded King Morningkill and refused to admit that things in North Country were getting worse the older the king got. Thinking about that while brooding over his earlier political missteps was quite enough for Albrecht.

So, waiting until SeaFoam was at the opposite end of the room with his back turned, Albrecht got up and turned to leave the feast hall. Mephi, who was busy scowling at SeaFoam's back, noticed Albrecht departing and hurried after him. They dodged a pack of warriors who came in from the hallway to hear SeaFoam's song, and slipped out.

Once out of the feast hall, they set off down the main hallway, moving upstream against the current of folks who were heading to dinner. Albrecht walked with his thumbs hooked into his pants pockets, holding his leather jacket open. Mephi kept pace on Albrecht's right side, his hands stuffed into the pockets of his gray duster. The Strider was annoyed, too, apparently.

"I don't get why people like that song so much," Mephi said. "It isn't *that* good."

Albrecht grunted. He didn't especially want to like it either, but that was only because he was already in a bad mood.

"I mean, the rhyme and meter are so forced," Mephi griped. "It might as well be Emily Dickinson up there.

And that part about the Transylvanian vampire… how trite can you get? Creepy bloodsucker in a gloomy castle on some craggy mountain stealing virgins from the nearby villages and making them his slaves. Spoo-ky."

Albrecht grinned despite his annoyance.

"And oh, this vampire's got about a hundred zombie slaves manning his castle, of course," Mephi went on. "But is our margrave worried? Nay! He cuts them all down like cardboard and finds the vampire down in the basement, lying in repose in his velvet coffin. And when the vampire wakes up and throws himself at his intruder like an idiot, the margrave just cuts him to ribbons— one, two, three."

"I don't know," Albrecht grumbled. "I liked that part."

Mephi glanced at him and rolled his eyes. "Ahrouns… You know, it probably didn't even happen that way. Where were the margrave's warriors during all of this? His pack? Did he just *walk* from here to Transylvania? Sure! Realism, take the hindmost."

"It's just a song," Albrecht said. "You saying you never exaggerate to make one sound better?"

Mephi bristled. "I don't have to. When I tell a story, it's what the heroes do that makes them look good, not what I make up about them."

"Oh," Albrecht said. "I guess I can take that as a compliment."

Mephi looked a little confused at that, but he caught on quickly. "Yeah. Because of *The Saga*. You should. You came off great in that."

"Thanks."

After that, they walked on in silence for a while before Mephi spoke again.

"So, are we going where I think we're going?"

"Yeah," Albrecht said. "I thought we'd go ahead and talk some sense into this Tvarivich woman tonight while we're up. Provided you want to come along and translate, of course."

"Sure," Mephi said. "That's why I'm here. But aren't you worried you'll look like you're skipping to the margrave's tune, going out so soon after he… asked you?"

"Let him think whatever makes him happy," Albrecht said a little stiffly. "I've got my own reasons to talk to Tvarivich."

"I see. Well, let's go then."

Mephi led Albrecht to a door that opened out from the rear of the fortress, and they stepped outside into the cool, cloudy night. Right away, Albrecht fished a pack of cigarettes out of one jacket pocket and a box of matchsticks from the other. He offered one to Mephi, who declined, and they started walking. Before he could even light up, two of the sept's Guardians approached in Crinos form, demanding to know what they were doing.

"Delivering a baby," Albrecht said in English as Mephi started to say something else in Hungarian. He stuck his cigarette in his mouth and struck a match. "Where's the maternity ward around here?"

The guards didn't appear to speak English, but they figured out what he wanted to know. They gestured down a path that led to the expansive, rocky campground near the base of the mountain and told him to go smoke down there. He waved and lit his cigarette, and he and Mephi headed off in that direction.

It took them little time to find the campground at the rear of the bawn, and only a little more to find Queen Tvarivich's campsite. It was squirreled away in a corner of the campground behind a tumble of large boulders, reflecting the occupants' desire not to mingle with the warriors from other septs. Albrecht and Mephi exchanged a glance and headed that way.

When they reached the two tallest boulders blocking off the Silver Fangs' camp, two Russian sentries materialized from the shadows to challenge them. The men were both tall and of medium build, with neck-length hair and thick beards, and they wore clothes made for colder climates. They stood shoulder to shoulder and rose into their larger Glabro forms, blocking off the path. They both held drawn klaives.

"Go no farther," the one on the right said in the Garou tongue.

"Who goes there?" the second asked.

"I really hope you can tell," Albrecht growled, refusing to show any sign of submission. The two sentries only looked at each other then back at Albrecht without any hint of comprehension. Albrecht rose slowly into his own Glabro form, repeated himself in the High Tongue and added, "Who the hell are you?"

"We are Silver Fangs," the one on the right replied. "Visitors."

"We hail from the Sept of the Crescent Moon," the other put in. "We serve Queen—"

"Tvarivich," Albrecht interrupted. "Yeah, that's who we're looking for. Where is she?"

"You are the recent arrivals?" the first sentry asked, peering at Albrecht and especially Mephi with skepticism. "The Americans?"

"Doesn't matter where I'm from," Albrecht said. "I'm also a Silver Fang."

"And not just any Silver Fang," Mephi added. By way of explanation, he looked significantly toward the crown on Albrecht's head.

As Albrecht glanced over at Mephi, the two sentries peered at Albrecht then began whispering to each other rapidly in Russian.

"It's true, isn't it?" the first sentry said in the High Tongue after a couple of seconds.

"Is it?" the second asked. "Are you he? Are you Albrecht?"

"Yeah, I am," he growled.

As one, the two Silver Fangs sheathed their klaives and folded down into their Lupus forms so that two gray-and-white wolves stood before him. They then stretched out onto their forepaws to touch their snouts to the ground and rolled over onto their backs three times. As they came to their feet again, their tails were swishing.

I knew, the wolf on the right indicated to his partner. *I told you it was him as he approached.*

Yes, the second said, letting his tail droop just a little before it resumed its quick beat. *I was wrong. He does have the silver circle.*

Albrecht stood up straight and started to relax a little. "It's good to finally meet some people around here who recognize it. Damn good."

The wolves rose back into their Glabro forms, and Albrecht once more hooked his thumbs into his belt. The two men hunched their broad shoulders and stooped slightly.

"We are very pleased to meet you," the first Silver Fang said.

"Honored," the second corrected. He then looked at Mephi. "And this is Evan Heals-the-Past?"

"*Nyet*," Mephi answered, looking a little embarrassed.

"Evan's at home with my other packmate," Albrecht said. "This is Mephi Faster-than-Death. He's a highly renowned Silent Strider from back home who's come to pay his respects to Queen Tvarivich."

The first Silver Fang nodded. "Yes, we have overheard some of the other visitors mention his name."

"So, maybe we can get down to business then," Albrecht said.

"Yes, King Albrecht," the first Silver Fang answered. "We will take you to Queen Tvarivich right away. Although she may be less warm than we have been with you. She and Arkady were close. She does not trust the margrave's judgment."

"I know. That's why I'm here. Take me to her."

As he commanded, they obeyed. They took the lead, and Albrecht and Mephi followed about ten paces behind. For the sake of civility, Albrecht shrank down into his Homid form as he walked. The sentries led them to a tall, broad tent flanked by several smaller ones. Behind that row, about fifteen Garou were practicing combat maneuvers in various forms. They didn't notice the visitors' approach. As Mephi and Albrecht caught up, one of the sentries opened the tent flap and called to those inside. A moment later, the tent's occupant emerged and stood before her visitors.

She was a slim, powerful woman, roughly of an age with Albrecht, and about half a head shorter. She wore a white cloak over white robes, and both garments were decorated in a fine silver tracery of runes from numerous cultures. A heavy mace hung at her hip beneath her cloak, its weight seeming not to bother her in the slightest. Jet-black hair was carefully coiled and piled on top of her head, and a coronet of silver filigree settled right in the front. The woman looked Mephi up and down coolly then directed her attention to Albrecht. Her gaze found the crown on his head, and her eyebrow arched. With a look, she dismissed her two sentries to their posts.

"Welcome, guests," she said in Russian-accented English. "Gaia's grace be upon you. I am Queen Tamara Tvarivich, defender of the Sept of the Crescent Moon, scion of House Crescent Moon and Theurge of the Ivory Priesthood."

She then bowed and looked expectantly at her visitors.

"Hey," Albrecht said with a quick nod. "Nice to meet you. We need to talk. This is Mephi Faster-than-Death of the Silent Striders tribe, and if you don't know who I am, you're not a Silver Fang."

Tvarivich blinked. "I have heard of Mephi Faster-than-Death, and I do, indeed, recognize you, Albrecht of House Wyrmfoe," she said, trying to mask a bloom of distaste. "Your reputation precedes you."

"So it seems," Albrecht growled. "I bet you already have an idea why I'm here."

"You have spoken to the generals of the other septs who gather inside," Tvarivich said. Her eyes were thin slits, and her jaw grew increasingly tense as she spoke. "They told you that Arkady told me something about Jo'cllath'mattric, but that I will not share it with them, despite the fact that I have come all this way at Margrave Konietzko's invitation. Doubtless, they told you why. So now you have come to plead with me on their behalf and compel me to change my mind."

"That's mostly right," Albrecht said. "Except the last part."

"Then you have not come to dispute my personal judgment concerning Arkady of Firebird Sept?" Tvarivich asked with a sardonic lilt. "I understand that you disdain him."

"I'd say revile," Mephi mumbled.

"I hate him," Albrecht said. "That's no secret."

"Yes," Tvarivich replied. "Many here chose to feel that way after those inside passed judgment."

Albrecht snorted. He knew very well what judgment the queen was referring to. The kangaroo court proceedings that had pronounced Arkady anathema were the same ones Mari had been so intent on attending before she'd gotten herself tangled up with Jo'cllath'mattric.

"But you don't believe Arkady's guilty," Albrecht said. "Even hearing it from Count Dracula in there."

"I do not," Tvarivich confirmed. "His 'trial' was a mockery. Arkady was not allowed to speak for himself. No Silver Fangs were allowed to sit in judgment. Those fools even took the word of three Black Spiral Dancers over all common sense."

"Well, there was the matter of him commanding a Thunderwyrm…" Mephi added in a small voice.

"That?" Tvarivich snapped. "Arkady's blood is the purest in twenty generations. He stood with us against the Wyrm-dragon Gregornous Deathwing, and he fought the armies of the Baba Yaga by my side. The Wyrm knows Arkady's name, and all of its vile spawn have reason to fear him. That is why he was able to stop even a Thunderwyrm's rampage. Yet, still those others all turn on him and cast him out. The margrave fears Arkady's power as a threat to his own, so he engineered this travesty of justice solely to disgrace him. And until Konietzko admits that—"

"Lady," Albrecht said, stepping in front of Mephi, "I remember how strong Arkady used to be, and I've seen better leaders than Konietzko do exactly what you're talking about. The best king to ever come out of House Wyrmfoe even did it to *me*. But that isn't what's happened here, I promise you."

"Wyrmfoe is a house of decadent American children," Tvarivich scoffed. "Don't try to cloud the issue, Lord Albrecht. It was your house and your 'best king' who betrayed us. You turned your backs on us when we needed you most. Your promises carry little weight."

"Turned our backs how?"

"Arkady told us about you," Tvarivich said. Her voice rose in volume, mirroring the buildup of incredulous outrage that Albrecht had to fight down. "Before the Shadow Curtain fell, the ancient Baba Yaga rallied her six armies against us. Brave Arkady volunteered to fight his way out of Russia all alone and bring reinforcements from without. He fought all the way to your great-grandfather's caern, but King Morningkill only stalled him and led him on with vague promises.

"When that king died still without committing any forces to our aid, Arkady seized control himself. Yet no sooner had he done so than you returned from exile, claiming to have found the long-lost Silver Crown. You tricked everyone into following you, and they chased Arkady away in disgrace. He barely returned with his life to let us know that we had no allies to count on in the West. You may have hoped that Arkady would perish on his way back to us and take the tale of your treachery with him, but he was too strong. He did return, and he told us everything.

"And now you've come to me, supporting those who conspire against him. You've come all this way to dance to their tune and endorse the lies they tell. You, who could not be bothered to come to help your own tribe! Do not tell me I'm wrong or about how much you want to believe me! No more lies! I won't hear—"

"Damn it, lady, that's all bullshit!" Albrecht roared, no longer able to bear the queen's tirade. "Every bit of it. If Arkady told you that, he's been lying to you since he got back. He didn't come to King Morningkill looking for help; he came in fear. He was a wreck when he first showed up. He begged King Morningkill to take him in. Sure, I wasn't there when it happened, but I've heard the story plenty of times. Arkady was one of Morningkill's bravest warriors after that, but when he first got there, he was a desperate man running for his life."

Queen Tvarivich opened her mouth to protest, but a thought flashed behind her eyes, and she stopped herself.

"Did you see Arkady when he got *back* to Russia?" Albrecht asked. "I bet he was in a pretty sorry state then, too."

"He was dismayed that no help was coming," the queen said without as much conviction as she'd mustered a moment ago. "He despaired."

"I'm telling you, he never asked anybody to send help," Albrecht said. "He did try to take over, though. Right after King Morningkill died, Arkady tried to seize control. That's all true. What he didn't tell you was that *he murdered* Morningkill. He compromised the king's defenses and let an attack force of Black Spiral Dancers right into the caern. They tore Morningkill apart, and that's when Arkady tried to replace him. But before Morningkill died, he revoked my exile. The king's last wish was for me to take over."

"A convenient story, that. He had cast you out himself," Tvarivich said. "Why would he—"

"I guess he suspected," Albrecht said.

"So why the ruse with the crown if Morningkill had named you his successor?" Tvarivich replied.

"Because Arkady challenged me," Albrecht said. "He challenged me to a duel, and then he cheated so

I'd lose. The only recourse I had left was to find the Silver Crown. And as hard as Arkady tried to stop me after that, I did. This isn't a ruse, Tvarivich. I tracked this thing from one end of the Umbra to the other, and I put myself through hell and worse just to touch it. And after all that, Falcon himself judged me worthy to wear it. It's the real thing."

"So you claim," Tvarivich said. "But any pretender would."

"Do you really think Falcon would've let me get away with that... *blasphemy* all this time? I'd get caught, and I'd be worse off then than when I was in exile."

"Perhaps..." Her eyes were still narrow with skepticism, but her anger was fading. "And yet you just let Arkady go back home once you had the crown? I doubt that."

"Oh, I wanted him to die," Albrecht growled. "You were right about that. But more than that, I wanted to punish him. I wanted him to go through what I'd gone through because of him, and I wanted him to know that it was all his own damn fault.

"So I did. I stripped him of everything he had. His honor, his nobility and even his birthright. I banished him from the tribe, and I commanded him to go crawling back where he came from. And just like in all the old legends about the crown, Falcon bound Arkady to my command. That's why he even bothered to come back to you guys at all. His true king commanded him to."

Tvarivich was quiet for a long time. She opened her mouth to speak several times, but she hesitated as doubt gnawed at her long-held belief in Arkady's purity. At last, after several more false starts, she said, "This is only your word. You, like Konietzko, have plenty of reason to envy Arkady and every opportunity to profit from his disgrace."

"God damn it, woman!" Albrecht bellowed. "Are you really that blind? I'm here to remind you of your duty! There's a Wyrm-spirit eating away at us and you're sitting on information out of sheer bullheadedness."

"Don't dare tell me my place, false king!" Tvarivich's words turned to snarls as she rose to her Crinos war-form. Albrecht followed suit without missing a beat and the towering werewolves locked gazes in a challenge for dominance. One that could become an all-out battle at any second.

"Wait!" implored Mephi, interposing himself—still in his lithe Homid form—between the hulking Silver Fangs. "Isn't there a way you could verify some of what Albrecht is saying?"

Albrecht looked down at the Strider and, a beat later, shrank back to Homid. He addressed Tvarivich. "You're a Theurge, right? Ivory Priesthood and all that jazz?"

"Yes…" She remained in Crinos but took a step back.

"Well, what about the Silver Crown? Can you verify its authenticity?"

"Perhaps." She shrunk down to Homid and turned on her heels. "Follow me."

She led them to a clearing just outside her camp, one dominated by a single tree with high branches. Albrecht was no spirit-seer, but he'd had enough dealings with his tribe's totem to recognize Falcon's preferred perching ground when he saw it.

"Kneel," Tvarivich said to Albrecht. She sat at the base of the tree, her back to the trunk and her legs tucked under her. "Do not worry, King, you bow for Falcon, not for me."

"Yeah, whatever you say." He did as he was asked and knelt on one knee. He didn't lower his gaze from the Russian's eyes, though. He watched as she closed her eyes, entering a trance of sorts, and began to speak in Russian. Mephi began to translate, but he waved him to silence. Albrecht knew the words, from the invocations his own Theurges at North Country had performed.

I call to the father of honor and truth, to the great Falcon who soars above all lies. Your children have need of your discerning eye and request your aid.

The high cry of a bird of prey came from the sky above, and before he knew it, Albrecht could feel sharp talons on his shoulders and scalp. Spirit servitors of Falcon Himself flew down from the tree, perching on and around him. It wasn't long before the entire clearing was covered in the silvery birds. At first, they seemed to mill about, but soon they had all oriented themselves toward Albrecht and the crown on his brow. Then, all together, the spirits performed the very unbirdlike act of bowing, their wings spread forward and heads lowered. After a beat they all exploded into flight, like pigeons disturbed while feeding.

The environs took on the solidity of the physical world and Albrecht saw that Tvarivich was staring at him or, more properly, at the crown on his brow. "That truly *is* the Silver Crown. And you… You're its king. *The* king."

"Yeah, I sure am," he said. "Glad we got that cleared up."

"But Arkady…"

"Arkady lied to you."

Mephi stepped forward this time. "Think carefully, Queen Tvarivich," he said. "Arkady survived a journey that none of your bravest soldiers of any auspice had been able to before or since. He must have had help, and we all know what kind I mean. He made some kind of deal with the Wyrm, and from that one moment of weakness follows all the tragedy King Albrecht described. Is it so hard to believe that, when the alternative is so ludicrous?"

"Ludicrous?"

"If you believe Arkady," Mephi explained, "you also have to believe that five perfectly reasonable sept leaders from across this region all conspired to disgrace one of the greatest warriors any of us has ever seen. And for no real reason. *Then*, you have to believe that King Albrecht would come all this way across the ocean from his own protectorate just to lie to your face.

"Which is easier to believe, Your Highness? That one desperate warrior made the wrong decision in a moment of weakness or that some of the brightest luminaries of the Western world want to trick you into believing he did?"

When Mephi finished speaking, Albrecht mentally breathed a sigh of relief. He would have trusted Evan to fly solo like that in his defense, but he had no idea whether the Strider saw things the right way. For an outsider, though, Mephi had probably one of the best objective views Albrecht could have asked for. And it seemed to be having an effect, too. The queen sighed aloud, and her shoulders sagged under a weight of despair and broken faith.

"I don't want to believe you," she whispered. "Arkady is the best of us. How could he betray us? How could he fight so hard to make us believe him and not collapse under the shame of it all?"

"I don't know," Albrecht said. "But he knew his foolish pride had ruined everything. Maybe he was hoping he could start over again if he got far enough away. Or maybe he just hoped that if he threw himself into the fire often enough, he'd eventually get burned up. That's the sort of thing that goes through an exile's mind, anyway. I know."

"Perhaps," Tvarivich sighed. "And now you wish me to bow before his accusers and recant my support for him?"

"Now hold on just a minute," Albrecht said, stepping closer to the queen. "I never came here to pressure you for those pricks. I just wanted you to know the truth about what really happened between Arkady and me, because you deserve to.

"I'm here to get you to put what Arkady told you on the table so we can fight this Jo'cllath'mattric thing like the warriors Gaia made us to be, not bickering politicos. That's the duty I was talking about: not licking Konietzko's ass, but fighting the Wyrm with him.

"Those guys had no right to pass judgment on one of ours without our say-so. You were right about that. But that doesn't even matter, because I'd already branded Arkady a traitor when I banished him from the tribe. That's what made it a reality in Falcon's eyes. That's why Arkady hasn't showed up to defend himself. He knows he can't. It's not our fault it's taken the other tribes so long to get behind us and make it 'official.'"

"Have you said this to the others?" Tvarivich asked, looking a little more confident. "Do they know what you've just told me?"

"Not yet," Albrecht said. "It's more important that word gets out through the tribe first. We all have to get on the same page before we can assume our rightful position leading the Garou Nation again. For the time being, we can let them believe what they want as long as they're on the right track. We've got more important and immediate concerns to deal with, anyway."

"Yes," Tvarivich said solemnly. "Such as telling the council what I have learned about Jo'cllath'mattric."

She seemed to be over the shock of everything Albrecht had told her, and she was coping well.

"Actually, I'll tell you what, Queen Tvarivich," Albrecht said. "Why don't you tell us what Arkady told you first. That way Mephi and I can tell you if anything doesn't jibe with what we know and then we can walk into that council like Silver Fangs ought to: strong and united."

"I don't know," Mephi said. "How do we know we can trust any of what he might have said?"

"I don't see as we have much choice," Albrecht said. "You heard those guys in that council. They've got nothing else to go on, and things aren't getting any better. Even if everything Arkady told Queen Tvarivich is a lie, maybe if we get enough heads thinking about it, we can figure out the real truth behind it. Either way, we can't just assume it's all a lie and keep it to ourselves. We have to take the chance that at least some of it might be true."

"So now we're back to relying on long odds."

"Hey, anything's possible, remember?" Albrecht said.

"All right," Mephi conceded. "Fair enough, I guess. Let's hear it."

"Very well," Tvarivich began. "Keep in mind, of course, that Arkady told me all of this some time ago, before anyone had called his integrity into question, so it was in good faith that I discussed it with him. This occurred when he was visiting my caern in the Ural Mountains for a celebration in honor of our defeat of the Baba Yaga's armies. One morning during his visit, he woke me before dawn, seeking my counsel on a dream he claimed to have had.

"In this dream, he walked in a dark mockery of the Silver Fang Umbral homeland, where he was attacked by winged, serpentine Banes like none he had ever seen, and which matched nothing I had ever heard of, either." Albrecht and Mephi exchanged a look over that but said nothing. "They coiled themselves around him and wounded him, but he slit their bellies open and tore them apart. Yet, as those Banes' carcasses disintegrated in his hands, other spirits were given birth from within them. Not Banes like the serpents, Arkady claimed, but spirit-servants of Falcon."

"No shit?" Albrecht said.

"No. He described these falcon-spirits as decaying and mutilated, as if the Banes had been digesting them, but they were still recognizable, and they could still fly. Once Arkady freed them, they flocked together and flew away across a blasted steppe, over a forest of rotting trees. They called to him in his ancestors' voices, he said. Following them, Arkady eventually found himself at the stagnant moat of an enormous basalt castle with his family's crest inverted above the gate. The gate then lowered for him, and he went inside. Once inside, he followed the sounds of the falcon-spirits' wings through twisting corridors, past confused, wandering ghosts, to the castle's central spiral staircase.

"Arkady climbed the stairs to the roof of the castle's tallest tower, and there the falcon ancestor-spirits circled around him and began to whisper stories of times long past and the caerns at which they took place. As he listened to these stories, some of which he even remembered in waking, Arkady looked down from the tower on a world in miniature that responded to the falcons' whispered words. As the spirits would mention a caern, a light shone from the spot below where that caern was. Soon, the land all around Arkady's castle was aglow with them in a bright matrix of light.

"Yet the shadow of the Wyrm, he told me, fell over many of these caerns as Arkady watched, dimming their light. One by one, all the lights fell into shadow, until they were almost too dim to see. Arkady despaired at this, and he asked the falcon-spirits how he could remove that shadow and alight the caerns again. But the falcon-spirits all turned away from him and told him it was impossible. Then they all lifted higher into the air together and called out, 'The light of hope has gone. Here the forgotten son will remain. Ever here. Forgotten son.' (He remembered that part very well.) The spirits then disappeared into the distance, stranding Arkady atop the tower, until a shadow fell over him from behind. He woke at that point, before he could turn to see what cast it.

"After he did, he tried to dismiss the entire vision as a simple nightmare, but he found blood on his pillow and even more dried on his bedclothes, where the dream-Banes had wounded him. Seeing that, he came to me at once and told me of the dream exactly as he remembered it. It was then that he admitted to me— and perhaps to himself as well—that he had had the same dream on other occasions, although never with such a tactile aftermath.

"Regardless, as a Theurge, I am always intrigued by dreams of Falcon, especially when they appear to members of our tribe. When Arkady told me of his vision, we discussed it at great length, hoping to find some meaning in it. Arkady believed that it was some mental trial Falcon had devised for him to test his faith and resolve, much like the biblical legend of Abraham and Isaac."

"I don't know about *that*…" Mephi said.

"I had never heard of Falcon testing another Silver Fang that way myself," Tvarivich went on, "but a different part of the dream piqued my interest even more than divining its general interpretation. The part concerning the caerns the falcon-spirits revealed to Arkady seemed of especial importance. Some were ones we Garou hold now; others are in the hands of Wyrm-spawn. Some have not been used or even awakened in centuries. Some I had never even heard of. But what I found especially interesting was the fact that the ones I recognized are all in basically the same region of southeastern Europe."

"The Balkans," Albrecht said. Mephi nodded.

Tvarivich did so as well. "As you may already know, many caerns have been lost to us there over the years, to the Weaver and the Wyrm, as well as to simple neglect. And for whatever reason, many of those were the ones Arkady told me he saw in his dream from atop his basalt castle. So, at my urging, we plotted them all out, starting with the ones we knew by name, then triangulating the rest relative to the landmarks Arkady could make out. We worked on it for days, seemingly without pause. When we finished, we had mapped out as many of the caerns' positions as we could and even interpolated almost exactly the position of Arkady's dream vantage relative to his vision of the world in miniature below his tower."

"Why did you do that?" Mephi asked.

"Arkady asked me to," Tvarivich said.

"Okay," Albrecht said. "So you had that. What did you do then?"

"We then turned our minds back to deciphering the dream's general message," Tvarivich said. "As I said, Arkady was convinced that it was a message directly from Falcon, designed to test him. He grew morose and tried to convince me that Falcon had turned his back on him. The fact that the falcon-spirits all abandoned him and kept calling him 'forgotten son' made him believe it. He even claimed to think he deserved it since he had been unable to bring us reinforcements from the West."

"He did deserve it," Albrecht said. "But not because of that. Otherwise, he was dead right."

"So it might seem now," Tvarivich said. "But then, I could not agree with him. I had no reason to. In fact, I blamed you for his failure, Lord Albrecht. But try as I might, I could not convince him that he was blameless.

"Arkady believed that Falcon was offering him some avenue of redemption for his failure. He believed that the dream was a command for him to go to the place he had seen, and that we had mapped out together, which corresponded to a granite mountain in what is now the buffer zone between Kosovo and Serbia."

"AKA, Wyrm country," Mephi said.

"Yes," Tvarivich answered. "He said he felt that if he were to make it to that place, he could commune with Falcon once again and learn what he must do to redeem himself. And by the time he had convinced himself of this, his conviction had affected me as well. I did not think that he was in any need of redemption, but it did seem to me as if Falcon had indeed called out to Arkady and set him on this quest. I wished him luck and offered him any help he needed. All he asked of me was that I keep what he had dreamed a secret until he returned. He did not want to set off a wildfire of paranoia and panic among our tribemates, who considered him the best of all the tribe. Or so he said at the time."

"Because if they knew Falcon had turned his back on Arkady," Albrecht sneered, "they'd freak wondering which one of them was next, right?"

"That was his concern."

"And, of course, he had to do this alone, because he didn't want to take warriors out of the fight back home while he chased his personal demons. I'll just bet he told you something like that."

"He did," Tvarivich confirmed. "You know well how he thinks."

"I just know the type," Albrecht grumbled.

"I see. In any event, when Arkady finally left, he intended to stop briefly at the Sept of the Dawn to attend a relative's Rite of Accomplishment before moving on in earnest. He claimed that he wanted to see Falcon bestow his favor on someone who deserved it one last time before his long journey alone. Yet, it was while he was there that he confronted the Thunderwyrm and condemned himself in others' eyes. No one has heard from him since."

"Right," Albrecht said. "I don't get what any of this has to do with Jo'cllath'mattric, though. They said you knew something about him specifically, but I haven't heard anything like that yet."

"Actually, you have," Mephi said. "Just not as such."

"What? When?"

"Perhaps you should explain," Tvarivich said with a small nod to Mephi.

"Sure." He turned to Albrecht and said, "When I was here last at the Tisza Hellhole, I witnessed some Black Spiral Dancers performing a ritual. I didn't work it all out until later, but they were using it to try to break Jo'cllath'mattric out of his prison by snapping the bonds that are holding him down. And the whole time they were doing it, they were calling Jo'cllath'mattric the 'Forgotten Son.'"

A light went on in Albrecht's mind, and he took a long deep breath. "And that's what those spirits were saying in Arkady's dream. The forgotten son is right here. They weren't talking about Arkady; they were talking about Jo'cllath'mattric."

"I heard the story about Mephi Faster-than-Death's mission into the Tisza Hellhole for the first time when Konietzko sent his runners to invite as many sept leaders as would come to follow him and work with him here at Night Sky. As the runner told me the story of the margrave's efforts thus far, I recognized not only the name of the Owl's Rest Caern—which was one of the ones in Arkady's dream—but the name Forgotten Son as well."

"And you figured," Albrecht said, "maybe it wasn't Falcon who'd called Arkady after all."

"Yes," Tvarivich said. "It occurred to me that, in his self-reproach, Arkady had allowed himself to be tricked, and that he had been walking toward a trap."

"But wasn't this after the whole Anvil-Klaiven deal?" Albrecht said. "Didn't it occur to you that maybe Arkady had known all along who it was that called out to him?"

"It did," Tvarivich said. "But I refused to indulge those thoughts. Instead, I came to fear for Arkady's safety. I knew that the council's ruling would send him into hiding, but I feared that he would continue to make his way to his destination, never realizing what danger might be waiting for him. And it's for that reason that I came here and made my demands to the margrave's new council. I had hoped that by leveraging my knowledge against the Anvil-Klaiven ruling, I could draw Arkady back into the open."

"With a new trial," Mephi said.

"Yes. Where he could clear his name and I could warn him about the peril he had almost faced unawares. He could then renew his quest, but this time with an army behind him. Perhaps then he would no longer doubt himself and his faith in Falcon would be restored. That was my desire from the beginning."

"I hate to say it, Queen Tvarivich," Albrecht said, "but it doesn't look like that's going to happen any time soon. Arkady went bad a long time before he started having these dreams. Matter of fact, that's probably why he started having them in the first place."

"Maybe," Tvarivich said quietly. "That may be."

For a long moment, none of them spoke, and Tvarivich's breathing a heavy sigh of disappointment was the only sound. Albrecht knew what she must be going through inside. Thinking about King Morningkill had made him sigh like that in the early days of his exile, once the anger at the injustice of it all had worn off. But, for Gaia's sake, she'd known where Jo'cllath'mattric was all this time, and she hadn't *told* anybody?

"I've been foolish not to share what I know," Tvarivich said at last. "I see that now. I should not have withheld it from the others, regardless of how I thought I could use it to help Arkady. But knowing how unworthy of my help he has been from the beginning, how can I go back now and face them?"

"You can because it's the honorable thing to do," Albrecht said. "You have to. Sometimes, you've got to admit you made a mistake and take your lumps for it. That's just the way it goes. Then everybody gets over it, and the war goes on. And if those guys in there *can't* get over it, well…"

"The hell with them," Mephi finished.

"Yeah," Albrecht grinned. "What he said."

"Very well," Tvarivich said. "I will speak to them, as honor demands, and tell them what I know."

"Good," Albrecht said. "Better late than never. The margrave wants to reconvene the council tomorrow afternoon for another go-'round of planning, and I'm pretty sure that what you're bringing to the table is going to blow them away."

"I will be ready," Tvarivich said a little sadly.

Chapter Seven

It was roughly one o'clock local time the next day before Albrecht actually joined the margrave and the other sept leaders in council again. Throwing the doors open, he walked into the room with Tvarivich one step behind him on his left and Mephi one step farther back on the right.

The chamber looked more or less as Albrecht expected it would. Houndstooth, Slow-to-Anger, Swift-As-the-River, Dawntreader and Konietzko were all in there standing around the large table in the center of the room. Fewer of the warriors and advisors who'd helped fill the room last time were here, though. Those who were missing, Albrecht figured, were either exercising with Konietzko's soldiers, touring the fortress or still hanging out with their own at their campsites.

Everyone looked up at their sudden entrance, and thankfully, less annoyed impatience greeted his arrival today than yesterday. The others looked fresh and eager now, and a little more ready to listen. They were also eyeing Queen Tvarivich with surprise and a look that could have been a hint of grudging respect. The impression lasted for only an instant, but it was a more dignified reception than Albrecht had gotten last time.

"Lord Albrecht," Konietzko said in English as Mephi closed the door behind him. "We have already begun. Please join us."

Albrecht, Tvarivich and Mephi made their way to the table, and the other leaders made room for them.

"It seems that you were more successful than any of us anticipated," Konietzko continued. "Queen Tvarivich, we are surprised that you have decided to join us at last."

Sergiy Dawntreader echoed the sentiment with good humor, and the others made noises ranging from noncommittal grunts to sighs of bleak acceptance. Swift-As-the-River and Guy Houndstooth seemed the least thrilled.

"What does she want now?" Swift-As-the-River growled.

"Have you come to discuss your terms in person, Tvarivich?" Houndstooth asked, crossing his arms over his chest and glowering at the queen. "I'm sorry, but we don't have time for more games."

"No more games," Tvarivich answered in Houndstooth's native German. "We're here now in the spirit of alliance and honest cooperation. As we should have been from the beginning."

"Indeed," Konietzko said with even more surprise. "Then you are willing to abide by the Anvil-Klaiven council's ruling?"

"That ruling no longer matters," Tvarivich said, serenely and in English. "The danger posed by the Wyrm-beast Jo'cllath'mattric outweighs any other concerns. King Albrecht has discussed this matter with me, and we are in agreement."

"That's right," Albrecht said slowly enough for the translators around the room to keep up. "And the three of us are still here to help."

"Of course," Helena Slow-to-Anger said with a sweetly venomous smile. "You want to do your part. You have done yours, Lord Albrecht, and now, thanks to some providential reversal, young Queen Tvarivich wants to as well."

"I do," Tvarivich said, refusing to rise to Slow-to-Anger's sardonic bait. "I was wrong not to."

"Then please, Queen Tvarivich," Dawntreader said, as murmurs of surprise orbited the table. "We would all like to know what you considered so vital to our efforts that we would change our judgment of a traitor to hear it."

"Did she already tell you what was so important, Albrecht?" Houndstooth sneered. "Silver Fang to Silver Fang."

Albrecht was inclined to let Tvarivich keep handling these sniping ingrates herself, but even still, he had to resist the urge to give Houndstooth the finger. Or a bloody nose.

"I have," Tvarivich answered. "But I prefer to share what I learned from Arkady with the entire council, rather than only one of its individual members. Even King Albrecht."

As Tvarivich swept her gaze around the room to stare down any challenges to her assertion, Albrecht found himself locking gazes with Konietzko across the table. The margrave's canny eyes peered into him, mining for any weakness of character or spirit, gazing into him unflinchingly. Albrecht felt rage bubble deep inside him at the audacity of this old man—this Shadow Lord—but he kept his cool and gave Konietzko's appraising look right back. At last, the margrave inclined his head a fraction of an inch to the side.

"Of course, Queen Tvarivich," he said. "Now, if you please, tell us what you know."

Queen Tvarivich did just that, relating to the assembled almost verbatim what she had told Albrecht and Mephi the night before. She recounted Arkady's dream and the decision she believed he had made regarding it. She then told them what she had put together later on, and her motivations for her subsequent actions. She had to stop more often to answer questions from her larger audience, but inside of an hour, she had told them everything she had been withholding since her arrival. She then went on to produce a map she had made of the region based on Arkady's information and her own extrapolations from it. She laid it out on the table among the charts of Wyrm infestation and Umbral storm activity that the various sept leaders' scouts had created over the past months.

"There," she said at last, indicating a mountain in the center of the diagram she'd drawn. "This, I believe, is the physical link to where Jo'cllath'mattric was imprisoned in the spirit world, based on everything Arkady told me and what I have deduced since."

"How convenient that Arkady would give you just enough to figure out just what we needed," Helena Slow-to-Anger sneered, earning an approving nod from Guy Houndstooth. "Everything you've pieced together is based on information rooted in that traitor's lies. How can you expect us to trust any of it? How can *you* trust any of it?"

"All these maps and charts confirm what I have discovered," Tvarivich said, picking up several papers and flipping through them. "They all show that Banes are massing around these mountains in greater numbers than ever before. And these Umbral storms you've been tracking appear to be moving in the same direction. The evidence seems to support what I've said."

"All *I* see is evidence of the making of an ambush," Guy Houndstooth said. "One orchestrated by Arkady himself and set to commence with you relating his lies to us. However innocently."

"Did it ever occur to any of you that these Wyrm-spawn are massing in this region because they've been trying to find this place, too?" Albrecht said. "I mean, look at everything they've been doing over here lately. They know Jo'cllath'mattric's around here somewhere, and they're trying to dig it up before we even know to look for it. Now, don't get me wrong. I do believe Arkady was lying to Queen Tvarivich, but I know he isn't *that* good a liar. He would have kept any lie he told simple and as close to the truth as possible."

"Perhaps," Dawntreader conceded. "But where was the lie, and what should we believe?"

"Well, for starters, I believe that dream he told Queen Tvarivich about happened just like he said it did," Albrecht said. "I think he saw those caerns and was supposed to infer where his position was relative to them just like he did. I even think he saw the shadow of the Wyrm like he claims. But I think there was more to the dream than he said. I think in the end when that shadow fell over him, he didn't just wake up in a cold sweat. I think he saw what it was that sent that dream to him, and I bet he talked to it. I bet it wanted him or needed him somehow, so it called to him the only way it could. And when it called, Arkady went to go find it."

"Possible," Houndstooth agreed with a wicked grin. "It would not be the first time Arkady consorted with minions of the Wyrm."

"It's still too easy," Swift-As-the-River barked in the High Tongue, thumping his knuckles on the table in irritation. "It's a trap."

"I'm sorry, Queen Tvarivich, Lord Albrecht," Dawntreader said. "I'm inclined to agree. Arkady could have given this information with the intention of then faking his own disappearance in the course of 'investigating' it. Then, since he was so renowned and prominent a figure, surely the best of his comrades would rush into this Wyrm-contaminated region to determine his fate. Only to meet their own by his devising."

"A ruse he could have perpetuated potentially without end," Helena Slow-to-Anger said. "Sacrificing his would-be rescuers to his newfound master until Jo'cllath'mattric's rebirth into the world."

"Except that a certain incident outside my protectorate got in his way," Dawntreader finished. "The one that exposed his treachery to us prematurely and forced our hand at Anvil-Klaiven."

"Or maybe," Albrecht said grudgingly, "Arkady knew what he was getting into, and he was trying to warn us. He didn't give us everything he could have to completely double-cross the Wyrm, but he gave us just enough to figure out what we needed to for ourselves. Maybe he had just that much honor left in him at the end. *Maybe*."

"So even as he sold his soul," Slow-to-Anger said, "some lingering vesper of it cried out for redemption? How romantic."

"I don't know," Albrecht admitted. "None of us can really know for sure. But if the possibility's there, you can't just ignore it out of hand. I'm living proof of that."

"So the story goes," Houndstooth said. "But those concerns aren't why we came here. We came here to take what we know and decide what to do based on it. So let's decide. What will we do with this new information laid out before us?"

All eyes turned in Konietzko's direction for an answer to that, rankling Albrecht. Only Tvarivich had the courtesy to look his way first. Even Mephi automatically deferred to the margrave.

"The simple truth," the margrave said after his long, thoughtful silence, "is that, despite Queen Tvarivich's revelations, we still have no more hard evidence than we did. We have traitor-dreams, speculation and inference, but no solid facts. Even if everything we've just learned is completely reliable, the best we can do now is organize a reconnaissance mission and send it into—"

"No!" Albrecht shouted, drawing all eyes his way. The margrave actually flinched in surprise. "You've already lost too many people trying that. I didn't come all the way here to sit on my ass while you throw away even more perfectly good warriors a handful at a time just to confirm what we're telling you we already know." He stabbed his finger down onto the map Queen Tvarivich had opened on the table and rose into his Glabro form to address everyone in the High Tongue. "Jo'cllath'mattric is here. The forces of the Wyrm have been converging around this mountain, looking for him. If we give them any more time, they're going to find him, and they're going to set him free. Do you understand me? That can't happen. I won't allow it. And if any of you love Gaia enough to fight for Her, you won't allow it, either. This is your damned duty I'm talking about, and I'm sick of you all ignoring it!"

Silence descended in the wake of that proclamation, and dumbfounded expressions ringed the table. The only exception was the margrave's face. For the first time, Albrecht saw true emotion there, and it was seething, indignant outrage. Albrecht knew this look very well. It was the last expression he had ever seen on his great-grandfather's face, and it burned in his memory, trying to leach his nerve. This same anger had filled King Morningkill's eyes the afternoon he'd finally snapped and exiled Albrecht from North Country. The old man had just sat there on his throne that day, surrounded by his court, daring Albrecht not to back down. Daring him to say one more word and cross the point of no return—which Albrecht had. It was the look of a king who will not be challenged at the foot of his own throne.

But now, as then, Albrecht refused to be intimidated. Just as he'd challenged his old king so many years ago, he did not back down now from Konietzko. Barking at Morningkill had been nothing but headstrong arrogance, of course, but he'd learned how to pick his battles since then. This time, he knew he was right, and he couldn't cave in. Too much was riding on it. Besides, Albrecht told himself, Margrave Konietzko was not King Morningkill; Morningkill was dead. Neither man had any power over him other than what he gave them himself.

And as they stared at each other, it appeared that Margrave Konietzko recognized this conviction in Albrecht. At last, the skin around his eyes tightened and the corner of his mouth rose a fraction of an inch.

"You are right, Lord Albrecht," he said slowly. "Perhaps we have been overcautious. Perhaps we are hesitating when we should be acting. No longer, then. We have a duty to Gaia to keep Jo'cllath'mattric from going free. We are obligated to do everything in our power to fulfill that duty."

"Damn right," Albrecht said. "And we need to get started right away."

"Then we shall," Konietzko said. He then turned and looked at everyone else in the room with one sweeping glance. "I recommend everyone gather the warriors who accompanied you, prepare them for battle and assemble them on the bawn below the fortress. When they are assembled, return here so that we may begin planning our offensive. It seems the time has come, at last, to take this battle to the enemy."

All around the table, eyes glowed with eagerness, and warriors wore predatory smiles. This was the sort of news they had been waiting for. This was why they had come to begin with. They'd come to fight, and now it was finally time.

"All right," Albrecht said. "Now we're talking."

***

"A moment of your time, Lord Albrecht," Margrave Konietzko said a few minutes later as the councilors left to prepare their soldiers as he had recommended. "I would speak to you."

Albrecht had no soldiers of his own to address as such, but he'd intended to accompany Tvarivich back to her campsite. When Konietzko called him, he stopped, waved on Mephi and Tvarivich—who'd stopped with him—and held his position by the door as the other sept leaders and auxiliary werewolves filed out. In another moment, only he and the margrave were left together. Even then, the room still felt small and cramped.

"What is it?" Albrecht asked, hooking his thumbs in his pockets. He and Konietzko stared at each other across the cluttered table.

"Those things you said just now," the margrave replied with deliberation. "It has been some time since a Silver Fang dared speak to me thus. It has been even longer since *anyone* has lectured me about my duty to Gaia."

Albrecht kept his own counsel on that. The only things he could think to say in response were things that had earned him sharp looks from Evan and Mari in the past.

"I want you to know," the margrave continued, "that this time—this *one* time—is quite enough."

"I hear you," Albrecht said with an almost-smirk. "I figured it would be, too."

And with that, he turned on his heel and left the margrave alone in the audience chamber.

***

Albrecht caught up with Mephi and Tvarivich outside a few minutes later, halfway back to Tvarivich's camp. Mephi was the first to hear him as he jogged up to them, and they both stopped to meet him.

"Trouble inside?" Mephi asked.

"Not hardly," Albrecht grunted. "Just some friendly encouragement between allies."

"Uh-huh," Mephi replied.

Albrecht shrugged. "Before we get back to the campsite, though, I need to talk to Queen Tvarivich alone for a second."

"Sure," Mephi said. "I'll go on ahead and tell your people you're coming."

Albrecht nodded, and Mephi jogged off away from them.

"What is it, King Albrecht?" Tvarivich said as they started walking again, side by side. "Is something wrong?"

"Maybe not right now," Albrecht said, looking straight ahead, rather than down at her. "But something you said last night got me thinking. Something Arkady said, too, before I sent him back to Russia. He told me I had no idea what it was like over there. That I didn't know the Hag's power."

"It defied description," Tvarivich said, scowling at the memory of it.

"Yeah. And last night, you made it sound like you were counting on some help from outside to deal with it. You said we betrayed you because we never sent any."

Queen Tvarivich shook her head. "Those were Arkady's lies. I thought you had consciously chosen to abandon us."

"Still," Albrecht said. "I used to wonder why Arkady was the only one to ever make it out of there in one piece, and only then because he'd consorted with the enemy. I couldn't imagine how bad it really must have been for you."

"If you still wonder, our Galliards can tell you many stories. Would you like to hear some before we leave?"

"No," Albrecht said, stuffing his hands into his jacket pockets. "That isn't why I brought this up. I brought it up because all I ever did was wonder. I never *did* anything about it or got personally involved. But now—"

"Now you are here," Tvarivich said, looking away into the distance.

"Exactly," Albrecht said. "I'm here because I've got a personal stake in this. One of my packmates is down. Arkady's involved. I had to come. But when you guys needed help in Russia, I didn't see it as my fight like now." He paused, took a deep breath and said, "I guess what I'm trying to say is I'm—"

"Don't," Tvarivich said, coming to a stop and crossing her arms under her cloak. "What could I say in reply, King Albrecht? That I understand? That it doesn't matter because we eventually found victory on our own? That a king should not have to apologize to his subjects in the first place?"

"Not unless you think any of it's true," Albrecht said, trying not to sound too hopeful.

"Good, because I do not," Tvarivich replied. "We needed your help, and it never came. Many Silver Fangs died who might have been saved. I cannot forgive you for that. That kind of absolution can only come from Falcon himself. In time."

"So what about until then?" Albrecht said. "What do we do?"

"You and I?" Tvarivich asked. "Our duty. That's all we can do. The war goes on regardless."

"Yeah," Albrecht said. "I guess it does."

Chapter Eight

Several hours later, all the sept leaders returned from the fortress to address the men and women assembled on the rocky plain outside. Of the almost sixty warriors chosen for the offensive, one-third of them were the margrave's soldiers. Houndstooth and Tvarivich had supplied the next two largest groups, and the rest had come with Slow-to-Anger, Swift-As-the-River and Dawntreader. They mingled while awaiting their leaders' return but stayed near their traveling gear and weapons so that they'd be ready to deploy at a moment's notice. When those leaders at last made their way through the middle of the group, the soldiers quieted down and made ready to listen.

Margrave Konietzko walked in the lead, carrying a large roll of paper that was wound onto two long metal poles like a scroll. The other leaders followed him single file and arrayed themselves around him when he finally came to a stop before the assembled warriors. He unrolled the paper and stuffed the poles into the hard-packed earth. There displayed was a topographical map of southeastern Serbia. Near the center of it was marked the location Queen Tvarivich had provided, and two more locations were marked to the north and south of it as well. When the map was arranged as he wanted it, Konietzko turned to the warriors and spoke.

"For some time," he began, "we have known that this region crawls with the spawn of the Wyrm. Many of you have followed me in raids against the fringes of this massing evil, yet the Wyrm-spawn never stop coming. Long-range reconnaissance deeper into this region has proven ineffectual and costly in comrade blood. And all the while, the reason the enemy masses here has been a mystery."

Angry grumbles from the audience followed this pronouncement.

"But at last," the margrave went on, "we have solved this mystery. Through combined efforts, we have uncovered a heretofore-unknown spiritual presence hidden in these mountains—" he touched the map where the middle mark was "—that has been imprisoned since time immemorial. The name of this spirit is Jo'cllath'mattric. We have seen evidence over these last months that it is awakening and that its prison is weakening, which has directly inspired the rise in Wyrm-spawn. These servants of evil are looking for an access to Jo'cllath'mattric's hidden Umbral prison with the intent of freeing him and unleashing him on an unsuspecting world."

Many of the grumbles turned into full-throated growls.

"It is, therefore, the decision of this allied council that we take the initiative and attack before our enemies do so. We know that our enemies' ultimate destination is here—" he indicated the center mark on the map again "—and that this mountain is the key point in an extensive prison ward binding Jo'cllath'mattric safely away. Taking control here is necessary to maintain the integrity of that ward. Therefore, we will storm this region in force, break through our enemies' ranks and establish a strong defense, such that the enemy cannot break Jo'cllath'mattric free. This is our overall objective."

As the warriors took that in, the margrave turned to Guy Houndstooth, who stepped forward with arms akimbo. His warriors cheered lightly, and he nodded to them.

"This is no easy task," the Swiss werewolf said when he had everyone's attention. "Wyrm-spawn are thick where we are going. There are no clear lines of approach or supply, and we can expect no reinforcement once we are fully deployed. What is more, we have no stable moon bridges established into any tenable stronghold in the contested area. Yet, moving a force even our size overland would attract the notice of not only Wyrm-spawn but of Serbian troops, the KLA and UN peacekeepers. Thus, we will stage our forces at a recently recovered Shadow Lord caern in Szeged." He pointed to the northernmost mark on the map, up in southern Hungary. "From there, Margrave Konietzko, Queen Tvarivich and Helena Slow-to-Anger will coerce captured Lunes into opening temporary moon bridges for us. We will take these bridges in two waves to the foothills here and here." As he continued, he touched the map to indicate the locations he was talking about. "Our objective is somewhere within this mountain. Queen Tvarivich speculates that there is a caern somewhere within it anchoring Jo'cllath'mattric's prison. We must find our way into that caern and seize it. Geographical data suggests that a series of caves leads underneath from this point, so we will open our moon bridges into this valley leading up to it and begin our search there. If that effort proves fruitless, we will regroup and start sending search parties up the sides to investigate the mountain's summit." Houndstooth paused and turned to Konietzko, "Margrave."

"Thank you." Konietzko stepped forward once again. "We have little further tactical information on the enemies' strengths and weaknesses on this battlefield. We have examined the terrain, the climate and the Umbral conditions for their most accurate strategic significance, but we do not know if the enemy has had time to establish defenses or is still searching the area with an attack force. In the former case, we must break through and rout them from the field. In the latter, we must establish a strong defense at once before the enemy can attack. In either case, we must move immediately, as any further delay only adds to our enemies' advantage."

The margrave paused to let that sink in, then carried on gravely.

"As you all know, you are the only warriors who can be spared from the defense of our other important holdings around this region. There will be no reinforcement or avenue of retreat. It is up to us to keep the enemy from freeing this great beast, even if some of us must give our lives to do it. But if we are brave and strong and have faith in Gaia, we will succeed. We will have victory. We will kill our enemies, and we will live to fight another day in Gaia's name."

Applause broke out at that, and Red Talons and other wolf-born Garou howled their assent. The margrave smiled, pleased at the zeal growing in his audience. He turned to Albrecht and nodded once. Albrecht nodded back then looked at the audience himself.

"All right, ladies and gentlemen," he said to them. "Let's do this. We've all waited long enough."

Chapter Nine

"How is this possible?" Gashwrack demanded of the metis scout cringing before him. He grabbed a fistful of the malformed bastard's shirt in each hand and all but shook him in agitation. "This place has been lost for centuries. How did they find it so quickly after us? Is there a traitor in the ranks? A spy? If there is, I'll—"

"Does it matter?" Bile-Claw said, staring into the void just in front of his feet. He and the two others stood in the heart chamber of the Forgotten Son's prison caern. His arms were crossed, and he wasn't looking at Gashwrack at all. He appeared to be staring into the Abyss-pit, as if looking for a reflection there. He'd been organizing the connection of moon bridges from here to allied hives all week, and the puckered, sphincterlike orifices that stood in midair all around the perimeter of the void testified to his work. He was now gathering strength anew for his ritual to attack the chains of the Forgotten Son's prison. "I don't see how knowing that would help."

"It matters to me!" Gashwrack shouted, shoving the metis to the floor and turning toward Bile-Claw. "I told Arastha this place would be safe. I told her it would be secure."

"Arastha wasn't worried about our enemies finding this place, Gashwrack," Bile-Claw said. "Remember? Maybe she trusts you."

"Yes," the scout said from the floor. "There's nothing to worry about. There aren't even that many on—"

"Nothing to worry about?" Gashwrack shouted. "They know we're here! They're looking for us, and more may be on the way."

"But we have plenty of Guardians," the metis whined. "We're well defended."

"Then you tell the Guardians to make ready!" Gashwrack screamed. "*Now!* An attack is coming! I promised Arastha this place would be safe, and it will! They will not get inside!"

The metis scurried out without even replying, leaving Gashwrack shaking and clamping his hands into fists at his sides. When the metis was gone, Bile-Claw turned to face him at last. The Theurge's amber eyes deep in his shadowy hood seemed amused.

"Is her opinion so important to you?" he asked. "She represents but one head of the hydra in one hive. Why do you care for her so much?"

Gashwrack shuddered and boiled into his brutish Glabro form, seemingly without realizing it. He charged over and got in Bile-Claw's face. "It isn't about her!" he screamed. "It's about what she promised me!"

Bile-Claw tilted his head casually, then said, "Ah, your sacrifice. I forgot."

"Arastha promised," Gashwrack spat. "I will not be denied it by weak, deluded fools who think they're saving the world."

"Ones who don't share your enlightenment," Bile-Claw said. "Of course not."

"And I will not be mocked," Gashwrack growled. "Don't make me kill you before your allies get here to help you perform your vaunted ritual."

"Don't threaten me, Gashwrack," Bile-Claw said. "You know well what Arastha would do to you."

Gashwrack backed off then, grinding his teeth and flexing his short Glabro claws. "Then get into the pathstone chamber and get to work," he said. "Don't give me reason to test her forgiveness. Do what you must and wake the Forgotten Son. For all our sakes."

"Don't worry," Bile-Claw said. "The time has almost come. When I am but a little more rested, and the others have arrived, we will begin."

***

Albrecht was the last to emerge from the moon bridge from Szeged, and a riot of noise pressed in on him from all sides when he did. And along with the noise, a storm gale carrying a vicious Wyrm-thing with it hit him in the back. Even though he was already in Glabro form, the impact spun him around and pitched him down a steep ridge so that he caught only glimpses of the terrain. Livid clouds roiled in the night sky. The ground was already bloodstained and claw marred. Banes thronged, and winged serpents dodged through the sky.

Albrecht tumbled through the chaos for a second then grew into his huge Crinos war-form. He dug his claws into the rocky ground and skidded safely to a halt. The Wyrm-creature that hit him —a spine-covered thing called a Scrag—slid a few feet down the incline itself then leapt at him. In one motion, Albrecht rose to his feet, drew his grand klaive Solemn Lord from his belt and jammed its point right through the monstrosity's face. The thing stopped with a wet, satisfying crunch and dropped to the ground.

Albrecht pulled Solemn Lord free and wiped the Bane's spirit-gore out of his eyes to get his bearings. Contrary to his expectations, he discovered, the moon bridge had dumped him into the Penumbra rather than the physical world. Yet, before he could wonder why, he heard a howl for succor from one of his warriors over the next hill, and he rushed off in that direction to help. When he reached the top, he surprised a knot of houndlike Ooralath Banes that were tearing at the unfortunate werewolf who'd called for help.

Before the Banes even turned his way, Albrecht leapt into the middle of them, swinging Solemn Lord and snapping his own massive jaw. He chopped two of them into oblivion before the others knew he was coming, and he broke another's neck with his jaws before any of them could attack. Another one of the dog-things jumped on him then from his blind side, but he rolled on his shoulders and flipped it into the air with his feet. As he came up into a four-point crouch, the Bane collided with its only remaining fellow, and both went down in a heap. Albrecht bolted forward and skewered the pair of them.

As they disintegrated and the pieces of their armored bodies disappeared into the storm, Albrecht checked the werewolf the Banes had been attacking. The victim was a woman named Ilanya Silverfoot, one of the first of Konietzko's people. She lay flat on her back in a pool of blood, split open from sternum to crotch. Her mouth and eyes were wide open, and the storm winds whipped the ragged ends of her savaged flesh. She was already shrinking into her breed form, the werewolf's equivalent of a death rattle. He reluctantly backed away and spotted a knot of his fellow Silver Fangs coming together in the lee of a high ridge. No other werewolves were anywhere in sight. He joined the Fangs, and they formed a quick defensive ring for mutual strength against the storm. Queen Tvarivich was among them, also in her Crinos form.

"What the hell happened?" Albrecht shouted over the storm. "How did we end up here?"

"This was the best the Lunes could do through the storm," Tvarivich answered.

"Well, how far are we from where we're supposed to be? Which way is it?"

"That way," Tvarivich said, pointing with her mace, which dripped some sort of blue gore. "It's not far."

"Then let's go."

The Russian nodded and relayed the directions to the others. They hunched together and moved in the direction Tvarivich had indicated. They fended off a few lone Banes that dropped down on them from above, and made a long, curving trek through the Penumbral hills. Eventually, though, they knew they could go no farther thus against the mounting fury of the storm. So they stopped, and Albrecht and Tvarivich peered across the Gauntlet into the physical world.

Relative to the physical world, they now were about two hundred yards from the high granite mountain that Tvarivich's information said hid Jo'cllath'mattric's prison caern. More immediately, however, they were just on the edge of a ravine between two tall foothills, in which a pitched battle was raging. A force of Black Spiral Dancers and several packs of fomori and materialized Banes were swarming over the rocky expanse like maggots on a corpse. The warriors who'd already arrived—mostly soldiers who'd accompanied the margrave's guests from their respective septs—were scattered and fighting poorly, as if reacting to a surprise attack. Individual packs defended themselves well enough in the short term, but the Wyrm-spawn were more numerous and more coordinated. The enemy was driving the isolated knots of invading Garou farther from each other. If they kept at it, the Wyrm-spawn were going to win the field then fall back into a position of strength closer to the mountain. Albrecht would be damned if he'd let that happen. He rose to his full Crinos height and held Solemn Lord up in front of him for everyone around him to see.

"Spirits of war, sharpen my blade," he howled over the volume of the storm. Some of the Silver Fangs standing near him echoed him. "Spirits of Luna, sharpen my claws and grant me your protection. Mother Gaia, let your wrath live in me."

The spirits he invoked awoke and responded one by one, granting King Albrecht and many of his warriors the blessings they'd asked for. Then, when it was done, Albrecht and the Silver Fangs vanished from the spirit world.

Albrecht was the first to appear in the physical world seconds later, and people noticed. Solemn Lord shone bright in his right hand, seeming to vibrate in excitement. His left hand was tipped with five long silver claws that reflected the lightning in the sky. He was clad in what appeared to be a suit of gossamer-thin plate armor, which seemed to be made of silvery moonlight and weigh nothing. He took a step forward and roared, shaking the stones with the power of his fury. Lightning struck somewhere nearby, and the crash of thunder echoed his call to battle as more warriors materialized around him.

Chapter Ten

Gashwrack rushed into the caern's heart chamber and found five men in black robes like Bile-Claw's, all kneeling at the edges of the Abyss-pit and chanting monotonously. The Theurges had arrived shortly after the attack started, and they'd begun their ritual immediately. Now their words echoed in the pit, and the moon bridge portals seemed to quiver in syncopation.

"What is it?" one of the figures asked. Gashwrack couldn't tell which one.

"Where is Bile-Claw?" Gashwrack demanded.

"With the pathstone," another of the Theurges answered.

Gashwrack hurried around the chamber's perimeter to the antechamber opposite the way he'd entered, where he found Bile-Claw within, bending over the basin with the pathstone in it. With utmost care, he was placing extremely thin glass rods across the basin in a complicated pattern that resembled the Forgotten Son's prison ward. Gashwrack remembered the design well.

Without looking back, Bile-Claw asked, "Yes, Gashwrack?"

"I came to check on your progress," Gashwrack said. "How close are you to being finished?"

"I have only just begun," Bile-Claw answered. "My allies are calling on the Forgotten Son's servitors now to attend their master when he emerges."

"We're under attack, you realize," Gashwrack said. "How long will this take?"

"The Umbral storm is helping fray the chains," Bile-Claw said, "but I can only break them one by one as the ritual permits. It takes time."

"We have no time!"

"Don't worry," Bile-Claw answered. "As I break specific chains, the entire pattern will weaken. In time, the unbalanced forces will do our work for us. But until then, the energies I must channel require delicate control. If you must monitor my progress, do so in silence. I must concentrate."

"Just see that it's done," Gashwrack said, turning to leave. "And quickly, before the whole Garou Nation gets here."

***

Albrecht rushed onto the battlefield, and an entire pack of Black Spiral Dancers broke from its position in the center to meet him halfway. Although they were fierce Ahroun warriors, he knocked one aside with his silver claws and batted down the next with Solemn Lord like they were cubs. The Silver Fangs right behind him pounced on the Spirals as they fell. Three more Spirals encircled him and alternated trying to tear away his defenses, but the armor Luna had granted him turned aside their claws. Albrecht hacked at their arms and slashed them with his claws as they came close. One switched to Hispo and tried to bowl him over, but he shoulder-rolled across its back and chopped the legs out from under its packmate. A vertical backhand slash of his silver claws gutted the next Spiral, and Tvarivich charged in behind him to crush the one in Hispo form's skull as it started to charge again. Albrecht howled out orders as the five Black Spiral Dancers landed all around him, spasming, whimpering and sinking into their birth forms. The other Silver Fangs acknowledged his commands and followed him toward their embattled allies.

The first soldiers they made it to were those surrounding Guy Houndstooth. They had surrounded the Theurges who were commanding the materialized Banes, but they were having trouble finishing them off. Albrecht joined them and chopped down a Psychomachia from behind. On the other side of the nightmare-Bane, Houndstooth had his jaw clamped on the throat of a thrashing Black Spiral Dancer. His back was to Albrecht and he wouldn't have seen the Psychomachia until it was too late. As Albrecht approached him, Houndstooth looked around with a bloody muzzle and rose to his feet. Before either could say anything, another Dancer collapsed between them, his skull caved in by Tvarivich's mace.

"To the center of the ravine!" Albrecht commanded, pointing with Solemn Lord. "Fight your way across!"

Without waiting for a verbalized agreement, Albrecht pulled another Spiral off one of Houndstooth's men and broke its back over Solemn Lord's edge. The warrior returned the favor immediately by taking up the fetish halberd he'd dropped and spitting a Bane that had been charging up from Albrecht's blind side. Albrecht batted the screaming thing off the end of the halberd then helped the prostrate warrior to his feet. They then separated to help other comrades as Houndstooth howled the order that Albrecht had given him. As one, his soldiers and Albrecht's carved up the rest of their immediate enemies and began to push their way to the opposite side of the narrow valley.

Diametrically across the battlefield, Sergiy Dawntreader's soldiers were dropping quickly. Only the enormous Child of Gaia seemed to be having any luck holding his ground, but as huge and powerful as he was in relation to the pack of Ooralaths that was harrying him, he still looked like a baited bear. He stood before the grievously wounded bodies of a pack of his warriors, bobbing and weaving and twisting as quickly as a mongoose despite his size. Although he had no opportunity to attack any of them, the Banes around him could not take him down to get to any of his wounded men. Some of them broke off as more of Dawntreader's other warriors fell, but he was still forced to hold off too many for even one so powerful as he.

When it seemed that Dawntreader couldn't possibly take any more, the Silver Fangs and Houndstooth's soldiers crashed into the Ooralath pack from behind. Free to cut loose at last, Dawntreader hit the smallest Bane in front of him so hard that it flew over the heads of his saviors and broke its back on a rock. After that vicious blow, dispatching the rest of them was short work. In the sudden lull that fell around them, several warriors of Houndstooth's and Dawntreader's now-combined force started to relax and try to catch their breath.

"The Red Talons are falling!" Tvarivich shouted at them before their blood had any chance to cool.

"This way!" Albrecht said.

The warriors howled and did as he said without question. Even Houndstooth and Dawntreader obeyed. As one, they all converged on the spot where Swift-As-the-River and his remaining Red Talon comrades were fighting desperately for their lives. The Black Furies surrounding Helena Slow-to-Anger took up Albrecht's orders as well and fought their way to the Talons' side. The last of the Wyrm-spawn on the field found themselves surrounded in short order, and they died before they knew just how completely the tide of battle had turned.

Quiet settled over the field after that, broken only by the low whimpers and moans of the wounded. Albrecht ordered the warriors around him to "make sure," and they spread out all over the battlefield, finishing off any Black Spiral Dancers who weren't quite dead yet. They then started helping wounded Garou into a weary congregation in the center of the ravine. The wounds these warriors had received from the Banes healed quickly on their own, and a group comprising three of Dawntreader's surviving warriors, and both Red Talon and Black Fury Theurges made the rounds. This group healed some of the more seriously wounded by laying on hands and making prayers to Gaia.

No one really saw fit to howl or celebrate victory in this battle—everyone still seemed to be in shock, in fact. Albrecht just crouched and tried to catch his breath. His mystical armor was rent and broken in several places, and the claws of his left hand no longer gleamed silver. The wrath of Gaia that had flashed in his eyes, driving weaker foes back from him into the arms of his allies, had now abated.

Finally, it was Tvarivich who broke the silence. "Where are Konietzko and his men?" she asked as she bent over one of Dawntreader's dead men and closed his eyes.

Albrecht stood up, towering over the tired warriors all around him, and performed a quick head count. Indeed, even accounting for the dead and wounded, a good third of the force was missing.

Swift-As-the-River pointed in the direction of the mountain.

"That way," Houndstooth said at the same time, pointing with a bloody claw. "But the Wyrm-spawn are better entrenched than we estimated."

"They mined this pass," Helena Slow-to-Anger said through gritted teeth.

"They tried to bury us in debris then rode the landslides down into the midst of us," Dawntreader added.

Albrecht looked around and saw that, indeed, the ground seemed much more broken and rocky than its Penumbral reflection had.

"They were waiting for us," Dawntreader went on. "This place is already thicker with Wyrm-spawn—"

"So they're that way?" Albrecht cut in insistently.

"The margrave's men ended up closer to the rendezvous point than we did," Houndstooth said, "but they may have walked into a trap of their own."

"So let's get moving, then," Albrecht said.

"Yes," Tvarivich growled. "Lead the way."

Chapter Eleven

Albrecht and his warriors approached the planned rendezvous point for the first time since they'd left Szeged some hours ago, and they could hear sounds of battle in the distance. Albrecht turned to the others, who stopped around him, listening to the howls and clash of weapons coming from up ahead.

"Houndstooth, Helena," he said, "take your warriors over that hill on the west side. The rest of you follow me around the east side. And hurry. The others are counting on us."

The others obeyed without question. They formed up into two units and split off as he'd indicated. They howled and rattled their weapons, both to give their allies confidence and to frighten their enemies.

As Albrecht's people reached the other side, having taken the shorter path by luck, they saw that a desperate battle raged in the valley before them. Konietzko and those of his soldiers who had survived thus far fought at the far end, pushed toward the granite mountain by rank upon rank of materialized Banes and the Black Spiral Dancers who commanded and supplemented them. Scattered corpses testified to where the defenders had established their line originally, as well as the bloody price they had paid to push the attackers back. Howls, cries, snarls and screams echoed in the air, and Albrecht could hear desperation in the sounds Konietzko's warriors were making.

With a roar, Albrecht thrust his weapon forward, ordering his troops to charge. They surged down the hill at his command and plowed into the thickest knot of Wyrm-spawn from behind. Dawntreader and Swift-As-the-River added their own warriors to the Silver

Fang charge, splitting the amassed Wyrm-spawn down the middle by surprise. The Gaian force then fanned out behind Albrecht and pushed harder, driving the wedge deeper into the enemy. Heartened by their arrival, Margrave Konietzko drove a phalanx of his men toward Albrecht and formed the rest into an opposing wedge. The two lines of werewolves forced their way toward each other, then passed each other by, covering each other's backs. When the maneuver was complete, the defenders had cut the force of Wyrm-spawn neatly in half and formed a tight circle between the halves.

That circle then split in two along the opposite axis on which it had been joined and pushed the divided Wyrm warriors against the walls of the valley. The force on Albrecht's side was easier to finish off, but he wasn't worried in the slightest about Konietzko's worn-out soldiers on the other side. As that force did its best to push back its half of the Wyrm-spawn, Helena Slow-to-Anger and Guy Houndstooth's warriors finally arrived, sweeping down their side of the interposed hill behind the larger force of Wyrm-spawn. Houndstooth's warriors and Konietzko's performed the same maneuver in miniature on their side of the valley that those following Albrecht had used to break the larger enemy force in half.

The twice-divided Wyrm-spawn stood no chance. The reinforced and reinvigorated Gaian attackers cut them down one by one until no creature of evil lived. No Bane still lurked, either in the immediate Penumbra or materialized in the physical world. No Black Spiral Dancer could stand under his own power, and the ones that yet lingered were dispatched in short order. None was shown the slightest mercy.

When the work was done, an odd, heavy hush fell over the valley. It was nicked here and there by the falling rain, the scuffing of feet, moans of pain and faraway thunder, but no one broke it by speaking. Everyone seemed to be holding his or her breath in anticipation of something important. As if in answer to that sensation, Margrave Konietzko made his way through the crowd toward King Albrecht, who was approaching from the opposite direction. Albrecht's mystical armor broke apart and rained down into useless ephemera at his feet. His sword was notched and bloody. His teeth and claws were sticky with remnants of the victims he'd put to death with them. And yet, only a little of the blood that was splattered on his body was actually his. He stood proud and tall, and the Silver Crown shone.

"You lead and fight better than I expected," the margrave said, stopping in front of him. "Your reinforcements were... well timed."

"Thanks," Albrecht said. "And you're welcome. But the fight's not over yet. We've still got to find the caern."

"Yes," Tvarivich said. Albrecht could see red staining her gray-white fur under her left armpit, and she seemed to be walking off a limp. "I can feel it inside the mountain. It is hidden deep within."

"Then let's get to those caves and get in there," Albrecht said.

"That won't do any good," Konietzko said. "They don't lead deep enough into the mountain."

"It's true," Mephi said, coming up behind Albrecht. He'd taken the same moon bridge Konietzko had. "They dead-end about a hundred yards down. That's where our moon bridge dropped us."

"The Spirals ambushed us after we crossed the Gauntlet," Konietzko said. "As we were coming back out, they materialized with a horde of Banes and set upon us."

"I wondered why they were on the side of you away from the caves," Slow-to-Anger said.

"So where did they come from?" Dawntreader asked.

"Wyrm tunnel," Mephi answered. "We saw it when our moon bridge dropped us into the Penumbra instead of here, but we didn't realize what it was. It opens up out here in the Penumbra and leads down under the mountain."

"That sounds like the way in, then," Albrecht said. "And it sounds like there are already Spirals inside."

"Yes," Konietzko said. "I could also detect moon bridges leading out. Reinforcements could arrive from other hives at any moment."

"Then we have to hurry," Houndstooth said. "Into the tunnels and into the caern."

"Yes," Konietzko said again. "But the Wyrm-spirits are more numerous here than where any of our moon bridges brought us. We must establish a defensive perimeter and send one contingent of warriors into the tunnels at a time," Konietzko said. "The rest can follow in waves to make sure the Wyrm-spawn don't follow us."

"So who should go first?" Dawntreader asked.

The European Garou looked around uncomfortably, and no one answered right away.

"We'll lead the way," Albrecht said finally. "Me, Mephi and Queen Tvarivich's warriors. Then yours, Dawntreader. Helena's after that, then Houndstooth. Swift-As-the-River, you're next, and the margrave's men will watch our backs."

Konietzko nodded and said, "Good enough. We will cross the Gauntlet in the opposite order to clear out a perimeter. When you enter the tunnels, do not wait for us. Move into the caern as fast as you can before their reinforcements arrive."

"Or they ruin Jo'cllath'mattric's prison," Slow-to-Anger added.

"Yes," Houndstooth said. "Cut them off."

"Got it," Albrecht said. "Let's move."

Konietzko's men formed up in a defensive circle and vanished into the spirit world to clear a path around the tunnel's mouth. Swift-As-the-River's warriors followed, as did the other European sept leaders' one set at a time in quick succession. As each group disappeared, Tvarivich watched across the Gauntlet and signaled when the next group should follow. Finally, Tvarivich gave them the signal to cross as well. With quick prayers to Gaia all around, they readied their weapons and stepped sideways into hell.

They tore their way through the pattern webs across the Gauntlet, only to be blasted with ferocious storm winds and flying debris once they touched down in the spirit world. The Umbral storm rendered visibility almost nil at the ground, but in the counterintuitive way of the spirit world, the Garou could see throngs of airborne serpent Banes swooping through the sky like black clouds, driven almost to frenzy by the intensity of the storm. Some of the warriors who'd already crossed over disappeared screaming into the storm, snatched away from behind by flocks of Banes they hadn't seen coming.

The condition of the spirit world was far worse than it had been when they'd arrived. The storm winds pulled at even their Crinos bodies, nearly knocking them off their feet. Banes covered the mountain and valley floor like ants on a disturbed anthill, and even more winged ones played in the storm. The first Garou through the Gauntlet were doing their best to hold back the press of them, and battlefield communication was all but impossible.

Yet, Albrecht and the others had to ignore this commotion and focus on the tunnel opening in the center of the margrave's unsteady defensive perimeter. The ground around the opening was an inky black and veined with deep fissures that wept a yellowish ichor. It seemed like a scabbed-over chancre in the Penumbral ground, with more of the puslike ichor seeping from the edges, but Albrecht could see how the ground between it and the mountain was mounded over the passageway beneath. It was definitely the way in, and the other soldiers had cleared a path to it.

Exchanging disgusted looks, the Fangs steeled themselves then jumped into the hole one by one. As they did, the blackened crust broke apart, and they disappeared. As bad as the initial plunge was, though, nothing could have prepared them for the reality of the tunnel proper. A collective shudder went through them as they landed and looked around.

The tunnel ran into impregnable darkness straight ahead, and it was tall enough for a Crinos warrior to just barely scrape the ceiling with the tips of his claws. It seemed wide enough for three warriors to stand shoulder to shoulder. Strips of glowing green fungus veined the walls and ceiling, providing limited visibility. Vile, dripping orifices opened up in the walls and the floor at random, whispering gibberish just beyond the threshold of hearing. The walls and ceiling throbbed like the inside of a blood vessel. Albrecht could feel Wyrm filth in the air, crawling on his skin, rolling into his mouth, coating the inside of his nose. The feeling made his eye water, but he was afraid to touch it, lest he rub in the pervasive taint.

"Okay, everybody," he choked out. "The best part's over. Let's go."

Struggling to remain as calm and focused as Albrecht appeared to be, the others broke into a distance-eating jog toward the mountain. As they moved, they could feel a disgusting sensation of peristalsis, as if the tunnel were swallowing them into the belly of some rough beast.

***

After what seemed an eternity of waiting, the moon-bridge portals all around the Abyss-pit finally peeled open and a fresh batch of warriors emerged. Gashwrack stepped forward eagerly. The ever-growing and fluctuating sound of the Theurges' chanting had grated his nerves raw, and the fact that none of his lookouts had reported to him in almost an hour certainly wasn't helping. He'd almost rather be outside fighting than stuck coordinating the efforts from inside. The fact that Bile-Claw's ritual was taking so long only made things worse. But at least the reinforcements he'd asked Arastha for were finally here.

"Gather around," he said as the warriors took in the room and scowled at the black-robed men encircling the Abyss-pit. "Welcome. You are sorely needed."

"Aye," a tall fellow with long red hair growled at him. "Y're in charge?" Gashwrack nodded. "Where y're wantin' us, then?"

Gashwrack pointed over his shoulder toward the antechamber. "Out that way. The tunnel leads to the chamber where we made camp. Just beyond that is the tunnel leading outside. Trill out for Theurges from your home hives. When you find them, help them hold back our enemies. We're already under heavy attack. Understand?"

"Aye," the fellow said. He then turned to his comrades and said, "This way, lads. Y' heard th' man."

The other warriors yipped and barked in excitement and followed the tall fellow out of the room. There were about twenty of them altogether, and Gashwrack breathed a sigh of relief. They'd be enough to safeguard the Theurges he'd positioned outside. The Theurges still had plenty of Banes at their command thanks to Bile-Claw's allies. The caern was secure. Plus, the earthquakes that had rocked the chamber twice now seemed to indicate that Bile-Claw's ritual was proceeding smoothly, if not especially quickly. There was probably nothing to worry about.

He just wished his lookouts would hurry up with a new round of reports on how the battle was actually going out there. His blind faith in his subordinates went only so far.

***

"Close in the circle!" Konietzko shouted to his men, defying the storm's fury and pinning an Ooralath to the ground with his sword. "Sergiy! Get ready to enter the tunnel!"

"Wait!" Slow-to-Anger shouted, ripping the leg off a Scrag and using it as a club. "Don't! Something is wrong!"

Before Dawntreader could even ask the obvious question, it was answered from above. The flying Banes suddenly surged upward and seemed to shriek with one voice, and an explosion tore the heavens above them to shreds. Those who witnessed it thought they saw a bright ribbon of energy twist itself into existence then arc high into the sky over the mountain for an instant before shattering into thousands of white-hot shards. The rest of the warriors got the gist soon enough, as those shards began to rain down from the sky all around them. They fell like meteorites or mortar shells, decimating the outlying ranks of Banes on the ground and almost scattering the Gaian warriors in instinctive panic. None of the warriors could hear anything over the redoubled cacophony of the storm and the explosions of crashes all around them. Whole packs disappeared, and the survivors had to dodge through an earthbound hail while still staying low against the storm winds.

Konietzko had been thrown several feet through the air, and he pushed himself up slowly. As the deafening ringing in his ears faded, he surveyed the scene, trying to figure out what had happened. More projectiles were still raining down, but it was the crater of the one that had hit nearest him that had his immediate attention. Penumbral debris was settling all around it, and a wail was emanating from it unlike anything he had ever heard. But as he ran back to investigate, he was almost bowled over by something coming out of it. It was a long, black ophidian body with membranous wings and a large, gaping maw. It was another Bane like the others up among the storm clouds, and it shot into the sky to join its fellows. As more of the Banes rose from other craters all around the valley, Konietzko realized what had just happened—Mephi Faster-than-Death had described a similar occurrence from his experience at the Tisza Hellhole. Another pattern chain over Jo'cllath'mattric's prison had just shattered.

What was more, some of the debris from the continuing bombardment had landed in the middle of his defensive perimeter, collapsing the Wyrm tunnel behind the Silver Fangs and cutting them off from any help.

***

Albrecht and his warriors had been running forward and ever downward for almost a minute—with Albrecht and Tvarivich leading the way by light of lambent flame—before they felt the explosion. It rocked the earth all around them and threw them, deafened, to the floor.

"What the hell was that?" Albrecht demanded, rising to his feet shakily and only with great effort.

"I've got a pretty good idea," Mephi said, propping himself up with his staff. "I think a pattern chain just snapped outside. It was kind of like that when it happened at Tisza. I remember it knocked us all dizzy and…"

At that, his eyes flew open wide, and he whipped back around the way they'd come. Tvarivich and her warriors, all of whom were trying to rise, looked at each other in confusion.

"What?" Albrecht asked.

"It collapsed the Wyrm tunnels there, too," Mephi finished. Albrecht and the other Silver Fangs looked back and saw that, indeed, the tunnel was blocked off by rocks and dirt. The collapse had occurred about a dozen yards back the way they'd come. They hadn't lost anyone, thank Gaia, but there was no way Konietzko or any of the others could reach them now.

"Well, shit," Albrecht barked, at a lack for anything more regal or inspiring.

"Now what?" Mephi said.

"We must try to get back," Tvarivich said. "I'll summon an earth elemental to help clear the—"

"We can't do that now!" Albrecht snapped. "Are you nuts?"

"Dawntreader's warriors might have already made it into the tunnel behind us," Tvarivich said. "They could be trapped. We have to try to free them."

"We don't have time," Albrecht said. "If that was a chain snapping outside, we've got to get to the caern and stop the Spirals from snapping another one."

Tvarivich opened her mouth to protest but got a hold of herself in short order. "Of course. Let's go."

When they could all stand and move again, they ran to the far end of the tunnel. It ended in a black earth-wound much like the one they'd entered, except this one was vertical. Albrecht nicked it with Solemn Lord, and a line of pus ran. He then nodded to his warriors, steeled himself again and burst through it. As he did, he crossed not only its threshold, but the Gauntlet as well, finding himself in a dingy, cluttered chamber of stone deep within the mountain, lit by flickering blue torchlight. The floor was covered in pallets and dirty blankets and several piles of burned-up wood. There was also blood on the floor around a pile of mostly devoured animal carcasses in a corner. This was apparently where the Spirals who'd found this place originally had chosen to make camp.

Mephi, Tvarivich and the other Fangs emerged behind him, and they all spent a second shaking dirt and Wyrm-filth from themselves. Only one tunnel led out of this large cavern, and it opened in the wall opposite them.

Tvarivich pointed to the stone tunnel with her mace, snarling. "The caern's heart is that way. And Wyrm… the stench of it is like heat from a diseased man's skin. We must—"

Mephi hissed for silence suddenly, holding a finger to his mouth. "Someone's coming. You hear that? A lot of someones."

Everyone fell silent, and after a second, Albrecht could hear it, too. It was the click of toe-claws on stone, the rattle of weapons and giddy growls of excitement, coming toward them.

"Spirals," Mephi whispered. "Good number of them. We've got about a minute before they get here."

"Probably reinforcements for their brethren outside," Tvarivich said.

"Way's blocked," Mephi said. "They're our problem."

"We don't have time," Albrecht growled. "Even if we kill them, they still win if they stall us long enough."

"Then we'll just have to cut them down quick," Mephi growled back.

"No," Tvarivich said. "Even that could take too long."

"We're still going to have to face them," Albrecht said.

"Then *we* will," Tvarivich said. "But *you'll* have to go ahead without us. We'll hold them here as long as we can while you stop whatever is happening at the caern's heart."

"I hate that plan," Albrecht said.

"It's all we've got," Mephi said. Just out of sight down the tunnel, the sound of approaching warriors was getting louder. "And we're almost out of time."

"I know," Albrecht said grimly. "I'm not arguing. I just don't like it."

"Get behind us in wolf form," Tvarivich said then, readying her mace. "We'll cut you a path."

Albrecht nodded and folded down into Lupus form as Tvarivich's warriors and Mephi formed a tapered phalanx around him in their Crinos forms. No sooner had they done so than the Black Spiral Dancers entered across from them. There were about twenty of them, and they stopped in a disordered knot on the opposite side of the wide chamber.

Before anybody could move, Mephi looked over his comrades' heads and said, "Every one of you ugly bastards is going to die."

And with that, the phalanx charged into the Spiral mob. They hit their enemies hard, pushing them back for just a second in surprise, as the Spirals hadn't yet boiled into their Crinos forms. The warriors made it all the way to the entrance to the tunnel, at which point they stopped and opened their formation into a reversed wedge. The Spirals were still somewhat off balance, and they allowed themselves to be swept back momentarily from the tunnel they'd just exited. And as the Silver Fangs turned and tore into them, Albrecht shot out from amongst them down the tunnel toward the caern's heart.

Chapter Twelve

The situation in the valley had improved only marginally by the time the hail of proto-Banes finished. The Penumbral ground was scorched and broken, and more Banes were in the sky, but the ones on the ground were scattered and disoriented. Konietzko's surviving warriors had cleared a swath of them from their immediate vicinity, and they were in a tight circle around the site where the falling Bane had collapsed the Wyrm tunnel behind the Silver Fangs.

"They've failed," Houndstooth said. A flap of skin was hanging open beneath his right eye, and he had to lean on one of his warriors as the bones and muscles of his mangled right leg forced themselves back into their proper shape. "They're probably dead."

"Crushed," Dawntreader said. His left arm hung useless at his side, and he was swaying slightly against the force of the storm winds.

"Unless they were already beneath the mountain," Slow-to-Anger suggested. "Maybe some of them even survived."

"We can't assume that," Konietzko said. "We have to go in and carry on the mission."

"How?" Houndstooth snarled. "The tunnel's collapsed."

"But not gone," Dawntreader said, stumbling in place. Slow-to-Anger had to hold him up until a Theurge could get to him and lay hands on him.

"No," Konietzko agreed. "It's not gone."

"That doesn't mean we can use it," Houndstooth insisted. He could stand under his own power now, but his face was still a bloody ruin.

"Yes we can," Swift-As-the-River said. His two packmates were gone, but he had yet taken no wound. "We can dig."

"Yes," Konietzko said. "We have no choice."

***

Switching into his Crinos form in midstep, Albrecht raced down the tunnel with Solemn Lord held low. The farther he went, the more he could make out a bluish glow spilling from a chamber in the distance, and the more he could feel the Gauntlet growing ever thinner. The caern's heart, he knew, must be right ahead. He couldn't hear any more voices or footsteps approaching from ahead, but as the blue light grew brighter, he could feel pulses of unclean energy throbbing through the stones all around him with increasing intensity. He didn't know what that sensation foretold, but he knew he didn't have time to wait around for its meaning to reveal itself.

Instead, he sped up, hoping to gain the chamber at tunnel's end before whatever Spiral ritual was progressing could proceed much further. He didn't have to be a Theurge to know that caerns weren't supposed to feel this way. He hurried through the last leg of the tunnel and stopped in an unadorned, semicircular antechamber. When no guards or sentry spirits harassed him, he advanced more slowly into the caern's heart proper.

There, he saw a circular pit in the middle of the chamber, surrounded by disgusting, sphincterlike orifices that were quivering in time with the pulsating energy in the air. A huge stalactite covered in black writing hung down through the pit, and the symbols on it also pulsed in time with the energy, like blood in veins. Albrecht could smell Wyrm-taint all over the place, like acrid, invisible smoke.

Investigating further, he saw five unmoving black shapes arrayed around the edge of the pit between the freestanding orifices. He walked up to one and saw that it was a black-robed human figure sprawled out on the floor with a pool of blood under its head. He stabbed it experimentally with Solemn Lord, and it didn't so much as flinch. He then flipped it over with his foot and saw a pitiful, dead human face. Its eyes had apparently exploded, and thick, black blood was clotted all around its mouth, nose and ears. The other figures he could see seemed to be similarly out of commission.

"Did I miss something?" he huffed uncertainly, backing away from the edge of the pit and frowning at the dead bodies. "Or did you guys just—"

Before he could finish that sentence, a shrill growl broke out from behind him on his blind side, and he heard footsteps sprinting toward him. He had just enough time to turn that way before a werewolf with a brindled coat plowed into him like a Harley-Davidson going flat out. The two of them rolled over snarling and snapping at each other, and Solemn Lord clattered out of his hands onto a stone beam that spanned the pit. The werewolf—the Spiral—must have been waiting right inside the chamber this whole time, Albrecht thought, and the lucky son of a bitch had chosen his blind side. Albrecht wrenched himself upright and threw his attacker across the floor. The Spiral was fast, and he got his feet under him before Albrecht did. The two of them rose and faced each other.

"I recognize you," the Spiral barked, causing Albrecht to check his lunge in surprise. "The eye patch. The circlet. The sword. You're Albrecht. The one Brother Arglach preached about at our hive."

"He should have told you not to fuck with me," Albrecht snarled.

"He did," the Spiral sneered, circling toward Albrecht's left so that Albrecht was between him and the pit. "But if I can kill you, that bitch'll have to respect me. She'll have to let the Forgotten Son reward me at last."

"Yeah?" Albrecht growled. "Because I've got a reward for you right here, motherfucker. Unless you'd rather go fuck your mother some more."

For some reason, those words incensed the Spiral more than Albrecht could possibly have hoped. Its eyes burned red, and it charged him with an insane shriek that sounded more like pain than pure rage. It ran right at him with its claws out and its mouth open. Albrecht met this uncontrolled attack without fear. He stepped forward, bringing his hands up with his elbows out. So doing, he turned his attacker's claws aside and drove his claws into the Spiral's shoulder. Then, still using the Spiral's momentum, he twisted at the waist and flipped him over his hip. The two of them went down with Albrecht on top, and he clamped his jaws down hard on the Spiral's throat. The Spiral jerked and tried to dig his claws into Albrecht's back, but Albrecht shook his head back and forth as hard as he could until the Spiral stopped struggling and started melting down into human form. When the Spiral lay still at last, Albrecht stood over him and spat a mouthful of blood and gristle down in his face.

"Motherfucker," he said again. "Should have listened to your Brother Ass-rack. Now where'd Solemn Lord go?"

He glanced around and spotted it on the beam out over the pit. He also realized that the energy pulse he'd felt in the air wasn't getting any lighter. He'd kind of hoped that the black-robed figures on the ground had been performing whatever ritual had snapped the pattern chain outside and that some sort of backlash from it had killed them. In his heart, though, he knew that nothing in life was that easy. He walked out onto the beam over the pit, picked up his grand klaive and took another beam across to the other side of the room. When he did, he saw a second antechamber across the room from the one through which he'd entered, and he heard chanting coming from over there. As he rushed up to the antechamber, he found a stone basin in the middle of it with a black-robed figure leaning over it intently.

The figure was chanting softly in a language Albrecht didn't recognize, but the tempo matched the energy pulses perfectly. And as he built up speed, he held a silver scalpel over what appeared to be a complicated spider web across the top of the basin. The scalpel twitched this way and that like some instrument of divination, and the robed figure lowered it carefully toward one of the strands of webbing. The thin blade parted that strand before Albrecht could stop him, and a blast shot up from the depths of the pit to shake the entire mountain. The Gauntlet itself seemed to rattle like a flimsy screen door, and a storm gust blew outward from the chamber. Albrecht had to grab the wall to keep his feet. As the blast washed over him, he knew intuitively that another pattern chain had just snapped in the Umbra outside. The energy pulse subsided briefly, then started building again, faster this time.

At the sound of claws on stone, though, the black-robed figure stopped chanting and turned partway around. "Get out, Gashwrack!" he shrieked over his shoulder. "The Forgotten Son is at the threshold. He needs me! I must not be disturbed!"

"No," Albrecht said, coming toward him with Solemn Lord held high, "I'd say you already are."

The man in the robe swirled to his feet faster than Albrecht expected. Bright amber eyes burned deep in his hood for an instant, and he leaped forward, growing into his jet-black Crinos form as he did so. Albrecht sidestepped and chopped off the black-furred Dancer's right arm with one swipe. This injury didn't seem to deter the Spiral much, though. He swung his tiny silver scalpel in his left hand while Albrecht was overextended and buried it deep in Albrecht's right side. The scalpel lodged between two of his ribs. Bellowing in pain, he clubbed the Spiral in the head with Solemn Lord's pommel then slashed his stomach open with a home-run swing that probably wasn't strictly necessary, considering the severity of the first wound he'd dealt. The Spiral flew back into the wall of the antechamber and slid to the floor in his Homid form. His remaining hand clamped across his midsection, trying in vain to hold his entrails in place.

With a grunt of even more pain, Albrecht grabbed the handle of the scalpel protruding from his side and tried to pull it free. The thing burned like a fireplace poker inside him, and it was stuck deep, so it actually took him two tries. After the successful second one, his knees wobbled and he had to grab the wall for support. When he could see clearly again, he looked over at the dying black-robed Spiral and flung the scalpel at him in petulant rage. The harmless impact inspired the Spiral to lift his head. The hood hung down over even his eyes now, so that his face was entirely hidden in shadow.

"What are you looking at?" Albrecht barked. "Aren't you dead yet?"

"Close," the Spiral whispered. "So close."

"Then get on with it," Albrecht said. The pulse of energy in the air was slow and steady now, no longer building in intensity, although it had not died out.

"I was so close," the Spiral continued. "I'm sorry, Father. But at least... the intruder... will die... as well..."

"Not today," Albrecht scoffed, watching as a ropy intestine slipped between the Spiral's fingers. "You've got to stick me with something a hell of a lot bigger than—"

"...when they come," the Spiral finished, almost too quietly for Albrecht to hear. That statement gave Albrecht pause. The reinforcements were still fighting Mephi and Tvarivich's men at the other end of the tunnel where he'd left them, and they could, realistically, head back this way any second. Of course, there was no way for this dying Spiral to know that they were trapped in the higher chamber with no other way into it or out. Therefore, even more reinforcements were probably on the way. That must have meant that the orifices around the pit in the other room were moon-bridge portals, and all hell could break loose again momentarily. Hoping he wouldn't be too late, he turned away from the dying Spiral and approached the basin he had been bending over when Albrecht came in.

The thin, transparent strands still covered the surface of the bowl, but Albrecht could see that the pattern they made was now warped and malformed, as if by unbalanced tensions. Several of the strands that might have helped balance them lay broken under water at the bottom of the bowl, and a smooth white pebble with a black paw print etched on top was in there, too. Since he ruled his protectorate from a caern of his own, Albrecht could tell that this was no mere object of ritual; the pebble was this ancient caern's pathstone.

He knew that the pathstone anchored the moon bridges to this place, so he figured that if he just got rid of it, the bridges (and the reinforcements who were likely inbound on them) would be cut off. He had a fair idea of what would happen if he broke any of the strands that covered the surface of the stone basin while he was trying to get it, though. He'd seen what happened when the Spiral cut one just a few seconds ago, and he didn't want that happening again. So, with the utmost care, he slipped a long Crinos claw into the largest gap between the fine, delicate strands and tried his best to scoop out the stone. He pushed it back and forth, hooked it, dropped it, then eventually managed to slide it up the side of the basin into his other hand, all without breaking or disturbing any of the glass rods.

Now that he had it, though, he didn't exactly know what to do with it. The pulse of energy had stopped radiating throughout the chamber, which seemed like a good thing, but the moon bridge portals were still standing around the pit, despite his hope that removing the stone from its basin would shut them down. In fact, as he watched, the one directly in front of him began to iris open with a wet, sucking sound. Seeing this, the black-robed Spiral on the floor twitched in agonized laughter.

"Soon enough," the man wheezed, "yet too late. My brothers… will finish my work… freeing… the Forgotten Son."

"You think so?" Albrecht growled, wishing the sucker would just hurry up and die already. He held up the pathstone, unsure if the Spiral could even see it. "Can they do that without this? 'Cause I say to hell with your brothers, and the Forgotten Son can stay right where he is."

So saying, he pulled the stone back and threw it as hard as he could through the now-opened moon-bridge portal at a high angle. He could just see a Black Spiral Dancer approaching the aperture when he did it, and the Spiral ducked instinctively as the pebble flew over his head. That brief sight was the last either ever had of each other. As the pathstone crossed the threshold out into the foreshortened Umbral space between this caern and the hive the bridge led to, it took its anchoring properties with it. The moon bridge right in front of Albrecht folded in on itself, sending the Spirals who were using it Gaia-knew-where out into the Umbra, and its portal disappeared. In an instant, the other portals around the room disappeared as well. Wherever the pathstone had ended up, it sure as hell wasn't here, and that's where all the moon bridges went now. The Spirals were cut off. No more reinforcements were coming any time soon.

Now all he had to do was get back to the other chamber before the ones who were already here killed any more of his tribemates than they already had.

***

Fortunately, Albrecht discovered, the matter had largely been settled for him by the time he returned. He also found that the room was a lot more crowded now than it had been when he'd left it. As he ran in, holding Solemn Lord high, the last Spiral fell dead at his feet, split nearly in half by a heavy broadsword. Opposite the corpse stood a large, black werewolf with a bloody muzzle, holding the broadsword in question. He and Albrecht looked at each other, then lowered their weapons respectfully. Albrecht noted with satisfaction that his was bigger.

"King Albrecht," Mephi said from a little farther away. He was standing in his Homid form, trying to work the cobra head of his staff out of the innards of a wolf who lay at his feet. "You're back. We were just about to come to you."

"Yes," the black werewolf before him said, folding down into the shape of Margrave Konietzko. "Why have you returned already?"

"What are you talking about?" Albrecht said as he shifted back into Homid form. The wound in his side blazed as he changed forms around it, but it stopped burning as soon as he was in human form. "I'm done."

"Done?" Dawntreader asked from near the Wyrm tunnel aperture with a deep frown.

"Sure," Albrecht said casually. "I stopped the ritual. I kept Jo'cllath'mattric from getting free. I cut off reinforcements. Everybody in the room's dead. Didn't seem like there was anything else to do. So I came back. Is everybody here all right?"

"Not everyone," Tvarivich said, limping toward him gingerly in Crinos form on a badly mauled leg. "I lost seven men. The margrave lost even more."

"We've all lost men," Houndstooth said. "And women. Good warriors all." Swift-As-the-River moaned in agreement.

"I'm sorry," Albrecht said. "I got back here as fast as I could."

Konietzko shook his head and held up a dirt-covered hand at that. "No, Albrecht," he said. "You couldn't have saved them anyway. You did what needed to be done. You traded their lives for ours. And for many more besides. You made the right decision."

"I know," Albrecht said. "I'm not arguing. I just don't like it."

Konietzko nodded and sheathed his sword. He then looked back at the other sept leaders and motioned for them to follow him. He stepped over the corpse at his feet and headed for the tunnel behind Albrecht. As he passed, though, he glanced at Albrecht and said softly, "Don't worry. It gets easier." And with that, he led the others down the tunnel to inspect the work Albrecht had done.

Chapter Thirteen

About a week later, Albrecht was starting to feel like he'd worn out his welcome at Night Sky. In that time, he'd made several trips between Konietzko's caern and the mountain caern in Serbia, helping ritually cleanse that place as much as was possible given its surroundings, then having himself ritually cleansed back at Night Sky before the ambient Wyrm-taint started affecting him adversely. He'd helped Konietzko's men establish some basic spirit wards around the place to keep out most of the Banes, then he'd even helped stand guard while Konietzko opened an experimental moon bridge from the prison caern back to the staging caern in Szeged. As the caern's original pathstone was gone, though, the margrave had had to use the one Mephi had recovered from Owl's Rest a couple of months ago. That seemed to work all right for the time being, and it allowed them to cave in the Wyrm tunnel they had been using and cleanse its infectious taint from the place.

After that, most of the work that needed to be done at the caern was Theurge work. Konietzko, Tvarivich and a handful of others started spending days in a row at the caern, checking on the stability of the remaining pattern chains and monitoring the Umbral storm's effects on them. They declared the prison's condition serious but stable, and they seemed confident that it wasn't going to get any worse on its own. Whatever the Spirals had been doing to break the chains from inside the caern, it had been truly stopped, not merely put on hold or temporarily suspended. That last revelation had earned Albrecht an evening's celebration in Konietzko's feast hall, but it had come off perfunctory and awkward, despite all the visiting sept leaders trying to praise him and give him glory for all the work he'd done. To make matters worse, Tvarivich had said her good-byes the next day and suggested that maybe Albrecht ought to take the opportunity to relax for a few days.

The trouble was, Albrecht didn't feel like relaxing. He felt like doing something important. Something *else* important, that was. He needed to be in the middle of something, making a difference and doing good. Not that he was a glory hound, of course, but he'd begun to feel useless these last couple of days, and he didn't know what he could do to assuage that feeling. He'd tried talking to Mephi before the Silent Strider had gone, but that hadn't helped at all.

"You're restless," Mephi had said. "I know that feeling well. I get it whenever I stay in one place too long. I constantly feel like I've got somewhere to be, but I can't quite put my finger on where. It's distracting. Kind of like the end of a long caffeine jag."

"Yeah," Albrecht had replied. "Like that. Kind of."

"Well, you know, you can come with me if you want," Mephi had offered. "I was planning on swinging through Morocco to the Silent Strider caern there in Casablanca on my way back to the States. You'd be more than welcome if you want to come along. My people love your story, I've got to say. The twice-exiled king who now wears the Silver Crown. You'd be a hit in person."

"Thanks, but I'm not sure that's what I need right now."

"Well, the offer's always open. If you change your mind and want to see it, put the word out through the grapevine, and we'll check it out."

"We'll see."

Mephi had left later on that day, as had most of the other visiting sept leaders. Albrecht had told himself that he'd stay as long as it took for all the leaders to confirm that their septs had not been attacked by treacherous Wyrm forces during their absence. As each of those messages had come and gone, though, Albrecht had finally been forced to admit that he'd been kidding himself. He wasn't waiting or resting anymore. He was officially stalling. Specifically, he was stalling by pacing around the halls of the margrave's fortress.

A large part of the reason he'd come so God-awful far from home to this sept was to help out with the Jo'cllath'mattric problem as best he could, and he'd done that. That just left two big goals still to accomplish on his agenda. First, he still had no idea where to start looking for Arkady. Everybody was on the bandwagon now, believing the Russkie was a Wyrm-worshipping traitor, but nobody seemed to have any clue about where he might have gone since he'd disappeared from Dawntreader's protectorate. Albrecht was no closer to putting Arkady down once and for all than he had been just after he'd banished him back to Russia.

Second, of course, was finding some way to help Mari. She was home, she was safe and she had Evan looking after her, but she hadn't gotten any better since she'd been brought to the Finger Lakes Caern almost two months ago. And even though Albrecht had come all this way looking for some means of curing her, he still had nothing to go on and no idea whom to even ask. The only person he hadn't tried was the margrave himself, and somehow, that didn't sound like the best—

"Lord Albrecht," a voice from behind him said, bringing him up short in the hallway and cutting into his reverie.

Albrecht turned around, realizing as he did so that he had no idea where he was. "Yeah," he said. "Am I off limits or something?"

"No, sir," the man standing before him said. Albrecht recognized the guy from Konietzko's feast hall. It was Gryffyth SeaFoam. "But I have been sent to find you by the seneschal of our most gracious host. My consternation at not finding you is exceeded only by my delight at overtaking you at last."

"Uh-huh," Albrecht said. "You need something?"

"Alas, no," SeaFoam said. "The irony is that it is I who am here for your benefit."

"Look," Albrecht said, sighing, "I know you're a Galliard and everything, but if you're looking to write some kind of ballad or whatever about me, now really isn't the time."

SeaFoam winked good naturedly and said, "Would that I but had the time and inspiration to do your legendary status its due justice, my lord. Especially now that your skill at arms has increased it anew. But, no, that is not the nature of my errand, nor am I its progenitor."

"Oh," Albrecht said, slightly crestfallen in spite of himself. "Then what do you want?"

Rather than just saying whatever it was that was on his mind, SeaFoam produced with a flourish from behind his back a slim PCS phone with the Shadow Lords' tribal glyph etched on the back of it. He extended it toward Albrecht, bowed, then backed graciously out of earshot.

Albrecht held the phone up to his ear and said, "Hello?"

"Albrecht," Evan's voice said over the line, bringing an unexpected smile to Albrecht's face. "Thank God it's you. I thought that guy was going to bankrupt me keeping me on hold forever."

"Yeah, he's a talker. It's real good to hear from you, kid."

"You, too. I hear you guys had some pretty big excitement there."

"Pretty big," Albrecht said. "I'll have to tell you all about it when I get back. Any developments I should know about where you are?"

"One," Evan said. "It's the reason I called. But just for the record, it's damned hard to get a cell phone number for a guy who lives under a mountain in the middle of nowhere."

"What's the news, kid?" Albrecht said. "It's your nickel, remember?"

"Oh, yeah. Well, see, the thing is this. I really think you should come home. Soon. Like tonight, maybe, if you can."

"Tonight? What's going on?"

"Um, I think you should be here to see for yourself. Over the phone, I don't know if I can—"

"What is it? Evan, what's this about?"

"Well, I didn't want to tell you this way," Evan said. "But if you insist. You see, it's about Mari..."

About the Author

Carl Bowen is a copyeditor and freelance author for White Wolf Publishing. He is the author of **Tribe Novel: Silent Striders** as well as two books in the **Predator & Prey** series. He lives in Stone Mountain, Georgia, with his wife, Ginnie.

#
GLASS WALKERS

TIM DEDOPULOS

author:	tim dedopulos
cover artist:	steve prescott
series editors:	eric griffin
	john h. steele
	stewart wieck
editor:	philippe r. boulle
copyeditor:	jeanée ledoux
graphic designer:	aaron voss
art director:	richard thomas

ISBN 1-58846-813-5
First Edition: August 2002
Printed in Canada.

White Wolf Publishing
1554 Litton Drive
Stone Mountain, GA 30083
www.white-wolf.com/fiction

For Penny,
Who believed, and waited as long as she could.

Lo! Some we loved, the loveliest and the best,
That Time and Fate of all their Vintage pressed,
Have drunk their Cup a round or two before,
And one by one crept silently to Rest.
—From the Rubaiyat of Omar Khayyam

GLASS WALKERS

TIM DEDOPULOS

Prologue

A sickening lurch tore through the blackness and woke her mind from torpor. *Come, girl.* Beneath its soft croon, the voice was slick with evil, and her hackles rose in automatic rebellion and anger. The darkness was absolute. Questions tumbled through the woman's mind swiftly, a whirl of confusion. What is it? Where? How? Who am I? There were no answers available, so she pushed them all aside. Time for that later, once the danger had passed.

She took a step forward, and the world faded back into view—a world, anyway. She was standing in an ancient forest glade, beside a dark pool, and her wrist hurt. Bulrushes and reeds clustered around the water's edge, lashing irritably in the breeze. They made the pond look hungry, as if it were trying to catch hold of something to eat. Breeze? The woman realized the air was absolutely still—and the water as flat as an oil spill—and automatically took a step back from the pool before she could stop herself.

The wood surrounding the glade absorbed most of the light, casting everything into dull, muted greens and grays. The forest appeared to be made of ancient olive trees, gnarled and twisted with age. They stood close to each other, closer than any other olive grove she'd seen, branches from one tree twisting around the next. Across the other side of the pool, though, the trees lightened. She could see a break, a path to head down, a way out. She circled the pool carefully, keeping to the middle of the patchy grass, out of reach of the rushes. As she got closer, she realized with a hot surge of disappointment that her eyes were playing games with her. The trees this side of the glade were locked as solidly as the ones she'd just left.

Must have been a trick of the light.

In fact, the woman could now see a way through on the far side, near to where she'd started. She made a careful note of the location, marking it by a particularly large clump of rushes. She sprinted round to those reeds as swiftly as possible, keeping out of reach—*just in case*, she told herself—and scoured the trees, looking for the break. Nothing. The closer she looked, the more tightly packed the trees seemed to be.

Her blood ran cold as she realized that it wasn't the light that was playing tricks on her. Just for a second, she had the very strong impression that the trees were laughing nastily at her confusion, and she stumbled back from their gloating, until she remembered the rushes snatching at her heels.

Was she dreaming?

This is no dream, girl. This is where you belong, but I can take away the pain. All you have to do is ask.

A burly, sweating cóp was in front of her. A moment before, he had not been there. The vivid pale blue of his uniform and the glistening red of his face were a brutal shock after the dark grays and greens of the glade. His face was flat with hostility and other, darker emotions. The thought that he might be there to help never even crossed her mind. The woman turned to run, but he was faster than he looked, and before she knew it he had her bad wrist twisted agonizingly behind her back. He shouldn't have been a threat—he shouldn't even have been worthy of comment—but somehow she couldn't remember what to do. The cop forced her down to her knees, and then a heavy boot on her neck pushed her down, face first, into the ground.

I can take away the pain. I can make this stop. Don't be stubborn. Just ask. Her attacker seemed oblivious to the wheedling voice. Maybe she was the only one who could hear it.

The cop was ripping at her clothes, mumbling vile obscenities and pathetic insults as he did so. *Spare yourself, girl. Ask.* The woman could feel her jeans coming loose and knew what would come next. Despair threatened to overwhelm her, and she could feel the voice urging her to surrender to it. The pain in her wrist blazed, and she crushed any thought of giving in. Any pain or indignity was better than that. White-hot rage boiled up inside her at her helplessness. She grabbed at it desperately, took hold of it and turned it against the whole sick reality, pushing it all away from her as hard as she could.

"Fuck you."

Spat out with the full force of her raging fury behind them, the words tore out into the glade and the voice lurking behind it. The scene rippled, and for a glorious moment the woman could feel her identity waiting to come back to her and give her back her name, her history, her weapons, everything she needed to win this fight once and for all. The voice screamed in frustration, and then blackness closed like a veil over everything, and awareness and memory fell away once more. Deprived of any stimulus, of any hints of thought or remembrance, she simply floated in the dark, oblivious of how close she had come once again.

A sickening lurch tore through the blackness and woke her mind from torpor...

Chapter One

Very gradually, Julia became aware of a dull, spitting, crackling sound. A familiar one. She froze, eyes still closed, trying to gather her thoughts enough to work out whether it was a threat or not. She sniffed, scenting the air, and the delicious smell of roasting venison snapped her straight into full wakefulness.

"Well, hey, Sleeping Beauty wakes up at last!" Carlita, of course. She was over by a new fire pit, keeping an impatient eye on the roast.

"Good morning to you, too," said Julia, too hungry to object. The venison smelled wonderful.

"Only just," said Carlita, grinning broadly.

"I needed to recharge. Yesterday was…" She flailed for a word to sum up the hours-long running battle, the doomed defense of the lore caern and then Cries Havoc's spectacular healing. She gave up. "Exciting."

"Don't let that little fraud needle you," said Cries Havoc with a smile. "She's only been awake ten minutes herself." The young Bone Gnawer poked her tongue out at him and went back to hungrily watching the venison. "How do you feel this morning?"

"Stiff as a board, actually," said Julia. "But very good despite it. You?"

"Glorious." He meant it, too. She could almost see his soul shining inside him, transcendent.

"Then it was worth it a hundred times over. By the way, does anyone have any idea how many Banes we killed in the end?"

"I wasn't keeping an accurate count." John North Wind's Son was over by the river, washing something. "I was a bit busy. I believe we got over two hundred between us, though."

"Fucking awesome!" Carlita looked stunned.

"We'll certainly have a tale to sing," said Cries Havoc.

"Yeah, it was a good day's work," said Julia laconically. She couldn't stop a huge smile creeping out onto her face, though. "Hey, where's Storm-Eye?"

"Scouting out the area back in the physical world, " said Cries Havoc. "She woke early, while I was still greeting the dawn. I think she wanted an excuse to work some knots out. She popped back with our share of breakfast about an hour ago."

"Did she say where we were?"

"In the hills. Which hills is anyone's guess, though."

"What's the matter, princess? Can't your computer tell you?" Over by the fire, Carlita was smiling to soften the jibe, and Julia found herself grinning back.

Julia arched an eyebrow at her. "When did you last see a GPS satellite in the Penumbra?"

"There is that, I guess." Carlita didn't sound at all chastened. She prodded the venison and nodded to herself. "Okay, who wants some food?" Somehow, she even managed to avoid getting trampled in the rush.

***

Full and relaxed for what felt like the first time in weeks, Julia lounged round the dying fire with the rest of the pack, gazing into the embers. A few flames danced here and there, licking at the scraps of wood that remained. Storm-Eye had returned a little while earlier, reporting that everything seemed quiet in the area, both within the immediate spirit world and beyond it. Julia was glad to see that the Talon was back and looking at ease and that she didn't seem to be in any hurry to get her pack underway. As much as she hated idleness, the quest to heal Cries Havoc had taken an awful lot out of her.

The quest had given a lot back, too, of course. Julia had been on the edge of the clearing when the Lore Bane had exploded into tale spirits, and then it had been like a halogen spotlight searing on her mind as all sorts of knowledge had poured into her. A swarm of halogen spotlights. She could feel the new information within her mind, almost as if the tale spirits themselves were waiting just below her conscious mind for a relevant moment to pop up and unfold themselves before her. Unfold?…

"The Lore Bane was *made* of tale spirits! Folded, twisted into muscle fibers…" The realization was so startling that she only realized she'd spoken aloud when the others turned round to stare at her.

Cries Havoc was the first to speak. "What do you mean?"

"It's…" She looked for a way to explain it that made sense. "It's about information. Information is like energy; it can't be created or destroyed. It can only be lost."

"Like the rest of us," muttered Carlita.

Julia sighed. "Okay, two plus two is four , right? If you somehow had the power to make everyone forget that, right across the world, even made them forget what numbers were, you still wouldn't change the fact that two plus two is four. No one would know it, the information would be lost, but it would still be part of the world. That's true for any sort of information. The story of Laughs-at-Pine-Cones will always be the story of Laughs-at-Pine-Cones, even if the time comes that no one knows it. There's always the chance that the story could be recovered somehow—a lost book, chatting to an ancestor spirit, glyphs in a lost cave, whatever—it doesn't matter. You can make people forget, hide the knowledge from them, lock it away, but you can't destroy it."

What has this to do with tale spirits? Even speaking in the growls and movements of the wolf tongue, Storm-Eye managed to sound slightly impatient.

"Don't you see? A tale spirit is the consciousness of a piece of information. If the information can never be destroyed, then the tale spirit must be as resilient. The Lore Bane wasn't feeding off the tale spirits, it was keeping them captive. When Cries Havoc killed it, it exploded. That's because it was made of hundreds of tale spirits, folded and wrapped around and spun together and bound with Wyrm essence. Imprisoned within that foulness, locked into a shape of evil and forced to serve the Wyrm. It must be hell for them. Literally. And when we killed the spirit that kept them bound together, they were set free again."

"That's monstrous." The Children of Gaia were a famously empathic tribe anyway, but as a Galliard, a Garou tale-teller, Cries Havoc looked doubly sickened.

"Yes, but think of the implications. The Lore Banes must have been created as mobile prisons for tale spirits. When the Wyrm attacked the Silver Record, it needed to do something with all that data that it couldn't destroy. Hence Lore Banes. They're not there as soldiers of the Wyrm—well, not just, anyway—but to defend the trapped tales from rescue. What better way to keep something away from us than to turn it into a lethally dangerous enemy?"

"Can we use this knowledge against other Lore Banes?" asked North Wind's Son.

"Perhaps. I don't know yet. It's something we'll have to look into. If we could find a way to awaken the tale spirits inside a Bane perhaps, then they might separate out again on their own. That would make the Lore Bane disintegrate."

An ember popped in the fire, sending out a small shower of sparks. *You are our Theurge, our Seer, and if you say this to be true, then I believe you*, growled Storm-Eye. *I do not see that it changes anything, however. Once we are recovered, we must pass on what we have learned and then set about the hunting and extermination of more Lore Banes.*

Cries Havoc nodded slowly, then looked curiously at Julia. "How certain of this are you? Is it just a good guess?"

"I thought it was a guess at first, but now… no, I'm certain. One of the things I learnt when you killed that Bane. It is part of a tale ripped from the mind of an old Croatian Dancer years ago." As she said it, the story welled up within her, and for an irrational moment she longed for a Galliard's gift to tell it properly.

"That monster Jo'cllath'mattric picked a child to carry a clutch of Lore Banes out of the Eastern Bloc. Memories and tales about itself were bound up within the clutch, and it wanted them comfortably out of the way. That's how the old one remembered it. The child was some kind of chosen one." She sighed in frustration. "I never was any good at stories. Anyway, the child was given some horrendous pet Bane that would activate when he came of age, and sent off to establish a nest in…" She fell silent in amazement.

"Hey, don't wig out on us now, your highness," said Carlita.

Julia shook her thoughts clear. "His name was Mika Gerbovic, and he was to establish a nest in central London."

***

Doctor Robert Galland looked around his office and sighed. Expensive books lined one wall—reference works, medical texts, journals, even a valuable collection of ancient leather-bound occult grimoires and prophetic tomes. All useless. Behind him, a tasteful selection of classical artworks offset his degrees, awards and diplomas. They weren't being much help at the moment, either. The papers and reports scattered over the expensive leather surface of his mahogany desk were worse than useless. To his left, the view out over the Megadon corporate research facility's mist-shrouded Long Island park was as lovely as ever, but it didn't offer any inspiration.

Three projects, all of crucial importance, all of them going poorly. Project Aconite was the most frustrating of the three; they'd been so close until Roland Hall had managed to get himself killed on that trip to Seattle, the damn fool. By a dammed passerby, too. A good Samaritan. If he'd retrieved the child… But no, that would have been far too easy. Now the child was gone, and all their preparation lost. It would take years to incubate another.

Galland sighed again and pressed a button on his telephone. His secretary answered at once. "Yes, sir?"

"I'm going to get some samples from specimen 113, Lucy. I'll be in the usual lab, but don't bother me unless something critical comes up."

At this point in the early evening, the corridors were quiet. The regulars had mostly gone home, and none of the night staff had turned up yet. The few people whom Galland encountered spotted his mood a mile off and kept their mouths shut as they passed. Perversely, that only irritated Galland all the more; it would have been pleasant to tear strips off someone. Maybe even literally. Despite the lack of people, the

facility was far from idle. Machines hummed away to themselves in most rooms, cabinets and centrifuges and vats, with computers controlling all manner of automatic machinery, spooling the data from the experiments, crunching the results and churning out reports. It made him feel a bit better. With all this computational power at their disposal, it was just a matter of time before something gave and things got back on track properly. It was always the way.

Specimen 113 was right where he was supposed to be, in his secure lab in D-wing. Just to be on the safe side, the man was locked into a thorough set of restraints that held him down, naked and spread eagled, on a chilly metal operating table. The thick steel bands locked through the table at wrist, waist, knee and ankle. Even if he came to his senses suddenly, 113 wasn't going anywhere. Apart from the shackles, he was also fixed up to at least three different experiments, not including the automatic saline drip. The latest device was attached through his groin. If the werewolf gene in his gametes could be coaxed into dominance, it would be possible to greatly increase breed rate. The Lady was enthusiastic. It was the first time that Galland had seen the device fitted, and it looked extremely painful. He certainly hoped it was, anyway.

Whatever had happened to him, 113 was clearly brain damaged. Despite a certain knowing glint in his eyes that suggested at least the remains of intelligence, just about all he could do was growl the same unintelligible sound. Oh, and scream, of course. Galland decided to leave the samples until later and work out some frustrations instead. A small tray of shards and needles, some of surgical steel, some of thrice-blessed silver, sat in their accustomed place in a small furnace, heated to over two hundred degrees

Celsius. He picked one up by its insulated handle and stabbed it down into the corner of 113's right eye. The specimen screamed, and Galland smiled.

The good doctor would have been extremely disappointed to know that Mick barely knew that he was screaming and certainly wasn't really aware of his body's pain. Totally absorbed in his desperate attempts to remember the Name, he may as well have been lying on a golden Mediterranean beach for all the torments bothered him.

Chapter Two

The next morning, Julia woke early. She felt good, rested and healthy, and she was impatient to do something. A day off was all well and good, but there was still a lot of work to do. Her wards were undisturbed; nothing had approached them in the night. Off at the east side of the field, by the stream, Cries Havoc was still celebrating the dawn. He actually looked as if he were enjoying it, and Julia had a sudden intuition that he'd never sleep late again. Dawntreader would be delighted when he got to hear about it.

Half an hour later, everyone was up and finishing off the remains of yesterday's venison. It seemed the rest of the pack was impatient to get going, too—if only they'd agree on a destination.

"We know that Jo'cllath'mattric is in Serbia somewhere, or at least in that area." Cries Havoc sounded fairly determined. "If that horror is the source of the Lore Banes, then the chances are that there will be plenty of Banes in the vicinity, and probably ones that know something useful. I think we should head back to the Sept of the Dawn and use that as a base. The Dawntreader would make us all very welcome. I have no doubt that he would be able to offer some sort of assistance, too. It's got to be a good place to start. Time is critical, North Wind's Son."

The Wendigo was not going to be easily dissuaded. "Look, you're healed, and we're all bursting with all sorts of new knowledge. We ought to go and try to help Mari fight off whatever it is that's corrupting her. She's a good person, and if she doesn't get better, it will devastate Evan and Albrecht. Who knows what we might be able to do? We have to try. The Lore Banes have been around for Gaia knows how long; they can wait another week or two. Mari might not be able to. Just having you there next to her might wake her."

"You mean if he does that early-morning wailing in her ear?" Carlita was dismissive. "We don't even know if she still needs help. Even if she does, we don't know anything about what's wrong with her. That Stargazer, Tearjerker, told us that her problem was something different from ours, remember? Nope, I think we should head back to the Big Apple. We were onto something there. That Dancer with the wolf and his fomori had something against us specifically."

"Well, I think…" began Julia.

"That we should go to London and drink tea with the queen?" interrupted Carlita, putting on a dreadful Dick Van Dyke–style British accent.

"Yes, damn it," snapped Julia, irritated. "Or no, rather. About the tea, anyway." She sighed. "Look, we've got a clear lead. We know there's a nest of Lore Banes in the city and that they were taken out of the Balkans *because* they were storing information about Jo'cllath'mattric. We have the name of the person who is their guardian or controller or whatever. I *know* they might have moved on, Havoc, but they also might not have, and they're not going to be surrounded by miles and miles of hellhole, which is more than you can say for the bloody Balkans. My home caern is going to be within immediate range. Central London is really only twenty square miles or so even at its most generous, and if the story means the City of London, then that's just one square mile. Officially, anyway. Old City Sept is on the edge of that square mile. We'd be insane to overlook that resource. On top of that, I'm a Glass Walker, remember? We deal in information and human society. You do remember human society, yeah? We can find this Gerbovic arsehole and his nest. If he ever went to school, had a job or a business, used a credit card, learned how to drive, fell ill, anything like that, we can bloody well find him and go explain to him in very close detail why playing with Banes is a bad thing. I have networks in London. I don't have anything in New York, and that dancer could very easily have just decided to pick on us."

"And if he's not human, not part of human society?" asked Cries Havoc reasonably.

"If he's in London, he can't avoid it. Even with the best disguises and false identities, even if he's a Spiral, he'll leave traces. I can find them, and him and this nest. I know I can."

"But Mari…" said North Wind's Son.

"Tell you what. When we step back into the physical world, why don't you call Evan Heals-the-Past—you can use my mobile—and find out what the situation is?" The Wendigo looked rather grateful. Julia glared at Carlita and Cries Havoc, daring them to say something. The Bone Gnawer was about to oblige when Storm-Eye cut her off.

Enough. I have listened to you all yapping, and I am tired of the noise. I want very much to go somewhere clean and wholesome—Cries Havoc broke into a grin—*but I feel that Julia is right. The clearest trail that we have begins in London. We should start our hunt there.* Julia smiled at Carlita and Cries Havoc, then glanced into her reflection in her PDA screen and stepped sideways.

Naturally, it was raining.

She glanced around, quickly at first to check for threats, and then more slowly, taking stock of the vicinity. They were in an area of gently rolling foothills, green and pleasant. The immediate surroundings of field and stream were more or less identical to their

Penumbral counterparts, but the thick woodland where Cries Havoc had faced his demons was absent. There were trees, of course, but they were dotted around the grassy slopes sparsely. A few early-season wild flowers added a pretty splash of color. In the distance, the hills rose up higher and higher, dark with trees. In the other direction, the land seemed to think about flattening out and was clearly being farmed commercially. While there weren't any roads or towns in immediate sight, it was a fairly safe bet that they weren't particularly far away.

Julia opened her PDA and fired up the location-tracing program. New York State. They *had* come a long way. Suddenly, a nasty memory crossed her mind. She opened her emailer and started typing furiously. The rest of the pack joined her just as she was finishing the note.

"You preparing us a welcome committee?" asked Carlita curiously.

"Not yet," said Julia, feeling a bit embarrassed. "I… the car needs to go back to the hire company or it's going to get me into trouble. I was just asking a friend to return it for me."

Storm-Eye turned to look at her but didn't say anything.

"I'll let Nicola know we're coming and that we've got good news." She hated sounding apologetic. "John, do you want to check in with your friend?" She tossed the phone over to him.

"Thank you," said North Wind's Son, nodding. He caught her mobile deftly and started dialing. While he did so, Julia switched to the locator program's map facility and called over the rest of the pack.

"Look, this is where we are. We're still just about within the Appalachian Mountain region, if you're generous. We're right up the other end, though, on the edge of the Catskills. Here, between Greenville and Cairo. Not far from Red Hook. Oh, the horror…" She grinned, but none of the others even noticed, so she tried to gloss over it and moved on briskly. "We came a long way in a very short time on that bridge of yours, Cries Havoc. Almost full circle, in fact. The nearest place is going to be Antonine's. The Catskills Protectorate. I don't know if he's got a pathstone there or not, but he's got that bridge to Finger Lakes if nothing else."

"The Stargazer is a good person to pass on what we have found," said North Wind's Son, rejoining the others. "His station is respected, and—since his kind have fled—he is mostly above politics."

Julia nodded to him. "What did Evan say?"

"They are still at Finger Lakes. It is not far, but although Mari is weakening, he agrees with you that Jo'cllath'mattric is more important. King Albrecht has gone into Europe, and Evan is concerned for him."

Cries Havoc looked unnerved. "He's gone to Europe? Why?"

"He means to find—and kill—Arkady and Jo'cllath'mattric."

Carlita was the first to recover, and she snorted in disbelief. "That guy has some serious delusions of grandeur, even for King Fang."

"I can imagine the reception he's going to get, particularly from Margrave Konietzko and Karin Jarlsdottir." Cries Havoc shook his horned head. "And I can see why Evan is concerned, particularly if Albrecht actually manages to track Jo'cllath'mattric down. If we're going to be of any use, we'll have to hurry."

Then stop chattering and get underway, growled Storm-Eye in wolf speech. She shifted shape, bulking up from a normal wolf into the huge dire-wolf Hispo form, and cocked an expectant ear at the rest of the group. They changed shape to join her, and then the pack was off and away, running over the rolling hills at a mile-eating pace.

***

The Lore Bane flapped idly around the lower chamber of the nest, as restless as its brothers. It had been weeks since any of them had been properly fed. The injunction to obey the master's commands was strong, but not absolute, and hunger was a powerful force. As was boredom. Mighty Jo'cllath'mattric had ordered it to be obedient to the master, but not at all costs, and it *had* been obedient. They all had. Food was required, however. Several of the brood had ventured out to hunt over the last few weeks. Shared around, the food had been meager but sufficient. Finally hungry enough to ignore its orders, the Bane decided to find something to eat for itself.

It flew up to the ceiling of the room and through the small hole that led to the upper chamber. The two parts of the nest looked much the same—rough, fleshy caverns of slimy red, shot through with dark and pale veins. Soothing, but tedious after weeks on end of nothing else. Two-thirds of the Lore Bane's brood was up here—eight or nine in total. The upper chamber held the portal to the outside, and they were all tempted to break the prohibitions.

Ignoring the others, the Lore Bane flew straight out through the shuddering sphincter to the outside. Once it was clear of the nest, it slowly forced itself down into the physical world, feeling its body take on weight and substance. A disagreeable experience, like sinking into thick mud.

At this time of night, the city was relatively quiet. The Lore Bane kept above the streetlights and concentrated on scanning for food. It spotted a tempting prospect down a small side alley, not far away. The mind was hard and bright with violence and greed, deliciously seasoned with a haze of drugs. There was some depth to it, too—unusual in these times. A good catch. The Lore Bane made its way toward the target, dropping low as it got close. The target was a tall, muscular human with thick, matted locks of jet-black hair cascading down his back like tendrils. He appeared to be waiting for something.

As the Lore Bane got close, the human spotted it. To the Lore Bane's surprise, the man did not run or cower, but shook his head, growled softly and said, partly to himself, "I an' I not be puttin' up with this shit." As he spoke, he raised a weapon and fired three quick shots at the Bane. Amazed, the Bane didn't have time to dodge, and the bullets slammed into it.

Furious at the irritating pain, the Lore Bane screeched and dived at the man. He fired once more, wildly, and then the Bane was on him. It sank its teeth through his ear and into his mind and pulled brutally. The soft, glowing light of the man's deliciously savage personality came out easily, as if oiled by the drugs in his system. The Bane guzzled his mind greedily, absorbing him, pulling and pulling until nothing was left. The bullet wounds stung, and it was determined to drain all it could. It would have to regurgitate the meal and share it out properly in a few minutes, anyway.

When the Lore Bane had finished, it flew back up into the night, leaving the drug runner lying mindlessly fetal in the stinking alley.

"… and in that burst of enlightenment was he forged again anew, and the whole pack gifted with secrets and tales long thought lost—including the location of a nest of its fellows, holding information about the terrible Jo'cllath'mattric itself. Let the Banes of knowledge tremble, for the Silver River is in full flood, crashing down upon them, and Gaia's force will scour them out of all the worlds."

Cries Havoc fell silent and let his outstretched hands drop, breaking the spell, and Julia remembered to breathe again. Everyone seemed as stunned as she felt. Even Antonine Teardrop looked impressed, and his southern visitor, a Fianna reporter called Stuart Stalks-the-Truth, was clearly taken aback. Julia fought down a wild urge to cheer. Looking up at Cries Havoc, she saw the twinkle in his eyes and grinned at him. He knew the power that his telling had held.

Antonine was silent for a long moment, gathering his thoughts. When he finally spoke, it was slowly and thoughtfully. "Vegarda warned me that I would hear something important this evening, so I wasn't too surprised when you showed up this afternoon."

That was an understatement. When they'd arrived at his cabin earlier, the Stargazer elder had just that moment finished preparing them a meal. His timing had been exact, just like the number of portions.

"I'm glad you were able to hear it firsthand, too, Stuart," said Antonine. "You tell a powerful tale, Cries Havoc. I'm particularly disturbed by the notion that our lost lore is bound up into these vile Banes. I wonder if it is just our tales that are in there? Who knows what stories and secrets have been captured over the centuries. There may be information stolen from the other Fera… or from darker sources. The Wyrm can be indiscriminate, and you should take care." Julia thought about some of her caern's secrets getting into the wrong hands, and shuddered.

Carlita looked concerned, too. "Are you saying we should avoid killing these things?"

Antonine shook his head. "No. If there is information about the current crisis to be had, then it should be retrieved. You have a further role to play in the defeat of this corruption. You are going to hunt out this nest?"

"Yes," growled Storm-Eye, speaking in the universal Garou language. "Julia believes that it is in London, planted there by a boy or man from east Europe."

"It's there," said Julia. "If I had Cries Havoc's tongue, I could tell it properly, and you'd understand why I'm so certain."

"Well, there's one thing you can say for the Ragabash," said Stuart. " We're damned good at spreading gossip. I'm a newspaper man as well. I can make sure your story gets around and that it sounds good in the process."

"And I shall ensure that the right ears hear the truth about Lore Banes," said Antonine. "We need to destroy as many as we can find. Despite the risks, there is too much that we have lost for any other course of action to be reasonable. Rest here the night, and in the morning we'll all get on our ways."

Chapter Three

The journey back to the Old City Sept went surprisingly smoothly.

The group was on its way within half an hour of sunrise, even after pausing to have some breakfast. A moon path that passed near the Catskills Protectorate led the group north over to a small Uktena sept called Crystal Waters, just inside the Canadian border. The members were greeted with a certain amount of hostility, for the minute or so it took Antonine to politely point out that the Silver River Pack was chosen by Uktena himself, and brought news of a new source of Wyrm-cached secrets. After that, they were treated as if they were the tribe's favorite children returned from a summer-long hunting trip.

It took until early afternoon to satisfy the curiosity of the Crystal Waters elders. Almost every point surrounding the Lore Banes was picked over time and again, so much so that Julia was starting to feel a little like a rat on a dissecting table. The probing questions did force her to look at the whole matter from every angle, though, and by the end of it she was slightly startled to discover that she had a far better idea about the whole process than when they had started.

After the elders had finished questioning the Silver River Pack, the sept's Mistress of the Rite took Julia to one side. An elderly Theurge, Long-in-Truths spoke slowly and perpetually seemed distracted. It could take her up to a minute to complete a question, and Julia had to work hard to suppress her impatience with the old woman.

When she seemed sure that no one else would overhear, Long-in-Truths waved a gnarled finger at Julia and said, "I have one final question for you, child."

Julia nodded and tried to stay relaxed. The Uktena looked so ancient that Julia thought she would probably even call the Queen Mother "child," too.

"Know that this is not a question to which I expect an answer. Not now. Not ever." Long-in-Truths cackled to herself in grim amusement, then paused to get her breath back. "Raven will pick over my bones long before you will know how to respond. When the time comes that you need help in starting to find a solution, though, you may come to us. You are a child of Uktena now, as we are. You will find that we know many secrets…" She drifted off into a private reverie. Julia was about to wave a hand in front of the Uktena's face when the old woman blinked and continued talking. "You will receive the aid you need here. There are those that say the Weaver is mad, and that it is her crazed attacks that have maddened the Wyrm. Now, child. Think. If the Weaver lost her mind and drove the Wyrm to insanity, what was it that first maddened the Weaver?"

Julia just stared at her, astonished. Long-in-Truths chuckled wheezily at Julia's expression and left the tent. The old woman had taken almost five minutes to complete her speech, and it took Julia the same time again to pull her thoughts into order. It was a fascinating question—all sorts of possibilities whirled in her head—but surely the Uktena didn't expect her to solve a mystery of that magnitude? With a mighty effort, she put the whole thing out of her mind and went to look for the others.

She found them outside, near the pathstone. Antonine and Stuart were making travel arrangements with the sept's Gatekeeper. Carlita noticed Julia approaching, cocked an eyebrow at her and came to meet her.

"What was all that about? Some kinda witchy heart-to-heart?"

Julia shook her head. "I'm not sure, actually. Instructions, perhaps. For the future."

"Well, it must be working—you sure *sound* like a Theurge. C'mon, spill the beans. Anything interesting?"

"Trust me, you don't want to know. You *really* don't want to know."

"What's the matter, J? Ain't I good enough to be told?" Carlita wasn't entirely joking.

Julia smiled wryly. "Nothing like that, I promise. I just don't really understand it myself yet. If I ever make any sense of it, I'll let you know."

"Okay then," Carlita said, grinning again. "If that's the way you want it, Lady Di, you keep your secrets."

"Have I told you how tasteless that particular joke is?" Julia arched an eyebrow.

"Nope. Think it would stop me if you did?"

"Not really," said Julia, resigned.

"I wouldn't waste the effort then, if I were you. I'm sure there's all sorts of deep, mystical crap you could be thinking of instead with that gigantic brain of yours."

Julia looked at the Bone Gnawer. Carlita started giggling, and after a moment, Julia found herself joining in. They were still laughing when Antonine and Stuart started heading over to the rest of the pack. Seeing the Stargazer, Carlita looped her arm through Julia's and led her back to the others. "C'mon, princess, let's go hear what they have to say."

Antonine waited for them before he started speaking. "Stuart and I will be going southwards for a little before we go our separate ways. The Gatekeeper will open a bridge to the Old City sept for you, if that is what you want. At the moment, he feels that it is safe enough. The storm seems to have died down, or at least to be concentrated in eastern Europe at the moment, and others have been crossing the Atlantic successfully for the last few days. However, he can also open a bridge that will take you to somewhere near a major international airport. What would you prefer?"

If the Gatekeeper feels it is safe, then there is no reason to cower in one of those wretched metal tubes, said Storm-Eye, talking in wolf-tongue.

"Besides which," said Julia glumly, "our passports are already on their way to London from Waynesville, North Carolina. Along with the rest of our stuff."

The pack looked round at her.

"All right, all right, it's mostly *my* stuff. Either way, we'd have to get some more passports and other documentation made up."

We will use the bridge.

"Fine. Good luck with everything," said Antonine warmly.

"Yeah, it was good to meet you," Stuart said. "You've given me a lot to think about. Don't worry, we'll pass the word around."

"Absolutely," said Antonine. "I'll make sure that the right folk hear about your accomplishments."

They made their farewells, and then the Silver River Pack went to the pathstone and crossed over into the Penumbra. The Gatekeeper had the bridge open already, and it hung there shimmering off into the sky. Storm-Eye, already slipping into Hispo, bounded onto the bridge with a growl of thanks. Julia changed shape to follow suit with the others, and the pack sped off along the bridge.

The crossing itself was quiet. The bridge ran high enough over the ocean that Julia was unable to make out any activity down on the surface. She did spot the occasional spirit off in the distance, Airts and Lunes mostly, but nothing took any interest in the pack. Off in the far distance, a faint but continual rumbling of thunder reminded her uncomfortably that the storm was still in full force. The far eastern horizon looked dark and sooty, too. As the hours passed and they traveled ever eastward, Julia tried to ignore the storm's increasing volume and the ominous presence of Anthelios, the baleful red star that heralded the Apocalypse.

Finally, the bridge started dropping down into the familiar landscape of London's Penumbra. The moon bridge came down sharply, as if it wanted to avoid as much of the Weaver-dominated region as possible. The city of London was old even before the Warders of Men became the City Warders, let alone the Iron Riders or the Glass Walkers. Many of its prominent buildings had stood, unchanged, for centuries. Where old blocks had been torn down to give way to new, modern architecture, faint remnants of the older buildings often remained in the Penumbra. By the time they vanished completely, their replacements were usually starting to cast their own shadow, so—as was the case for most of western Europe—the city skyline looked much the same as it did back in the physical world.

There were some notable absences, of course. No London Eye blighting the view of the Thames. No Canary Wharf dominating the eastern sky with its gigantic glowing pyramid—yet, anyway. Every so often, an eerie empty patch of ground would play testament to a new development or unused space. But any tourist, if one were selected at random and brought over, would easily be able to pick out all the usual sights, from Big Ben's clock tower and the Houses of Parliament, past

Covent Garden and St. Paul's Cathedral, and on down to the Tower of London and beyond. Everything was much the same.

Except for the Weaver, of course.

Here, in the Penumbra, the only moving things—you couldn't really call them living—were the vast hordes of Pattern Spiders and Web Spiders that infested the webs strewn over everything. Every building was wrapped in layer upon layer of thick webbing. Gigantic strands linked buildings together, and cobwebs nestled in every corner. The Weaver had the city in a firm grip. It wasn't totally dominant, of course. There would be cockroach and rat spirits slipping through every crack, and all manner of other opportunists who knew enough to carve out a living. Old Father Thames thundered through the center of the city, ferocious and unbound, totally ignoring the bridges and embankments that hemmed him in.

For the most part, though, the landscape was controlled by the Weaver's minions. With the moon bridge shining down onto the caern, Old City was a welcome haven. Julia could practically feel Storm-Eye's distaste, and Cries Havoc didn't look much happier, even in his Hispo form.

In the Penumbra, Old City still looked much as it had for centuries. The caern had been a sacred site since time immemorial. Roman activity had originally kick-started the growth of Londinium, and when new development along the Old Street swallowed the site up into the city, a small keep was built to guard over the caern, and the land was surrounded by stone walls. As the city developed through the Dark Ages, the sept kept pace with the architectural fashions of the times, ensuring that the outside world did not get suspicious. By the Middle Ages, the whole site had become enclosed, with its lushly green central courtyard surrounded by an impressive manor styled to look like a guild house or corn exchange. It was redone again and again in the Georgian and Victorian eras, and once more after the war. All of the many changes had left their mark.

Old City remained firmly medieval in its appearance, with thick stone walls and roof and narrow windows. The buildings of the structure sprawled around the open central courtyard, with the moon bridge dropping narrowly down between them. There were no ostentatious carvings or decorations; although the sept looked little like the buildings around it, there was little to distinguish it from any of a score or more of other old structures across the Penumbral Square Mile. Few of the stone structures had inner courtyards, of course, but there were enough enclosed spaces in and around the city that it didn't stand out—places like Gray's Inn Fields, Lincoln's Inn Fields, and Temple with its circular church. Julia grinned. London's barristers did seem to like their greenery.

The sept presented an equally unremarkable appearance in the physical world. The current camouflage had been built in the fifties to look like a converted set of old red-brick warehouses. From the front, there was no real indication of how far back the buildings extended, or that the brick was merely a façade over far stronger protection. Part of the frontage was home to the sept's small finance company, partly for camouflage and partly because it was damn useful sometimes, and the profits were handy, too. The rest was the same sort of nondescript property that could be found all over the north and east sides of the city, generic buildings that seemed ready to switch between accommodation, storage facility, business premises and trendy wine bar almost at random.

As the pack bounded down into the caern's heart, Julia sped up slightly and pulled in front. She came down into the garden courtyard, stepped off the bridge and took a moment to just savor the familiar surroundings. It was good to be home. The rest of the pack joined her a few moments later. She smiled at them and said, "Welcome back to Old City." She shifted back into Homid, and the others followed suit—except for Storm-Eye, of course, who shrank down into Lupus. When they were all settled, Julia stepped over, bringing the others with her.

Her greeting died on her lips. Half the sept seemed to be gathered round, looking at them with mixed expressions. Nicola River-Runner, the Fianna Grand Elder and CEO of the sept, was in front, talking to Roger Blake, Warder and head of security. Geoffrey Taylor was with them, which wasn't a particularly great sign. Behind the three of them, a whole flock of people was milling about, watching. John Sullivan, the sept's Gatekeeper and network manager, must have announced their approach.

Geoffrey took full advantage of Nicola's momentary distraction. "Julia dear, nice to see you've deigned to grace us with your presence again. I must say you're looking particularly lovely this evening." There were a number of sniggers from around the courtyard, and someone laughed out loud.

Horrified, Julia realized that she was still wearing the same stinking rags that she'd been in when they all left North Carolina over a week ago, and she hadn't even brushed her hair once during the entire time. By the time they'd completed their quest, she'd been so drained that her appearance hadn't crossed her mind, and afterward she'd felt totally natural with the pack. Antonine's kind informality had also tranquilized her self-consciousness, and the Uktena hadn't been in the least bit interested in her hairstyle. It was only now, back in "sophisticated" London, that she realized she looked like a hobo.

A brief flash informed her that some cruel bastard had decided to immortalize the moment on camera. No doubt the picture would be out on the GWnet, the Glass Walker version of the Internet, within minutes. She flushed bright red and irrationally found herself looking around desperately for something to hide behind.

Carlita saved her. The skinny girl pushed past her briskly, grinning like a Cheshire cat. "Yeah, we've looked better. *We* haven't had much time to sit on our asses pampering ourselves recently. Don't worry, though, old man. She'll be looking young and beautiful again for you to letch at in no time. Which is more than I can say for you."

Geoffrey went pale, and his jaw moved soundlessly. Julia giggled helplessly at his expression, her embarrassment forgotten. It was difficult to know which implication was the most offensive: that he was lazy and self-indulgent, that he was old and ugly or that he had sexual desires for a fellow Garou. Several people in the crowd were laughing openly, and even Nicola was grinning.

"Little Yank bitch… never… all my years… such insolence…" He was so offended, he was actually physically spluttering.

"That's a hell of a long time," Carlita said, her voice patronizingly soothing. "Are you sure? You've probably forgotten."

For a moment, Julia actually thought the old fool was going to burst into his Crinos battle form and attack them. His eyes glazed, and she could see the rage surging inside him. With a supreme effort, he mastered himself, turned smartly on his heel and pushed his way through the crowd without any further comment. River-Runner glanced irritably in Geoffrey's direction, then went back to her conversation. Sniggering laughter followed him out of the courtyard.

"That was *superb*, Carlita!" Julia was grinning broadly, and she had to fight down the urge to give her packmate a massive hug. "I'm really sorry about Geoffrey. He's a…"

"Ragabash?" suggested Carlita helpfully.

"Wanker," corrected Julia.

Carlita laughed. "It's no big. I'm used to hecklers. No moldy old creep disses *my* sister."

"That's your privilege, right?" said Julia, smiling.

"Hell yeah!" Carlita smiled back at her.

River-Runner finished talking to her Warder and came over to the pack. Behind her, Julia could see Blake hurrying off on some errand or other. "Sorry about that," Nicola said. "Welcome back to Old City. I've heard the stories of your doings—" she looked at Cries Havoc "—and of your miraculous healing. It's very exciting. I look forward to hearing all about it, and you're all very welcome to stay as long as you want. There's plenty of space in the guest suites, and there are clothes in a range of sizes that you can use while your own ones are being cleaned. I look forward to talking to you all tomorrow after lunch—2 p.m. say, in my office. Julia, there's one or two things I need to go over with you first. Can we see you in Meeting Room Three for 9 a.m.?"

That was the room used for formal interviews. Julia's heart sank. She nodded, feeling slightly sick.

Nicola smiled breezily. "Wonderful. Great to see you. Enjoy your stay." She headed off, and the spectators started dispersing, talking quietly amongst themselves.

"What was that all about?" asked North Wind's Son.

"Well, it certainly explains the crowd; word must have got around, and they wanted to hear what she had to say. She came to tell me I'm in trouble and that I'm going to be hauled up in front of the board tomorrow morning."

"She did?" Cries Havoc sounded dubious.

Julia nodded. "You've spent too much time with the Get, Cries Havoc. The British prefer to hint around the edges of a problem rather than confront it straight on. Particularly Glass Walkers."

"River-Runner is Fianna," growled Storm-Eye in the Garou tongue.

"Yeah, but she's been with us a long time, and she was unusually subtle to begin with. That was fair warning of a reaming, for Nicola." Julia sighed.

"She's gotta get through me first," Carlita said fiercely. This time Julia did hug her, hard.

"Thank you, Big Sister."

"Hey! Get off me, you dumb, soppy Brit!" Julia ignored her protests, and Carlita hugged her back. "Look, seriously, are you going to be okay?"

Julia released her, smiled wryly, and stepped back. "Don't worry about me. I'll be fine. We need the resources that Old City has to offer. The worst they can do is sack me for misconduct. Come on, I'll show you all to some rooms. The thought of a hot bath is making me feel weak at the knees."

Once the others were settled in a set of rooms, Julia headed back to her own suite. She'd managed to persuade the pack that she was relaxed and calm about the morning, but really she was scared. The prospect of losing her home here was terrifying. She stalked along the corridor, fretting over what the morning might bring. She was so deep in thought that she didn't even hear her name being called the first time.

"Julia. Julia?"

She turned round and noticed Rob Thompson—kinfolk, and one of the sept's hackers. One of the sept's best, actually, and a pleasant guy to boot. She smiled. "Hi, Rob. Sorry. I'm a bit distracted. What can I do for you?"

He flashed a cute smile back at her. "I… I just wanted to welcome you back, and…" He paused again. Was he actually shuffling his feet? "… to say that I really do think you're looking lovely. You never look anything less."

Julia wondered for a moment if he was taking the piss out of her, but finally had to admit to herself that he wasn't. She realized that she was smiling, and she felt her cheeks color. "Rob, um…"

"Look, I bet you're tired. I'll see you about. G'night." With a last smile, he hurried off. Julia watched him go. All the sept's kinfolk kept in top shape, even the programmers—Old City had an excellent gym, and use was mandatory—but she'd never really noticed before what a good bum he had. She headed off for her long-awaited bath, humming quietly to herself.

Chapter Four

By five to nine the following morning, Julia was waiting, immaculate, outside Meeting Room Three. After a very long, very hot bath, she'd gone straight to bed. She'd been sound asleep by eleven and up again less than eight hours later. Sorting out her hair took the best part of an hour, and by the time she'd done some tasteful makeup, patched up her nails and found a suitably sober-yet-dynamic outfit, she'd missed any chance of breakfast.

She nervously checked her appearance in the frosted glass door one last time and was microscopically relieved to see that she still looked tolerable. She refused to admit to herself, even for a moment, that she'd been worried that she might have missed something or, worse, somehow mystically reverted to the filthy, dragged-through-a-whole-maze-of-hedges-backward state she had been in the night before. She suppressed a shudder and then nervously checked her appearance again.

Her PDA chimed softly on the stroke of nine to tell her it was time. She took a deep, slow breath and knocked on the door in front of her.

"Come in." Nicola, sounding neutral.

Julia tried to squash the butterflies in her stomach, opened the door and went in. Meeting Room Three was laid out for interviews and inquiries. There was a long mahogany desk to the left, in front of the room's window. It could comfortably seat four or five people along one side. Nicola River-Runner was sitting behind it in a plush leather chair, flanked by Blake on one side and, on the other, Julia's superior Theurge, Karen Oldbury, the personnel manager who served as the sept's Truthcatcher and Mistress of the Challenge. The grand council, and no one else. It was going to be a tough meeting, then. A pair of bushy potted plants of some sort or other—one at either end of the desk—and a few abstract artworks on the walls completely failed to soften the room's impact.

In the middle of the room, a simple plastic chair—orange, like the ones in the canteen—had been set out facing the desk. The message was clear. *We have the power, the status and the defenses*, it declared. *You are lowly and exposed, and your discomfort does not matter to us.* The room was always pretty much the same, of course, but it wasn't much of a consolation. Just looking at that chair was intimidating. Actually sitting in it…

"Good morning, Julia," said Nicola. "Sit down, please."

"Good morning," Julia said, keeping her voice as neutral as possible. She walked over to the chair and sat down, painfully aware of the elders watching her.

"I trust you're fully refreshed after your escapades?"

"Yes," said Karen, "if you're still tired, please let us know and we can do this some other time." Julia knew her better than to be fooled by her tone.

"I'm back in top form, thanks." She forced a smile. "It's good to be home."

Nicola looked at her thoughtfully. "Is it, now? I wonder." That troubled Julia. What did she mean? Before she could think of some appropriate answer, Nicola continued. "We have some concerns, Julia. There have been a number of complaints during the month or so you've been away." She glanced over at Karen, who nodded.

"Specifically," said the Truthcatcher, "we've had a formal protest about your behavior at Anvil-Klaiven from the Get—from their Warder, accusing you of recklessly summoning a hostile spirit into their bawn. We've also received an internal complaint about your conduct at Anvil-Klaiven, and questions of your suitability as an ambassador for the sept. In addition, there have been two formal complaints about the duration of your unscheduled leave, a request for a temp to cover your duties in your absence and, as of last night, a rather bitter accusation of gross misconduct on the part of one of your guests."

Seeing Julia's expression, Nicola made her voice slightly kinder. "Look, Julia, it's not that bad. The Fenrir were just going through the motions, lodging a protest because it was the thing to do. I've spoken to the Jarlsdottir, and she's fine. Privately, she thinks you acted well and bravely, although she's still calling you reckless if anyone asks. We all know that you and Geoffrey have a personality clash, and we've discounted both of his complaints about your conduct. Anvil-Klaiven is sorted, and he really was asking for what he got last night. I've implied I'll tell you off, though, and asked him to keep out of your way for a few days."

Blake chuckled. "That smart-mouthed little Bone Gnawer is a fierce one, and she's fond of you. Hang on to her. She might save more than your life one day."

"As for your unscheduled time off," continued Nicola, "well, I have a pretty good idea of what you've been up to. The Tisza River affair was brave, particularly since most of your pack are young. I think you did well. Antonine Teardrop spoke highly of you, and the articles coming out about your metis's healing are impressive. It's clear that your pack has bonded strongly and accomplished some pretty remarkable things, and I look forward to finding out what you have learned. Your time has been used constructively. That isn't the issue."

Julia blinked. Inquiries by the grand council didn't usually start off by dismissing all the accusations. "What is, then? I don't understand."

"We're not here to discipline you, Julia. You've carried yourself well through difficult times." Karen sounded sympathetic. "We're here to decide if you still have a place within this sept."

"You're okay with what I've been up to, so you're thinking about sacking me? Could you just run that by me again?" Julia was stunned.

"You're young, Julia. Skilled, insightful, a good worker—but you've been restless for a few months. You haven't let it affect your work, which I respect, but it has been noticed. Now you have a strong pack around you, and you've started venturing out into the world, taking on important tasks… You're beginning to make something of a name for yourself, and I wouldn't be in the least bit surprised if all sorts of people decide that they need the assistance of your Silver River Pack. Do you really think you're going to be able to put all that aside and go back to the routine nine to five of sept life?"

"There's a lot of work out there for a hungry young pack, my girl." Blake sounded almost wistful. "Even if your Silver River Pack splits up, you'll find another. This is your chance to make a significant difference in your own right, rather than as part of our little operation."

"But this is my *home*," said Julia, desperate and almost in tears. "The people I know are here. My friends are here. My things are here. My family is here—my father. He's so proud of my work here. It would break his heart if you kicked me out."

"Julia," Nicola's voice was a curious blend of kindness and insistence, and it cut through her surging emotions. "Be honest with yourself. Your friends and family are currently lounging about in Guest Suite C. I know you're scared. Change is always frightening at the best of times, and, well, these are the very worst times of all. But you're growing up—outgrowing Old City. Your father will be even more proud when you become renowned."

"I can't believe this is happening. I *need* you. I need your help." Julia sounded small and broken, even to herself.

"I?" said Karen pointedly. "Surely that should be 'We need your help'?" Julia looked at her, uncertain and confused.

"We're not going to throw you out if you really, truly don't want to go, Julia. And whatever happens, you'll always be welcome." Nicola's words were a degree of comfort. "You're popular here, and your work is good. Even Geoffrey is secretly rather fond of you, in his own way, even if he is jealous. But if you're too scared to make the jump you long to and need to be pushed, well, it would be cruel of us to let you stay here. It's the least we can do. In the meantime, we'll talk to the whole pack later, find out what you're up to and what you need, and decide what we can spare for your task."

"That help you mentioned just now. You've come back here on business. Silver River business," said Karen. "Doesn't that tell you anything? You have asked Old City to help your pack. You have not asked your pack to help Old City. I'm not criticizing that. I'm just pointing it out, to help you see for yourself where your priorities truly lie."

"You're letting your mind and your fear get in the way of your heart, kiddo." Blake smiled at her, presumably trying to soften his words.

"We're going to leave you alone for a while now," said Nicola. "Have a think, and be honest with yourself. If you want to talk things over, all three of us will be happy to help, any time. Think about it."

The elders got up, filed round from behind the desk and headed for the door. Blake was the last of the three, and before he left, he turned round and looked at her sympathetically. "Which prospect scares you the most, Julia? Leaving Old City behind, or leaving the Silver River Pack behind? When you truly know the answer, come tell us." Then he too was gone, and he shut the door behind him. Julia stayed exactly where she was, in the middle of the empty room on her uncomfortable plastic chair, and let the tears streak mascara down her face.

***

There was no way that Julia was going to meet the others looking like a comedy panda, of course. She dashed to the ladies' room by Meeting Room One, staying in Crinos—facial fur and a muzzle had their advantages at times like these—and thanking Gaia that her makeup wasn't attuned. Ten minutes with some soap and water got rid of the worst of the damage, and she felt safe enough to venture out in Homid again. She dropped by her room briefly to pick up some replacement makeup and then, driven by the need to be alone for a while, quickly made her way up to the roof, keeping away from the main corridor and rec area.

The caern had several floors, but the ground and first floors were by far the busiest. The second floor was mostly storage and technical space—the server room, a data safe, the library of newspapers, magazines and financial reports and so on—and the third floor was really unused most of the time, overflow accommodation for moots and emergencies. There had been many centuries when the sept had taken up all the available space, but a lot of people had fallen by the wayside. The worst times of all. Nicola was on the mark there.

A small, easily missed staircase led up to the roof. Like most of the neighboring buildings, the caern had a flat, concrete roof split into sections. One part was quite a bit higher than the rest, but it was easy to get to if you shifted into Crinos for the extra three feet or so of height. There was a small hut up there—part of the lift mechanism—with an indented alcove on the far side. From the alcove, you could look out over the city in relative peace. There were sensors everywhere, of course, but the alcove wasn't covered by the caern's closed-circuit television cameras. Julia had been coming up here for years, and Blake had never disturbed her or made any comment.

Old City was on one of the quieter roads off Old Street, and the ever-present roar of traffic was muted even at ground level. Up here, it was almost peaceful. People bustled around in the streets below, businessmen and -women mostly, in smart suits. Londoners had never been the most friendly or outgoing people on the planet, but even just a few years ago, they'd walked around carefully ignoring others, staying in their own little private cocoon. Nowadays, everyone seemed to have a permanent snarl of aggression plastered on his face, and if anyone made eye contact, the glares they exchanged were ferocious. *Just try it, asshole*, seemed to be the only thought on anyone's mind. They were terrified, all of them. Maybe they didn't actually know what it was that frightened them—they probably thought it was work pressure, or money worries, or emotional problems or just the speed at which the future was rushing toward them—but they could sense the coming destruction.

Every warrior has been born who will fight in the last battle. Lupus Garou matured as quickly as normal wolves and typically took no more than two years to reach their First Change—sometimes as little as just one year. Some precocious cubs were promoted to full cliath within a year or two of First Change, too. Unless all the lupus and their kin had suddenly become barren or celibate, there was five years left at most. Maybe as little as eighteen months. She could feel her rage stirring at the prospect. No wonder the humans were scared.

It did rather put being asked to resign into perspective, too. It wasn't as if she could really plan on a long career.

Julia let her eyes wander over the city skyline, and slowly, gradually, her emotions settled. Hours later, at quarter to two, she made her way back down to the first floor. After stopping in a handy lavatory to repair her makeup again, she headed to Nicola's office. Her packmates were already there.

"Where have you been? We looked for you." For a wonder, Storm-Eye had assumed Homid form. She was even wearing clothes.

"Is everything all right?" asked Cries Havoc.

Julia smiled at them. "Yeah, I'm okay. It was a tough meeting. I needed to go and take care of a few things afterward. Sorry I missed lunch." Her stomach reminded her that she'd missed breakfast as well.

"Is it time?" Storm-Eye asked.

"Yes," said Nicola River-Runner, coming up the hall toward them with Blake and Karen close behind her. "It is."

After a general round of friendly greetings and introductions, everyone went through into Nicola's office. It was a large, comfortably cluttered room. Most of the space was taken up by a rough circle of comfy chairs and sofas surrounding a tastefully expensive coffee table. Her desk, at the far end of the room, was a sea of paperwork. Nicola's famous bottle of Knappogue Castle '51 stood out proudly from the mess—she was generous with it, and rumor said she had several cases of the vintage whiskey stashed somewhere.

Nicola quickly settled everyone around the coffee table with a minimum of fuss and formality and called the meeting to order. "Right. Now we're comfy, who wants to tell me what this is all about? I've heard the tale of your healing, Cries Havoc. Very impressive." Julia would have missed the tiny pause as Nicola's eyes flicked over his horns if she hadn't been looking for it. "I'm glad that you're back to being as whole as ever, but I'm not really sure what the Silver River Pack is up to now."

Storm-Eye nodded to Julia to explain. "Cries Havoc was damaged by an obscure type of Bane that is able to eat memory, a Lore Bane. They are somehow linked to Jo'cllath'mattric, the huge Wyrm-spawn that's behind all this activity in the Balkans. The Lore Banes are literally made from tale spirits, spun out and melded together by the Wyrm, and infused with a strongly evil personality. I suspect that the Lore Banes get bigger and stronger with every piece of memory they steal. When Cries Havoc killed the Bane that had damaged him, it exploded into its constituent parts. The information was set free. All of it. Not just the bits of Cries Havoc that he had been missing, but the original spirits used in the construction of the Lore Bane, too.

"They had been trapped inside that monster for Gaia knows how long, and they were ecstatic to be free. Tale spirits need their stories to be known—how else can they have meaning?—so their first thought was to share themselves with us, and share they did. We all know things now that the Galliards never taught us. Things that the Galliards don't *know*. I can feel them in the back of my mind, waiting to be examined. It's going to take us all a while to absorb our new knowledge into our conscious awareness, but in the meantime, it's sitting there like an old, half-forgotten lesson, waiting for some conscious trigger to set it off.

"You can understand, I hope, why we consider it important to hunt down and kill as many Lore Banes as possible." The three elders nodded but didn't interrupt. "Well, there's more. I was musing over the nature of Lore Banes when I remembered one of the new stories. One that had been ripped from the mind of an old Black Spiral Dancer in Croatia. Jo'cllath'mattric wanted to make sure that information about itself was as safely hidden as possible, so it bound up all the tales about itself into a clutch of unusually vile Lore Banes, bulking them out with a load of other tale spirits. Then it had one of its top lieutenants select an agent to carry the Banes out of the East, to somewhere out of the way, but where they could still be very useful in controlling European policy. To London. I don't know if the agent was a Spiral, a fomor or simply kin, and I'm not sure of the dates, but I do know his name and that he was a child at the time."

Nicola River-Runner looked cautiously excited. "How certain are you?"

"The old Spiral was absolutely certain. He watched the child being briefed." Julia grinned wryly. "I'm not much of a tale spinner, but the information is crystal clear."

"I don't like the idea of there being a nest of Banes on the doorstep that none of us have ever noticed," Blake said, "but I suppose that if they were being stealthy, it's easy enough to remain out of sight in the city."

"We will hunt out this nest of Banes and destroy them," Storm-Eye said with a fierce smile. "There should be much lore released."

"Are you sure you are up to the task?" asked Blake.

Storm-Eye looked about to explode at him, so Cries Havoc quickly said, "We have experience fighting these things. They're not easy to kill, but we have done it."

"We have won some major skirmishes recently," said John North Wind's Son. "We fight well together, as a good pack should. We'll be up to it."

"Although, if you wanted to tell someone to tag along, I'm sure we could find a use for them," Carlita said, grinning.

"You're welcome to ask for volunteers, Big Sis," said Karen pleasantly. "We don't assign security outside of caern matters, though. It's sept policy."

"We will need your assistance in locating this person, so it is that aid that we are asking for," said Storm-Eye. "We are prepared to make restitution for that aid, and for your hospitality. Once we know the location of the Banes, we will deal with them."

"Not only should that allow us to recover all sorts of stories and other information that we've lost," said Julia, "but we should also get data about Jo'cllath'mattric that the monster itself considered important enough to hide off site—perhaps even a vulnerability. That would be a pretty major scoop."

Nicola nodded. "Blake? Karen? No? Okay then. Clearing a nest of Banes out of the area, recovering lost lore and helping to stabilize affairs in the East are all important tasks that will be of direct benefit to Old City. If the Balkans can eventually be stabilized somehow, that will also be excellent for business. Your quest itself is a more than generous chiminage, and you seem confident in what you're doing. After the battles you've fought in the last week or so, I'm not that surprised. I'll place some of the IT people at your disposal, and I'll see if I can persuade a couple of the security team to volunteer to assist you when the time comes."

"Thank you," said Storm-Eye. "Your help will be valuable."

"It's very generous of you," added Julia. "We appreciate it."

"I'd be a poor manager if I didn't help a valued team member realize her full potential," said Nicola with a glint in her eye.

Julia smiled wryly. "Indeed."

Chapter Five

The woman ran through the forest, ducking and weaving between the gnarled, densely packed trees, forcing her body through the knots and tangles of branches. She was bleeding from a score of scrapes and cuts. Behind her, though, she could hear the cop coming after her. He was bigger than she was, but he was able to take advantage of the spaces she had already crashed through, and he had his nightstick to help smash the way further open. No matter how hard she tried, no matter which narrow openings she squeezed through, she couldn't make any significant headway.

I can make this stop. Spare yourself. The voice was familiar, a sinister wheedling tone to it. Briefly, the woman found herself wondering how long she had been running from the cop. It felt like years. It felt like moments. If she could only find the way...

I can show you the way.

She caught her wrist in the crook of a branch, and for a short moment it blazed with agony. "Screw you!" she screamed at the voice, at the cop, at the obstructive, hostile trees. Furious resentment boiled up, almost as if it were out of the pain in her wrist, giving her the strength to defy the voice. "Fuck your way. I want *my* way."

The voice said nothing, so she kept on running, and the cop kept coming after her.

***

As soon as the meeting was over, Nicola River-Runner demonstrated that she was as good as her word. After a quick consultation with Karen, she settled on an office that they could use to coordinate the search, and took them up to the second floor. The room, C6, was as bland and functional as its name. A central pool of desks and workstations, all in institutional office gray, offered seating for up to eight. Every place included a telephone, a networked computer, a pad of paper and several biros and pencils. Large whiteboards covered one long wall, and a large coffeemaker—complete with spare filters, cups and even portions of sugar and creamer—sat on one desk. A yucca plant pretended to offer a natural touch, but Julia could see the dust on the leaves.

Nicola left them there—"To get settled in"—and went to get a couple of the sept's computer experts and some material they would need. Storm-Eye had reverted to Lupus, and the ripped clothes she'd been wearing were in the corner. She looked harried, claustrophobic even. Cries Havoc was clearly unhappy as well. Julia had an idea.

"Storm-Eye, may I make a suggestion?"

The pack leader turned to look at her, warily. *Speak.*

"It would be good if as many sept members as possible could hear about what's happened to us over the last couple of months. You are our leader, and Cries Havoc is a Galliard; together, you would make a strong impression on the sept. People here usually gather in the courtyard when they're not doing anything urgent. Would the two of you mind going down there and talking to some of them? I know that if Cries Havoc got to tell that saga of his healing a couple of times, all sorts of Garou would be interested in listening. Glass Walkers are always interested in learning something new."

No one was fooled for an instant, but Storm-Eye and Cries Havoc exchanged glances, and then Storm-Eye nodded acceptance graciously. *Act as envoy? It cannot hurt. Very well. Send message when we are required.* Cries Havoc looked like he was about to protest—they probably could have been of *some* use— but after a moment, he followed Storm-Eye out of the room. John North Wind's Son nodded approvingly at Julia.

If Nicola was surprised to see that they were down from five Garou to three when she returned, she gave no indication of it. "Julia, I'm assigning Jared Pelling and Lisa Webber to your project team on this." She waved a pair of familiar faces into the room, laden with directories and references. "Jared, Lisa, you know Julia Spencer; her companions are Big Sis and John North Wind's Son. Julia dear, if you need any extra help or there's anything I can do, just let me know. Good luck." She bustled out, leaving the hackers behind.

Jared was a rumpled-looking man in his midthirties with a shrewd, ferrety face and a shock of dyed red hair. Kin, if she remembered correctly, but eidetic, and an expert with both GWnet and the Internet. Lisa was almost half his age, a slender Ragabash cub with an obvious taste for Nu Metal, black makeup and spiky facial piercing. She was a rather quiet, pleasant girl under her war paint, and Julia liked her. She was also the sept's best major systems infiltrator bar none, due at least partly to her incredible social engineering skills—she was an amazing actress and mimic.

"Greetings," Jared said, grinning broadly at them and scattering his pile of directories across the tables. "I hope we're all well on this fine afternoon."

"Yeah, hi," added Lisa, placing her huge stack of paper down carefully.

"Good afternoon," Julia said with a smile. "Let's all get seated and see what we can uncover, shall we?" When everyone had settled down, and Carlita and

North Wind's Son had been successfully logged in, Julia outlined the plan of action.

"Okay, we're trying to locate a Caucasian male called Mika Gerbovic. He might be as young as fourteen or fifteen or as old as fifty-five to sixty, but I expect him to be in his twenties or thirties. He's originally from Croatia and may be an official immigrant. He was about twelve when he moved to London, whenever that was. I'm not even totally sure he's still alive, though, so we may need to check death certificates, too. To start with, I think we should work independently and then pool our information after a few hours. We'll be able to cover more ground that way, and it'll help avoid cross-contamination of initial leads. John, Carlita, you're not really that familiar with our computer systems, so if it's okay, I'd be grateful if you would check records."

She waved a hand at the large stack of printouts that Lisa had deposited. "That's the electoral register for London, by constituency and then year, over the last decade. For each year in each constituency, the voters are sorted alphabetically by surname. Gerbovic probably doesn't have much interest in politics, but he'd need to register before he'd get approval for a credit card or loan. John, do you mind checking through it?"

North Wind's Son looked at the stack of paper and sighed. "Not the most heroic day's work I've ever faced. How many different sections are there?"

"Exactly seven hundred and fifty, I'm afraid. We have to get each part from public library photocopies every year, and no one has got round to typing them up yet." She smiled sympathetically. The hulking Wendigo warrior groaned but pulled the stack of printouts over to his desk.

Carlita eyed Julia nervously. "What have you got lined up for me, your highness?"

"Hospital," said Julia, grinning broadly. Carlita looked puzzled. "I'd like you to phone around the various doctor's surgeries in London. Pretend you're calling from St. Bart's Hospital, and tell them that Gerbovic has collapsed and is unconscious, is in your intensive care, and you need a fax of his medical records urgently. Imply he's from their area, or else they won't look for you. Even if he's a Spiral, he'll have been encouraged to have the standard vaccinations and checkups at school, and refusing is always suspicious."

Carlita cocked a quizzical eyebrow at Julia. "Don't you think the good old Florida accent will get in the way? Surely I won't know the right terms, either."

"That should be an advantage, actually," volunteered Lisa. "Tell them you're a temp. It'll give you an excuse to be a bit clueless with them. With any luck, it should make them ask you less questions."

"Okay…" said Carlita, dubiously. "I'll give a couple a try and see how it goes."

"Thanks," Julia said, smiling. "You'll find doctors' surgeries listed in the various yellow pages directories that cover the city. Most of them will have someone to answer phones until 6 p.m. or later, so you've got several hours."

"Gee, thanks."

"Jared, I'd like you to see if there's any trace of him on the net, either ours or the commercial one. It's worth checking news and magazine sites for their archives and having a look on the Companies House on-line databases. He could crop up in any context."

"Way ahead of you," said Jared, already typing away furiously.

"Great." Julia knew better than to be irritated by what many other Garou would have perceived as an insult. "Lisa, you've got the heavy stuff—driver records on the DVLC database in Cardiff, the Sherlock system at Scotland Yard, air travel logs to the Balkans, registrar's offices for deaths. Do you think you might be able to get into financial records?"

Lisa looked a little hurt. "Of course. Clearinghouses are easy. It's only tricky if you want to steal money. Basic customer records are kept in comparatively low-security areas. That won't be any problem at all. I got into the Home Office's subversives list last week. They change the phone number every day, but I'm sure I can track it down if you want me to check there, too."

"Is it risky?"

"Sure. They're a bit twitchy. But if this guy is dodgy, he'll probably be down there somewhere…"

"How do you define 'twitchy'?" asked Julia.

"Well… let's just say that if they spot me and trace the line, they'll be over here with half a dozen squad cars from two districts, the nearest Trojan ARV and a spotter in a helicopter."

Julia blinked. "Better not, then. I don't think Nicola River-Runner would be too pleased to have a small army of police gatecrash the evening meal. How do you know the response policy, by the way? Was it in a file?"

Lisa smiled sweetly. "As a matter of fact, a yucky old creep hassled me to take his phone number in a club two weeks ago, so I bounced my first attempt off his phone loop. When they noticed me, they traced the call back to his place. I used the CCTV network to watch them raid his flat."

Julia laughed. "That's one way of dealing with it."

"They had to let him go in the end. The HO are now being extra thorough about tracing calls into that server, unfortunately, so it might not work again."

"So we steer clear of them, for now, anyway. We can always come back to them if we need to."

"Okay, I'll get started."

Carlita looked up from the yellow pages. "You going to tell us what you're up to, oh mighty queen?"

"Me?" Julia smiled. "I'm going to surprise a few old friends of my father's and call in a favor or two… once I've taken care of a little urgent business. I'll be back in a couple of minutes." She was out of the door and on her way down to a very late breakfast before anyone had time to comment.

Half an hour later, and feeling considerably less light headed, Julia was ready to start in on the search herself. The others seemed to be getting on okay—eliminating possibilities, if not actually tracking down concrete leads. Across the table, Lisa was talking earnestly in a frighteningly accurate Glaswegian accent: "Aye, doll, I know, but we've no got a manual here in payroll and if I dinnae get that account name he'll be outwith his pay come week's end. It's no his password I'm askin' y'for." She flashed Julia a quick wink. Lisa could be very persuasive when she put her mind—and her gifts—to it.

Julia picked up her phone and dialed a number that wasn't even in her fetish-protected PDA. It was answered on the second ring.

"What?" He had a rough, gravelly voice with a thick East End accent.

"Uncle Bill? It's Julia." He wasn't a real uncle, of course. Bill was a childhood friend of her father and had been around a lot while Julia was growing up. He wasn't even kinfolk, in fact, but he had been a good friend over the years, and he had a lot of very useful contacts.

"Julia! Hello, girl. I haven't heard a peep out of you for donkey's. How's tricks in with all those merchant bankers?"

"Busy, thanks. Got a major project on at the moment. It's taken me over to the States for a bit recently. How about you?"

"You know the score, girl. Some's as up, some's as not. Had a spot of bother back a couple of weeks ago, but it's all sorted now, and only Epping Forest is the wiser. When you've got this project of yours put to bed, maybe you'd prise your old man out of his lovely mansion one Sunday and let Iris practice her roast-burning skills on you again."

"I'd love to, Uncle Bill. As soon as this project is out of my hair and I have a Sunday I'm not working."

"They'll work you into an early grave, my girl, if you let 'em. Mark my words."

"Yes," said Julia ironically. "I know."

"So to what do I owe the pleasure of hearing your lovely voice again, my girl?"

"I was hoping you might be able to help me with a little problem."

"A problem, eh? We're good at solving problems, round here. It'll be lovely to help out. How big a problem are we talking? Swimming lessons?"

"Nothing that serious, Uncle Bill. I need to find someone. Someone bad."

"You mean someone specific, I hope. I'd be all hurt like if there was a problem you didn't think I was up to solving."

"A specific someone, yes. He's... well, he's planning some pretty nasty things."

"All right, my girl. Let me know what you have, and I'll put the word out."

"Thank you. I really appreciate it."

"You just wheel your old pa out and come round for the afternoon. That's all the thanks I need."

"I will, Uncle Bill. Promise."

"Good. Now, this bad man…"

"His name is Mika Gerbovic. G-e-r-b-o-v-i-c. Mika as in the Formula One driver. He's Croatian, arrived here in London when he was eight. I don't know his age, I'm afraid, or what sort of business he's using as cover."

"Croatian, eh? Well, now. Can't say I know him myself, but I know a man who might. There's a gang of Serbs up on Muswell Hill. Wild lads, not the sort you'd take home to meet the family, if you know what I mean. Still, they know better than to cause trouble where it's not welcome, and they've always been polite—not that they had much choice, but still. Seems to me as if they might be a good place to start. You leave it with me, girl. If the Serbs draw a blank, there's plenty of other people I can ask."

"Thank you, Uncle Bill. You're a life-saver."

"That I am, my Julia. That I am. You still on your old number?"

"I am, yes."

"Then I'll call you as soon as I get word. Good talking to you, girl."

"Good talking to you, too, Uncle Bill. Thanks again. I'll see you soon, I promise."

"That's my girl! We'll sort this little issue out, see if we don't. Talk to you soon."

And so it went. Her father said that he'd question his colleagues and counterparts at other banks for any information about Gerbovic and promised he'd take a day off to visit Bill with her one weekend. Mac, one of the sept's kinfolk programmers, agreed to ask his partner, a forensic psychiatrist, about any clustering of mystery amnesia cases in London. A distant nephew of her father, who worked for a large newspaper conglomerate, said that he'd sniff around in the story archives in return for a little overtime "bonus." A friendly Child of Gaia—formerly an Old City fosterling and now back at the Rollright Sept in Oxfordshire— had a cousin who worked in the council's planning department and had checked records in the past.

Julia drew on every contact she could think of, and by the time she'd managed to get hold of them all, she had agreed to three social visits, one favor owed, two minor cash bribes and one date. She sat back, exhausted, and let herself enjoy a moment of peace and quiet. After she'd gathered her thoughts, she looked up at the others. "So how are we getting on?"

"I thought you Brits were supposed to be polite." Carlita sounded tired. "I've never come across a more complacent, small-minded, bureaucratic bunch of assholes in my life. And that's saying something, coming from Tampa. Lisa was a real help, though." Carlita grinned round at the cub. "You are one sneaky, underhanded, devious son of a bitch, girl. I'm impressed."

Lisa actually blushed—although it was mostly hidden by hair, makeup and steel—and mumbled, "Thank you, Big Sis."

"Thank *you*. Anyway, I got excited for a minute or two when a little old grandma in…" She checked the notes in front of her. "In a place called Camberwell found some of those immunization notes your were talking about. They were eight years old, though. I got her to fax them over anyway. I don't know if they'll be any use."

Julia smiled. "South of the river. That figures. That's amazing, Big Sis. Thank you! That tells us he's late teens or early twenties. The notes will probably have his hair color and eye color listed, and even an old address can be enough to track him down from. It's just a matter of putting in the legwork. A neighbor might remember something about where he moved on to, or there might be someone who knew him at the local school, or there are all sorts of other possibilities. It may take a couple of days per place he's lived in, but eventually we can run him to ground. I'd imagine that a pack of Lore Banes complicate things when you're moving, so he's probably living in the same area still. Camberwell gets pretty rough, and Peckham and Brixton—which are either side of it—are practically the human equivalents of Wyrmholes."

"You've done a lot better than I have, Big Sis," said John North Wind's Son. "I'm not really the paper-shuffling type to begin with, either. I've been through about half the records. I have not managed to locate anyone called Gerbovic. Plenty of Gerbers, some Gerbissons, even a Gerbov or two, but no Gerbovics."

"That's still important information, John," said Julia. "It helps us eliminate a number of avenues that might have taken up time. Thank you very much. Jared?"

"Hmm?" The red-haired kinfolk didn't even look up from the screen.

"Jared, have you found anything out?"

Finally, he looked up. "Oh. Yeah. Perhaps. He seems to be involved in the music scene. He's had a couple of passing mentions in 'zines and gig write-ups. Dance stuff—hip-hop or garage or something. I don't think he's an artist. Maybe he's a promoter, or a fixer, or has a venue or something. He's calling himself Mick rather than Mika. No one says much, though. I get the feeling they're scared of him."

"That could mean he's a Spiral," said North Wind's Son.

Julia nodded. "Yes, perhaps. That would explain why Carlita only turned up vaccinations for him. There's also plenty of things going on in the music scene in Brixton, from what I understand. And the drugs scene. Thank you, Jared."

"It was nothing." He beamed at her and then immediately sank back down behind his computer.

Julia grinned wryly. "What did you uncover, Lisa?"

"I found him in the DVLC database, license number GERBO-811071-MC5RD. He's the registered owner of a black Mercedes SLK 320, which he bought new, personalized registration number M1CK G. He passed his driving test two years ago. Both the test and the car registration have him living in Stockwell, but the building was gutted by fire eighteen months ago and pulled down shortly afterwards. He has a bank account with one of the big four, and very healthy it is, too. Suspiciously so, for his age. He probably paid for his Merc in cash. The address listed on the account—in Herne Hill—was demolished to make way for a drive-in burger restaurant four years ago. He's 22, and his birthday is November 7."

"That's incredible work, Lisa. Thank you so much. We'll have the little bastard in no time. He seems to be staying in the Lambeth and Southwark districts. Camberwell, Herne Hill and Stockwell are clustered all around Brixton, so that's going to be the first place to start looking. We know how old he is, what he's calling himself and what car he drives—and it's a flashy one, so it may be noticed—and we think he's involved in the music industry. He's probably a Spiral. Six hours ago, we didn't know anything about him at all. Good work, people. Very, very good work. I suggest we hang our hats up for the night and go relax a bit downstairs."

"Just hold on there a second," said Carlita as everyone started to file wearily out of the room. "What did you find out, team leader?"

Julia smiled. "That some of my friends miss me, and that some of them aren't that friendly after all. Don't worry, I've got a lot of people working on it. I can't really start pestering them for updates just yet."

"Okay, I'll let you off." She grinned.

"Thanks," said Julia, turning off the light and closing the door. "You're all heart."

"And don't you forget it."

Chapter Six

Later that evening, Julia was in the courtyard with her packmates, relaxing and unwinding a little. She was about to start trying to explain about Peckham—Storm-Eye had difficulty understanding why anything would live like that, even humans—when the phone rang. She answered it quickly, grateful to avoid the subject. "Julia speaking."

"Hello, Julia, it's your uncle. I do hope I'm not disturbing anything."

"Uncle Bill! Hi. Everything okay?"

"Sweet as a nut, my girl. Sweet as a nut. I've tracked down your mystery bad man."

"That's wonderful news!"

"Yeah. Them Serb lads I mentioned were very keen to help. They know of him, all right, and they don't like him one little bit. Turns out he's hand-in-glove with the Yardies down in Brixton. He's a part-time fixer with a nice little side in moving the white stuff along. A bad fella, bad as they get. I want you to promise me you ain't going to do anything stupid, my girl. If the Muswell Hill contingent are scared of him—and they are, for all they were bragging at me—then he's a very dangerous lad."

"I won't go anywhere near him," she lied. "Promise."

"I do hope you mean that, girl. I'd hate to get cross with you."

"I just need to find out where he is, Uncle Bill. Other people will take it from there. Specialists."

"All right, lass. I'll believe you. According to the Serbs, he's got a garage about halfway up Coldharbour Lane. Been laying low recently, but that's where he's at."

"A garage?"

"That's what the boy said. I'll admit his English wasn't the best I've heard, but it wasn't that bad."

"Do you think he meant a mechanic's garage, or somewhere to park a car?"

"Oh, it must be a body shop of some sort. The bloke said it was a business, some sort of private auto club or something."

"That shouldn't be too hard to find. Thanks a million, Uncle Bill. Oh, that reminds me—I've spoken to Father, and he promised to take a Sunday off soon and let me bring him round."

"That's what I want to hear, my girl! You get yourself round as soon as you can."

"I will."

"Look, Julia," said Bill, sounding serious for a change, "be very careful, okay? This Croatian of yours is a real piece of work. Very dangerous. Your old dad wouldn't be able to cope with losing you, too. You keep out of the way of this cockroach."

Cockroach? She mentally smacked herself in the forehead.

"Do you hear me, girl?"

She wrenched her thoughts back into gear. "I'll keep out of the way, Uncle Bill. Don't worry about me. I'm not going to get myself killed, I promise. I'll see you soon. And thank you."

"It's a pleasure, twinkle. Bye."

"Night."

She hung up. Cockroach. There wasn't anywhere in the city that his brood couldn't go, including into the very data streams themselves. She'd been so busy playing Glass Walker, she'd forgotten to think like a Theurge... She leapt up, and barely pausing long orce ghosted away from her finger, stirring the Umbra. She spoke to it, knowing her words would become part of the ripple in the spirit realm.

"This is Julia Spencer, Glass Walker of the Old City Sept. I call to the brood of Cockroach. I am trying to hunt the agents of corruption, a man named Mika Gerbovic who lives on Brixton's Coldharbour Lane. Are there any who can tell me about him?"

She heard a whispering rustle, and a moment later a sense of presence hit her like a hammer blow. She opened her eyes and bit back a scream. Thousands of cockroaches were surging from the vents all around her, a tide of nearly silent carapaces blanketing the rooftop around her. They didn't stop at her legs, either. The cockroaches swarmed up over her, too, and she had to fight down a rising tide of rage and panic. They left her hands and face alone, but within seconds they had covered the rest of her body, like a living, clicking suit of medieval armor. They even climbed around in her hair, and she could feel their tiny, feathery legs running lightly across her scalp, their long antennae probing and exploring.

Only years of training in trance states and extensive experience in the often surprising ways of the spirit realm kept her from bursting into her Crinos war-form and a berserk rage. That and the oppressive aura of power surrounding her, of course. She shuddered involuntarily and saw the bugs covering her ripple and matter as they held on to her clothing.

Her PDA grabbed her attention. A cursor was blinking away in the top left corner of the screen. As she looked at it, words appeared.

"WHO ARE YOU, TO CALL ME AND MINE?"

enough to tell her packmates that there was
she had to check out, headed for the kitch

Five minutes later, she was up on the r
second time that day. The caern's extractor s
a number of vents up there, in with a tangl
machinery. The air was always warm and h
natural result of all those people living
proximity, and the tangle of vents and pip
that there were plenty of dark, confined space
of the vents led straight from the kitchen's
fans. It was perfect cockroach territory, the b
caern.

She laid the scraps of food that she'd go
the kitchen around the mouth of the pipe that
to the extractor behind the fridges—that wa
that usually gave the best results—and sa
opening her PDA. Tapping away deftly with t
she opened her folder of work software and
her invocation program. The screen went bl
started slowly pulsing with a faint glow.

Julia closed her eyes and then started ca
mind. The mantra came to her automaticall
my thoughts, but that which thinks them. I
emotions, but that which feels them. I am no
but that which controls it. I am not my mir
which defines it. She forced away her th
emotions and stepped back from them, us
concentration to hold them outside of her.
dialogue—the mental voice that i
subvocalizing every thought—fell silen
turned to crystal as Julia let herself simpl

She reached out and touched the
PDA. She pressed, and her finger sank i
as if it were still water. She could feel t
of the Gauntlet parting around it. A ci

Julia paused, then typed out her answer on the PDA's keypad. "I am Julia Spencer of the Old City Sept."

"THAT IS NOT ENOUGH. I ASK AGAIN, WHO ARE YOU, TO CALL ME AND MINE?"

She frowned, concerned and confused. "I am Julia Spencer of the Silver River Pack."

"THAT IS WORSE, AND AN INSULT BESIDES. I ASK ONCE MORE, AND ONCE MORE ONLY… WHO ARE YOU, TO CALL ME AND MINE?" The response snapped whole onto the screen, and the roaches covering her rustled and clacked.

Julia suddenly felt very vulnerable. Getting the wrong answer again didn't bear thinking about. After several moments of careful thought, she typed a nervous response. "I am a Glass Walker."

The atmosphere eased, and the roaches swarming her settled down. "YOU WOULD DO WELL TO REMEMBER THAT FIRST AND FOREMOST, THEURGE. THE DATA YOU SEEK IS ALREADY WITHIN YOUR ACCESS."

Julia thought for a moment but couldn't make sense of the pronouncement. She typed out her answer on the PDA's keypad. "I don't understand."

"SUFFICIENT UNDERSTANDING IS A PASSWORD."

Her mind whirled. It was obviously some sort of test. "I see."

"YOU WILL. DO NOT EVER HARM MY CHILDREN, DAUGHTER OF THE RIVERBED."

"I will not harm them." She wasn't about to defy an Incarna's avatar.

"SWEAR IT."

"I swear I will never harm a cockroach." She spoke the words aloud as she typed them, aware that they were binding her.

"THEN I WILL LEND YOU A BOON, ONCE AND ONCE ALONE, FOR WHEN YOU WISH TO GAIN ENTRANCE TO THE LAIR OF THE BEAST. THIS MATTER IS OF IMPORTANCE. DO NOT CALL ON IT BEFORE."

Before she could even offer thanks, the presence was gone—as were the cockroaches covering her. She blinked a couple of times in confusion, but there was no getting around the fact that they had simply vanished. Her PDA had reset, but in the bottom corner of the screen she could see an unfamiliar icon that looked like a broken keyboard on strings. Below it, the descriptor read *Summon Net-Spider*.

She stared at it in disbelief. Several minutes later, it still hadn't changed, and her eyes were starting to hurt. She blinked a couple of times to clear them and then found herself fighting the insane urge to leap up and down whooping. She looked around at the empty roof, making sure no one was around, then smiled broadly and gave in. A minute or two later, when she'd calmed down a bit, she sat down again and thought about the riddle. If she went downstairs, she'd get bogged down in questions and explanations.

Sufficient understanding is a password. The phrasing was clumsy, even awkward. Unusual for a spirit. They almost always spoke cryptically, but usually their words had a certain rhythm to them, almost an internal poetry. "Sufficient understanding is a key" would have been a more accurate and elegant metaphor. Then again, Cockroach had seemed particularly obsessed by computing terms. *Password. Access. Data.* Julia racked her brain but couldn't remember anything about the spirit usually talking in techno-jargon. She hadn't had the privilege of talking to it before, and her particular specialty was the Weaver and its spirits. Karen, though… She was the sept's strongest Theurge and a specialist in city spirits…

Julia grabbed her phone and called Karen's mobile. The elder answered almost at once. "Julia, is that you?"

"Hi, Karen. Yes, it's me. I'm really sorry to bother you at this time."

"No, it's perfectly all right." She sounded sympathetic. "I'm happy to help. Have you come to a decision?"

"Eh?" said Julia, puzzled. *Decision?* "Oh. That. No, it's nothing to do with that. This is important."

"Oh, really?" Karen sounded amused. "More important than your future?"

"Quite a lot more important, actually."

"All right," said Karen, sounding less amused now. "What is it?"

"Cockroach. Not the insect—well, not just the insect."

"You're losing me," said Karen, confused. "Slow down."

Julia recalled a bit of general sept gossip. "Cockroach, the Incarna, is your patron, right?"

"Yes…" said Karen, warily.

"Have you spoken to its avatar personally?"

"Julia, can't this wait until morning? It's past midnight. I'm in bed." Karen was starting to sound a bit pissed off.

"I'll explain tomorrow morning," said Julia, trying to sound placatory. "It really is important, though."

"All right," Karen said, stifling a yawn. "Yes, I have spoken to Cockroach on a number of occasions."

"Fantastic. Did it talk in computer jargon?"

There was a long pause on the other end of the line, and when Karen spoke again, she had on her official kind and sympathetic voice. "Are you all right, Julia? I know we put you under a lot of pressure this morning. It's okay if you've had a drink or two to take the edge off. We all do it from time to time."

Julia couldn't help grinning. "I'm not pissed or stoned, Karen. I promise. Please, humor me. Does Cockroach talk in computer jargon?"

Karen paused again. "Not particularly, no."

It all clicked into place. "YES!" Julia suddenly realized she'd shouted down the phone at her elder. "Oh, shit. Sorry, Karen. It just all makes sense now."

"No it bloody doesn't."

"Um, well, I was talking to Cockroach," said Julia, excitedly. "It kept using computer terminology, which seemed out of place, and it said that sufficient understanding was the password, but it was a play on words and it meant that a password would serve as sufficient understanding to get the answer…" She trailed off. "I'm not making much sense, am I?"

Stony silence told her that she was right.

"Right. From the top. I wanted to ask the roach spirits of the city if they knew anything about this Gerbovic guy," said Julia, making an effort to slow down and explain a bit. "So I did an invocation, but I got the boss instead. Cockroach itself—well, it's avatar, anyway, along with a couple of thousand pals. It left me with a riddle and an unexpected present. The riddle was phrased with computer jargon, and if it doesn't usually talk in computer jargon, then that's a clue, and I think it must mean that we have the information I need here, in the sept's own database."

"Okay," said Karen. "I'm with you now. I'm impressed, Julia. Cockroach is normally rather shy. What was the present?"

"A Net-Spider program. One-shot." Julia could feel the grin plastered over her face.

"Bloody hell!" Karen sounded thunderstruck. "That's one of the legendary routines. The power to take total control over any computer system is not one that's ever given out lightly. I assume it's got a designated time for activation?"

"Yes," said Julia, "when we need to get in to Gerbovic's place."

"Well, whatever you're going to be doing in there, it must be absolutely critical if Cockroach is providing that much intervention. Someone obviously thinks highly of you. I'll talk to you about it in the morning."

"Sure. Thanks for the help, Karen. Sorry to have woken you."

"That's all right," said Karen, sounding thoughtful. "Always a pleasure."

"Night," Julia said.

"Good night." Karen hung up.

The PDA had wireless access to the sept's internal servers within the caern's boundaries, thanks partly to the spirit bound into it and partly to a bluetooth flashcard. It took no more than a few seconds to log in to her account—*understanding how to use my own password is sufficient*, she thought with a grin—and run a search. It threw up a sequence of twenty or thirty image files in a subdirectory of the security folder. She flicked through them and was amazed to see that they were high-definition digital CCTV stills from the caern's own security system.

The pictures showed a black Mercedes parked on the road outside the front of the caern. The second in the sequence was a close-up of the personalized registration plate, M1CK G. There were several close images of Gerbovic, too. He was dark haired and dark eyed, clean shaven and muscular. Handsome, in an arrogant, self-satisfied way. He looked almost familiar. His suit, what could be seen of it, was clearly expensive. As the sequence progressed, "Tiny" Tim—a brawny Child of Gaia who was part of the sept's Ahroun security team—went over to the car and exchanged words with Gerbovic, who was clearly playing businessman. Then, at last, Julia hit gold. Gerbovic tried to hand over a business card, and although Tiny Tim refused it, the CCTV got a good angle in one frame. She zoomed in on the card, and her viewer sharpened the image as best it could.

The result was not particularly pretty, but it *was* legible. His name and business were centered self-importantly in the middle of the card, *Mick Gerbovic*. *Club Release*, *Brixton*. A smaller, lighter strap-line below the club name declared *London's Hottest Garage Night*. A cell-phone number was in the bottom left corner.

"Gotcha," said Julia with a fierce smile.

Chapter Seven

From the outside, Club Release looked pretty unimpressive. It was large, there was no doubt about that; the frontage was easily fifty yards long. There were no windows or decorative features, though—apart from the entrance lobby, which was fronted in glass—and the building itself was painted a nasty dark gray color. A thick metal security grille had been pulled down in front of the entrance area, and the complex alarm box blinking away behind it indicated that the building's security system, at least, was in a good state of repair.

The place looked strangely dilapidated. There were a number of plastic-sheeted poster frames along the building's length, advertising special promotions and coming attractions. They were all well out of date, though, promoting events for the previous month. One of the lobby's glass panels was broken in one corner, presumably by someone with a broomstick. The large sign over the door that announced the club's name had been tagged by athletic vandals a number of times. The poster frames had been scrawled on, too.

The Penumbra was a very different matter. Peering through the Gauntlet at the building, Julia could see that the walls were dripping with acrid slime, oozing from the roofline. Pattern Spiders on the surrounding buildings were trying to spin webs onto the club, but the slime ate straight through them as fast as they could be laid. The Weaver's forces didn't seem to be able to make any impact on the place. The entrance lobby area looked like a revolting chancre, red and swollen. It was surrounded by an arch of sickly green glyphs. They pulsed and sizzled, as if they were radioactive. Perhaps they were. Inside the gaping entrance, further glyphs were woven together into some sort of ward. Julia got the disconcerting impression that the Umbral building was hungry. She switched her senses back to the mundane world.

According to several passersby that they had talked to in the center of Brixton, the club had suddenly stopped opening a couple of months ago. It had been quite the place, but it had just failed to open one evening. Several weeks had passed before would-be patrons stopped turning up in the hope that it was open again. The scene had moved on to the next hotspot. No one seemed to know anything concrete about why the club had closed. The pack had received a different answer from everyone. "Oh, the manager did a flit," said one man confidently. "My mate knows a girl who worked there. He grabbed the cash and ran." A couple of girls were certain that the police had closed the place down because some of the party goers were being abducted and forced into a sex ring. An old cabbie insisted that the owner had just gone on holiday and would be back soon.

Julia looked over at North Wind's Son in the passenger seat and shrugged uncomfortably. "It's a hellhole, all right. The Pattern Spiders aren't even getting close to it—and they're doing their best. The entrance is warded with some rather nasty-looking glyphs, too. We're not going to want to try it in the Penumbra unless there's no other choice. I can't tell for certain if the nest is there or not."

Storm-Eye was in the back, scrunched uncomfortably in human form between Carlita and Cries Havoc. "Is there any reason to believe that it is not?"

"Not particularly, no. Everyone seemed to agree that the place just shut down mysteriously, with no warning, when it was doing really well. That's always suspicious, so it's not the way to do it if you want to cover your tracks. Plus, according to Jared, most of the other places Gerbovic has moved out of have been destroyed, one way or another. This doesn't look planned. Maybe something happened to him."

"We are here for Lore Banes, not for their caretaker," said Storm-Eye. "So much the better if he is elsewhere. We shall proceed. Your vision last night indicates that this is the correct lair."

"Okay then," said Julia. "Shall we go back to Old City, or does anyone want to stay here any longer?"

Carlita glanced out of the window. "Actually, yeah, can you give me five?"

"What did you have in mind?"

"I've just spotted an old friend." She slipped out of the car. Julia watched her make her way to a small confectioners' three shops down. She emerged a couple of minutes later with a bag of stuff, munching on a chocolate bar and grinning broadly.

The return journey to Old City was mercifully short, only twenty minutes or so. The car was one of the sept's pool vehicles and was fitted with an identity chip fetish that opened the gates to the underground car park. Julia parked, and the pack headed back up to rejoin the sept. There was still the best part of half an hour before they were scheduled to report back to Nicola. Julia left the others in the courtyard and headed up to her rooms to get changed for the meeting.

When she opened her door, she noticed a plain envelope on the floor, her name handwritten on it. She picked it up curiously and opened it. Inside, there was a note along with a faxed sheet.

Miss Spencer, Sorry about leaving a note. I'm off for the rest of the day. Mary has run up a list of spontaneous amnesia cases in the last six months, as you requested. I've enclosed it with this note. I hope it's of some use. Thanks again for helping get my sister's CV in front of your father. Sincerely, Mac.

She turned to the fax, scanned down the column of data and grinned broadly.

By the time Julia had changed into something suitably smart and returned to the courtyard, there wasn't really time for her to explain about the fax. It was a couple of minutes before the whole pack assembled. Cries Havoc had been telling a small group of interested Garou and Kinfolk about his experiences of the horror that village life had become for the everyday inhabitants of the Balkans, and it had taken him a while to get away. He'd proved to be a big hit with the sept members—who were quite cosmopolitan, for the most part, and always interested in information—and was enjoying the chance to stretch his talents again. Carlita had been in the canteen, grabbing a snack and chatting to a tribemate who was based out of a small Gnawer sept down amongst the homeless cardboard city at Waterloo Bridge.

When everyone was ready, the pack made its way to Nicola's office. Storm-Eye stayed in her Lupus form this time, presumably unwilling to add further to the list of compromises she was being forced to make in the city. Her temper was starting to fray, and she was spending most of her time in the courtyard, by the bole of an ancient yew tree. Julia sympathized. The sept *was* strongly geared toward homid interests. When they got to Nicola's office, the door was open, and the elder called them straight in.

Karen and Blake were already there, sitting around the coffee table. The Silver River Pack joined them as

Nicola welcomed them in. When everyone was settled, Nicola started on an informal basis.

"Hi, everyone. Thanks for coming. I'm looking forward to finding out what you learned at the club. Before that, though Julia, could you tell me a bit about what happened last night?"

"It was something my uncle said. He had got hold of some information about Gerbovic and was trying to warn me off messing with him, the sweetie. Anyway, he referred to him as a cockroach… It reminded me that the one place I hadn't tried looking for answers was the spirit realm, so I went up onto the roof to see if I could coax out any cockroach spirits that knew anything."

Nicola nodded. Most of the sept knew—from long years of experience—that the outlet pipes on the roof were the best place for calling roach spirits.

"Anyway, I got a little more than I bargained for. An avatar of Cockroach itself turned up—along with a blanket of the insects—and left me a riddle and a Net-Spider program. I had to take a binding oath never to harm another roach, but I think it's worth it." She grinned. "I'm not the bug-squashing type as it is, and I can't really remember even noticing a roach before outside of dealings with the brood. If it had asked me to give up bacon, it could have been a very different story. After it had left, I realized that the riddle had used several odd bits of computer jargon. I phoned Karen." Julia grinned at the Truthcatcher. "I get the feeling you thought I'd been dropping acid, actually, Karen."

"I was getting quite concerned, yes," said Karen with a faint smile.

Julia turned back to Nicola River-Runner. "Karen was very patient with me and confirmed that

Cockroach wasn't known for its techno-babble. That gave me the answer to the riddle and led me straight to the CCTV image I showed you earlier."

Nicola looked thoughtful. "What did the spirit say about the Net-Spider program?"

"That it was single use, for when we wanted to get into the club. It also said that the raid was important."

"That's quite a tale building there, Julia," said Cries Havoc.

"It'll be even better if we can find some Lore Banes," Carlita said.

"Yes, it would be good to know for certain that they're there," said Blake.

It is the strongest trail, growled Storm-Eye in the Garou tongue.

"Plus, Cockroach's involvement and interest suggests that even if the Banes you're looking for aren't there," Karen said, "something else is. It's not a particularly sociable spirit at the best of times."

"Actually, I have some backup evidence." Everyone turned to look at Julia. "Mac left me a note that I just picked up a couple of minutes ago." She looked round at her packmates and smiled apologetically. "I haven't had a chance to tell you guys about it yet. His girlfriend is a forensic psychiatrist, and this morning she faxed over a list of unexplained amnesia cases in London over the last six months."

She handed the sheet to North Wind's Son to look at and pass around.

"As you'll see, there have been maybe fifteen or twenty cases in the city during that time, most of them presumed to be related to drug use, particularly cocktails of various Class As. Coldharbour Lane, where the club is based, is a notoriously drug-heavy area, but no more so than a dozen other districts. Four of the five cases in the last six weeks have been on or very near Coldharbour Lane—and three of those have been in the last ten days. The club has been closed for eight weeks, more or less, and Gerbovic himself is presumed missing. I think it's pretty plain that something in there is getting hungry. I'd guess there's three or four of them in there."

They are there, said Storm-Eye. *You follow a strange trail through places I do not fully understand, but you have followed it well.*

"Storm-Eye is right," said Nicola. "It seems pretty cut and dried. How easy is it going to be to get in?"

Julia looked slightly pained. "I'm not sure, actually. I don't really know what this Net-Spider program is capable of."

Karen shook her head. "Have you been skipping your classes, Julia? It'll hook you up to the system in the club. Full control. Anything you want it to do, it will. It's not known as a legendary Glass Walker routine for nothing."

Julia grinned. "Oh, I know. Don't worry. I meant I'm not sure how computerized the club is. I think the Spider will get us in, though. That's what Cockroach implied. Once we're in there, we'll just have to muddle along."

"Well, there are several people who would like to add to that muddle," Nicola said with a smile, "if you'll accept some extra hands on board."

Any who are prepared to fight will be welcome, said Storm-Eye.

"Great. The volunteers are Tim Bolyn, Pete Marment and Rochelle Harris. Tiny Tim is part of the security team, an Ahroun Child of Gaia. You may have seen him around—he's the one that looks like a mountain stuffed into a suit. I think he feels that he has something to atone for by not marking Gerbovic out as a bad'un when he spoke to him. Pete and Rochelle are both Galliards—I believe you've met them, Cries Havoc. They were inspired by your story of the death of your Lore Bane, and they're keen to get in on the act. Pete is a Glass Walker, and Rochelle is Fianna. They've both seen plenty of action, and I'm confident that they can cope. All three understand that you will be giving the orders, Storm-Eye. Lisa Webber wanted to be part of the group as well, but I've refused her request. She's still a cub—this week, at least. It's brave of her, though."

"They're all good people," said Julia, looking at Storm-Eye. "Particularly in a ruckus."

I will be glad to fight beside them, said Storm-Eye.

"Good, then it's settled," said Nicola. "When are you going to launch the raid?"

When we can quietly. We do not want to be seen entering.

"According to Old Herb," said Carlita, "the quietest time in that part of London is around dawn."

The Bone Gnawer?

"Yeah, that's right. He said that the early morning is by far the best time to go scavenging. No one gets in to work any earlier than they need to, and there are always people around in the middle of the night. Making the most of the night life."

"That would make sense," said Julia. "If there are other clubs in the area, it may be busy until three or four in the morning, even on a Thursday. The clubbers and other night people will all be in bed by six, and the office workers will just be getting up."

"We can plan things out tonight then," North Wind's Son said, "and get an early night so we're fresh tomorrow morning."

Very well. We leave at dawn.

"Can we make it ten minutes past dawn?" asked Cries Havoc.

Storm-Eye looked at him. *Yes. As soon as you have finished honoring the Sun's rise.*

"Thank you," he said and smiled.

After an early dinner, the pack gathered in a quiet corner of the courtyard to discuss the following day's battle. The three Old City Garou who would be going along joined them. Julia did the introductions, and then Storm-Eye took over, speaking in the Garou High Tongue.

"Our purpose in this fight is to destroy Lore Banes," said Storm-Eye, for the benefit of the new arrivals. "We can recover lost knowledge from the tale spirits bound up within them. If we find the human that is their keeper—this Gerbovic person—then it will be a bonus to kill him as well, but that is not as important. We think that the Lore Banes will have information that the great Wyrm-beast in the Balkans wanted hidden. That would be a very valuable day's hunting. The Lore Banes are strong and fast. Dangerous opponents, despite their odd appearance. We will need to fight them in the Penumbra so that they are truly destroyed and the tale spirits within them released."

"I'm not exactly experienced in the matter," said Cries Havoc, "but I have fought and killed one. They have fangs, clawed wingtips and a sharply spiked tail and can attack with all of them. The fangs can wound you in spirit as well as in body, particularly if the thing gets a clean bite at your head. The one I fought certainly liked grabbing hold with its talons and trying to bite me, and it was damn strong. It also grew long tendrils at one point, each one with a wickedly barbed hook on the end. These can damage your spirit as well, if you're not looking out for them. If you can disable a wing and get them on the ground, they're a lot easier to deal with."

"Do you know anything about the setup inside," asked Tiny Tim, "or what else might be in there?"

"I'm afraid not," said Julia. "However, the place is—or was—a nightclub, and a busy one at that. Its current period of closure seems to be accidental. I suspect that the Lore Banes will be shut up somewhere to keep them away from punters. I can't imagine how he'd keep more than four of them fed and quiet, so I'm guessing at that. It should be doable, as long as we keep our heads. If there are guards or other inhabitants, there can't be that many—the risks of keeping, say, a hive of Spirals in the same building as a thousand pissed-up clubbers would be way too great. I think the main defense has always been a low profile."

"That seems fairly sensible, I guess," said Carlita doubtfully. "I hope."

"Me too," said Julia grimly. "We might not have any power or light, either, so we should make sure we have torches, and walkie-talkies in case we get split up."

"The security team has plenty to spare," said Tiny Tim.

"So the plan is 'go in there and hope it's quiet'? Isn't that just a little sketchy?" Carlita sounded unimpressed.

"We have planned as closely as our information allows," said Storm-Eye. "We have discussed how the enemy fights. We are strong and resourceful. This is a raid, so we shall go in and raid. We will deal with threats as they arise."

"I don't see what else we can do," Julia said. "Lisa has been unable to find any information about the inside of the building. If we mount a surveillance effort, we may tip the Lore Banes off. At least this way, we should have surprise on our side."

Pete and Rochelle shared a look. "We just wanted to say thanks for the chance to come along," said Rochelle. "It's a great opportunity for any Galliard. We both know it's going to be a wild and hairy one, but it'll make a thumping story if nothing else."

"Your presence is welcome," said Storm-Eye.

"And if it all goes wrong," said Carlita with a wicked grin, "three Galliards should be enough to distract the Banes with a musical number or two."

***

The mistake had just been a tiny one, if indeed it had been a mistake at all, but now the trees had the woman penned in. The clearing had been miniscule from the start, just a few feet of clear space, but there had been a way through, a passage out the other side. As she had approached it, the heavy sound of hoarse breathing just behind her had made her turn. There had been nothing there, no explanation for the sound, but when she had turned back, the passage had closed up. The trees were a cage, interlocked and hostile. Disgusted with herself—she knew that you couldn't look away from the path, not here—she turned back, only to discover that the way she had come had sealed up, too.

She was trapped, her wrist burned like fire and something was getting closer. Distant still, but approaching.

A branch knocked against the small of her back, swaying in the breeze, and she knew that the trees had come in close behind her, harrying, confining. She almost looked round to see how near they were, but she repressed the instinct. It would be fatal to look away from the remaining foot or two of space ahead of her.

Behind you, said the voice, rich with slick malice. *It's behind you.*

She knew better—it was coming from the left. She could hear it. There would be a moment when the path would have to reopen as it approached, and that would give her a chance to make a break. So long as she kept the little of it that remained. She stared at it stubbornly.

A branch blew against her bad wrist, hard, and she got tangled up in it. She pulled at it, but it had her locked fast. It would go badly if she couldn't get away when the something came for her. She tugged harder, putting all her strength behind it. The branch seemed to be straining. Suddenly there was a deafeningly loud crack, and the tiny scrap of clearing was filled with light. Her wrist was free, and it had stopped hurting, too. After so long, losing the pain felt strange. Wrong. Still, it made things here just that little bit more bearable. In the burst of light, she caught sight of a way out of the confinement, through the trees, and she darted off again. The voice's gloating laughter followed her as she ran.

Behind her, a pair of fangs lay brokenly in the middle of what had become a broad, clear forest track.

Chapter Eight

Nothing appeared to have changed at Club Release. The extended pack had parked its cars a block away and approached on foot. At 5:45 on a Friday morning, the streets were almost completely empty. The occasional vehicle came past, but even those were few and far between, and no one seemed to take any notice. City dwellers quickly learnt not to pay attention to anything unusual around them—particularly in that part of London, where curiosity would quickly kill more than just cats. Storm-Eye had grudgingly agreed to stay in her Homid form until she made it into the club, and had even agreed to briefly wear a long coat and some sneakers.

The Garou clustered around the entrance, unpleasantly aware of the acrid stench of wrongness seeping out of the club. "So what do we try first?" asked Carlita.

"Julia uses her gift," said Storm-Eye. "The spirit said that she should use it when she wished to gain access."

Tiny Tim nodded. "That alarm system looks sophisticated. If we force our way in, we might find all sorts of nasty surprises. You would if you tried to strong-arm into Old City."

"Here goes, then," said Julia. She opened her PDA and double-tapped her stylus on the Net-Spider icon. The screen immediately blanked, then started pulsing with a soft glow. The glow intensified, getting stronger and stronger, until the light was actually shining into her eyes. Then it stopped pulsing and stabilized, still glowing brightly. A circle in the center of the screen darkened to a steady green, even though the PDA wasn't capable of displaying colors. Julia reached out and touched the green circle.

The world immediately peeled away, and she found herself looking into a landscape of data. The wall of the club was a sparse network of glittering strands of electricity. In front of her, the alarm box was a bright glowing cube, sending and receiving regular pulses of information along sparkling silver filaments. A thick beam of golden light, pulsing with packets of data, streamed out from her PDA and connected to a peculiar spirit clinging delicately to the alarm cube. The Net-Spider was an outline made up of sheets of golden light, floating on top of each other in widely spaced layers. Each sheet was an ever-changing tapestry of binary, tiny 1s and 0s flickering constantly. A high-tech doodle that almost resembled a perfectly symmetrical, squared off light-spider—if you squinted at it from a distance and ignored the fact that it was mostly empty space. The effect was strangely beautiful.

Without quite knowing how, Julia directed the Net-Spider to disable the alarm systems. It immediately merged with the cube of alarm data, sinking down into it. The cube turned gold, and a moment later so did the strands sparkling out of it. She could actually *feel* the spirit's control of the system, as if it were an extra limb she'd never known she had. The alarm circuits around the door were a tingling alertness, a momentary thought to ease into quiet rest. The security grille and front door locks were part of the system, too, tight, a muscular sensation like lifting a weight. She relaxed them, knowing that the locks were now open. Feeling slightly giddy, she closed her eyes and searched for the sensation of her finger touching the PDA screen. When she found her own sense of touch again, she lifted her finger off, and the normal world crashed back into focus. It was as if she'd been struck blind.

"Julia!" Carlita had her by the shoulders, shaking her. She looked worried.

"What? Stop shaking me!" Her cheek stung a little, too.

"Are you okay?"

"I'm fine," said Julia, puzzled. "Why? What's up? Did you slap me?"

"You've been standing there frozen still for almost five minutes. We couldn't get through to you. We thought something had gone wrong."

"It's like peering through the Gauntlet," said Julia distantly. "Only it's through the Net-Spider's perceptions. It… it's beautiful, Carlita. I could feel it all…" She looked at the appalled expression on the Bone Gnawer's face and grinned wryly. "Look, I'm okay. I can see why it's such a high-level routine. I've disabled the alarms, and"—she grabbed the grille and lifted it up smoothly—"opened the grille."

"Is the Net-Spider still running?" Cries Havoc sounded thoughtful.

Julia glanced at the PDA. The green circle was still there, inviting her back. "Yes. I'm not going to shut the machine down just yet, in case that ends the program. We might need it again."

"Is that safe?" asked Carlita doubtfully.

"It's fine." Julia smiled at her. "I know what to expect now. I was just taken aback with the power of it." She walked up the steps to the main door and pushed it open. "Last one in pull the grille down!"

As soon as they were within the shadowed lobby, the group grew into their hulking Crinos battle forms. The area was empty, just a small, narrow hall with a ticket desk and little cloakroom. Ahead of them, a pair of plush doors led into the main club. North Wind's Son took the lead, pushed the doors open slowly and stalked through. The others followed.

They were in a large open room. Some light filtered in through a set of small, shaded skylights, enough to make out the basic layout. A bar was to the left, glittering with glass panels, mirrors and spirit bottles. A few designer stools—tall and uncomfortable looking—were resting along the wall, underneath a thin metal drinks shelf. Doors indicating ladies' and gents' restrooms were at the far end of the bar. To the right of the group, the room opened up into a huge dance floor, complete with towering speaker stacks, dancing platforms, a DJ station and a mezzanine observation area. The ceiling, easily twenty feet high, was a mass of spotlights, projectors and other bits and pieces.

The room stank of decay and corruption. The air was thick with it. Rather than getting used to the stench, the pack thought it actually was getting worse. It seemed to be strongest over on the dance floor. Julia walked out onto it a little way. It was revolting, sticky with old drink and congealed sweat.

"Something's wrong," she said quietly. "I think something's coming. A guardian."

Carlita grinned at her and hefted her fang dagger. "Time for some fun."

Julia nodded and stepped back off the dance floor. It was difficult to see in the dim light, but it appeared to be rippling somehow. She started to point it out, but a slithering noise coming from all over the dance floor immediately silenced her.

"It's the floor," said Pete, amazed. "It's bunching up in the center."

The sickly smell of decay was getting stronger. The floor *was* buckling up. Then she realized with a lurch of disgust that it wasn't the floor that was collecting itself up at all, but the thin layer of filth covering it.

"It's the shit *on* the floor," she said. "It's knitting a body from the spilt booze and drops of sweat and drug-soaked vomit and piss and pheromones and god knows what else ends up on the floor here at the end of a heavy night."

They all turned to look at the form rapidly taking shape in the middle of the floor. It was bipedal, at least fourteen feet tall, with a broad chest tapering down to an incredibly thin waist. It took on definition as they watched, and Julia realized that it was a parody of a naked woman—a huge, long-armed, dirty gray woman with twelve-inch claws for fingers and toes, and hollow pits where the eyes should have been. Its skin churned in constant motion, giving the impression of a seething bed of maggots. An aura of dirty cravings and desperate lust oozed from it.

"What's the matter, baby?" Its voice was low and sultry, throbbing with evil. "Don't you want me?"

With a howl of defiance, the Garou leapt into battle.

The two Ahroun, John North Wind's Son and Tiny Tim, were the first to engage the corrupt spirit as the rest of the pack ran to move around it. It swung its claws at them, a lightning-swift slash at heads and necks. Its reach was immense. The two warriors barely managed to duck under the swing and barreled into the creature. It staggered back into a crouch as they slashed at it. North Wind's Son sank his claw tips through its abdomen, but the thin rips knitted back together almost as smoothly as he had cut them. The thing sprang straight up into the air and grabbed hold of a long rail of light fittings. It kicked out as it did so, and the sole of its foot caught North Wind's Son squarely in the forehead. He was knocked off his feet and fell backward. Tiny Tim managed to stay upright, but he had a nasty gash on his cheek where its claw had cut.

The Bane swung once, swiftly, and leapt backward off the light rail, landing outside the circle of Garou, behind Storm-Eye. She threw herself forward, hampering Rochelle and Carlita, but it slashed down with its claws as it dropped and scored bloody furrows along the length of Storm-Eye's back and thighs. She rolled out of the way with a snarl of pain and span round to face it. Cries Havoc slipped in from the side as it was dropping, and tore into its thigh with his claws and fangs. As he bit into the leg, it glanced down and punched him, hard, in the head. He was slung back, looking disgusted more than pained. He seemed to be having trouble clearing its mushy pulp from his mouth.

As Storm-Eye got to her feet, Julia and Pete slipped past her, the two Ahrouns close behind them. Julia moved in front of Pete as they got within the creature's range, then dropped into a crouch as soon as she saw it swing for her. She brought her arm up, focusing all her rage into the blow. As the thing's hand tore through the space she had been in, her claws cut into the gummy wrist. Simultaneously, Pete stabbed down into the vile hand. The creature screeched and kicked out, hand dangling limply, but Julia was already moving back. It took a half-step back and spun round, kicking Tiny Tim hard in the ribs where he was trying to flank it. Carlita used the moment to dart in and slash its flanks with her fang dagger before falling back. The thing flexed its damaged hand, and Julia realized that it was almost back to full use already. Her claws felt horribly sticky where she had cut into the Bane, and she spat on them without thinking, absent-mindedly rubbing the hissing muck off as she circled.

She caught a quick flash of movement off to her left, back in the bar area, and looked again, more closely. Six or seven newcomers were approaching the floor. They all looked much the same—tall with close-cropped hair, unnaturally long arms and impossibly bulky muscles. They wore expensive suits and sunglasses and were carrying pistols. Bouncers from the abyss. They had to be fomori, humans who had Banes bound within them.

She turned back to the center of the floor. The thing showed no sign of slowing down. It must have leaped again, because it was at the far end of the room. Cries Havoc's left arm was hanging uselessly, and Tiny Tim was slumped against one of the walls. Storm-Eye and Carlita were advancing on it.

"More company behind you," shouted Julia, dashing for the fomori. Pete Marment and North Wind's Son, at the rear of the pack, turned to join her. She flexed her claws, glad to have them free of the sticky muck again… She stopped dead in her tracks, then darted over to where she'd left her PDA, ignoring the startled look that the Wendigo gave her. No time to explain. Putting a pillar between herself and the fomori, Julia thumped a finger against the green spot and the world snapped out.

Even though she was expecting it, the sense of peaceful power was dizzying after the frantic chaos of the fight. It was like waking up from a dream and remembering what senses really felt like. An intoxicating sensation. She could feel the whole building now, sense its layout, its circuits and triggers. The Net-Spider must have fully integrated with the security systems. The temptation to explore was agonizingly strong. She managed to resist and felt for the internal fire control systems. It took a moment or two to work out which knots were alarms, but once she'd isolated those, she activated the rest, feeling the presence of both water and gas systems. They opened up. She could feel other parts of the data stream tantalizingly close. It might even be possible to bridge out to other networks—a link from security to the main system, from the main system to the Internet… Going for a look around would only take a few moments…. She fought the urge and won. She did have her friends fighting for their lives back in the physical world. Reluctantly, slowly, she sought out her own sense of touch from amid the tangle and lifted her finger off the dot in the screen.

Immediately, she wished she hadn't. She was sprawled wetly on the floor, her leg a blinding knot of agony. She felt the rage surge within her and clamped it down. Work to do. She glanced down at her leg quickly and unhappily noted the bloody, splintered mess that had been her left kneecap. She must have caught a bullet. The drizzle wasn't even really helping wash the blood off, either. Drizzle. Sprinklers. Bane. Her mind finally clicked back into gear, and she leaned up on an elbow and looked around. Dim red security lights had come on all through the club, looking slightly satanic in the watery haze. The remains of the Wyrm-beast were toward the back of the dance floor, melting in the water. It was losing shape moment by moment, dissolving back into the vile slime it came from. Carlita's fang dagger was planted deeply in what remained of the neck. The Bone Gnawer herself was down on the floor, writhing feebly. Cries Havoc was beside her. Tiny Tim was still against the wall, and it was too dim to see if he was breathing or not, particularly through the sprinklers.

The fomori were scattered across the bar area. In pieces, mostly. Everything seemed to be soaked in blood and water. Pete and Storm-Eye were just ripping the life out of the last one. They were covered in gore from head to toe, and it was impossible to tell if they were hurt or not. North Wind's Son was walking from the back of the bar, blood dripping from a scalp wound, and Rochelle was crossing the floor over to where Julia herself was.

"Cries Havoc, is she…" began Julia.

"She's fine," said Carlita weakly. "Damn thing tried to play hooky with my intestines. I'm regenerating normally, though. Garou healing really does have to be one of Gaia's smartest moves ever. Just give me a few minutes. Hey, was this cold shower your idea?"

"Yeah," said Julia, grinning.

"Smart move, princess."

Rochelle arrived and looked down at Julia's leg. "Are you okay?"

"Yes, thanks. I'll be fine. It's just the leg. If you could give it a tug for me though, I'd appreciate it. I wouldn't want it setting badly."

"Okay, brace yourself. After three." She put one hand on Julia's thigh and the other on her ankle. "One…" She wrenched the leg out hard, pulling the joint straight. It blazed like silver fire, and despite her best efforts not to, Julia howled. "Two. Three. There you go."

"Thanks," said Julia, when she'd got her breath back. "How's Tiny?"

"He's unconscious. It looks like his chest has been crushed. I think he'll be all right, but we'll probably have to leave him where he is for a while."

"At least he's alive." She felt a burst of relief.

"Hey," called Carlita, already sounding a little stronger, "someone near the bar area? I need help here."

"What can I do?" asked North Wind's Son loudly.

"You can get me a Coke. Please."

Ten minutes later, Julia's leg was good to walk on again, although it remained a bit sore. Carlita was up and about as well, and Cries Havoc's arm was back to normal. He had a spectacular scar down the entire length of it, though, and Carlita would have one across her stomach, too. Julia got up carefully, flexed her knee gingerly a few times and then walked stiffly over to where Storm-Eye was standing with Cries Havoc and Rochelle. "I think I know where the Lore Banes are going to be," she said.

"That is good news," said Storm-Eye.

"I half-expected to see them come at us here," Cries Havoc said.

"They'd have to be cut off from the main club," said Julia. "Probably insulated from the noise, too. It must be a hell of a racket in here when it's open. Anyway, there's a set of high-security doors upstairs, and the room behind them is rigged with all sorts of stuff. They're just off that room."

"Great!" said Rochelle, enthusiastically.

Carlita looked at her. "Yeah. More fun. Hooray for our side."

"Do you know how to get to the upper level?" asked Storm-Eye.

"Yes," said Julia, nodding. "The staircase is behind a door in the corner of the bar area." She pointed in the right direction. It seemed to be open. "I think the fomori must have come from there."

"Let's go then," Storm-Eye said.

They made their way through the slaughter. The door *was* open, so they continued on carefully up the wide, soaking staircase. Signed promotional stills of famous garage artists and producers—tinged red by the emergency lighting—lined the wall all the way up. At the top, the staircase opened up into a comfortable, intimate-looking lounge bar, considerably smaller than the area below. One-way glass walls provided a view out over the main club. Apart from another pair of rest rooms, the only door was next to the bar and clearly marked STAFF ONLY. It too was open.

The room beyond was a total contrast to the rest of the club. It was functionally fitted, brutally stark rather than tastefully hip. Two racks of triple-stacked bunk beds along one wall indicated where the fomori guards had stayed. Rudimentary cooking equipment was alongside it. A set of tall screens, folded back by the door, were probably used to section the quarters off from the rest of the room. The room also had sprinklers and was covered in water.

There were steel sinks along the back wall, but the room was dominated by a broad wooden table sitting in front of them. It was covered with a patchwork of stains—black in the red light—and thick leather straps at the four corners gave Julia an unpleasant notion of what the stains were. There was a tray of implements in one of the sinks, but Julia stopped looking when she realized that it included a bone saw, garden clippers and a power sander. A thick metal door with a glass panel was at the foot of the table. Through it, Julia could see a number of pieces of computer equipment.

She tried the door, which opened smoothly. "So far so good," she said and stepped in. This room was dry and the air smelt unpleasantly tinny. She waved the others in. Several large computers, a rack of server modems and a wide range of peripherals clustered in with a set of CCTV screens and other bits and pieces of equipment. There was a simple white door at the back of the room. "Right, I guess this is where we get down to business. When I was last in contact with the Net-Spider, it was fairly obvious from the security systems that the Lore Banes were in a chamber off this one. That means they're through that door at the back."

Carlita gestured at one of the CCTV sets. "Look." She sounded subdued. "That must be where they're normally fed."

They clustered round the monitor. It showed a large, sparsely furnished room. A row of chairs sat along one wall. Wrist clamps on the arms and ankle clamps on the forward legs made it perfectly clear that they were used for restraint. At the far end of the room, the wall bristled with several rows of wooden bars— perches, presumably, for the Banes. "Let's do it," said Julia. "Just give me a second..." She peered through the Gauntlet and into the Penumbra, looking for Banes or other threats.

In the Umbra, the room was a large, fleshy cavern. The floor was wet and sticky and unpleasantly yielding underfoot. The walls were bowed out rather than straight, and made of the same red, dripping material as the floor. Thick veins of green-white and purple were worked through the uneven red tones. Slime was everywhere. The walls and floor seemed to pulsate gently, and an unpleasantly warm, damp wind blew through the chamber. It looked like the inside of a gigantic piece of lung. A large, spastically shivering open sphincter had replaced the door to the next chamber. Through it, Julia could see four of the Banes, three clustered together, clinging onto a section of the wall, and one flying idly around the room.

The Lore Banes looked a bit like bats and a bit like winged mouths. They were black and rubbery with wide, hairless wings. Wicked-looking claws extended from the wingtips. The span was probably five or six feet in total. Their bodies were a couple of feet long, simple ovals with eyes at the top where a head should have been, and broad mouths in the middle of the torso. The teeth looked like needles, long and vicious, with a faint metallic glint to them. Below the mouth, the body tapered off into clawed feet and a long, ratlike black tail six or seven feet in length and tipped in a razor-sharp barb. "Okay, it's not pretty over there, but it's clear. There are four of them, but we'll be partly hidden until we enter their room. We should be fine. Gather round, and I'll take us sideways."

One of the computer monitors was switched off. Julia looked into the blackened glass, finding the hints of reflection within it. She let her mind sink into it, seeking the echoes of the Penumbra within it. She felt her thoughts clear and focus almost instantly, and mentally aligned the faint physical reflection with its Umbral counterpart. The two images melded and matched, like a puzzle piece clicking into place. The Gauntlet fell away, and she let herself slip out of the physical world, feeling the others come across with her.

"What do you recommend, Cries Havoc?" asked Storm-Eye, speaking in the Garou tongue.

"I'd suggest pairing up, two on one. Keep out of the way of them, taunt them into closing with you— but for Gaia's sake be cautious—and then, when you get a chance, one person grab the wings to restrain it, the other slash it to ribbons until it bursts. You'll need to keep a firm hold on your concentration, because killing one can be a dizzying experience when the tale spirits hit. Be careful of the teeth—they bite into your ear and eat your mind out. There's seven of us, so I'll keep the fourth one busy. They use those long tails just like whips, to entangle. They're strong, too. If it starts getting nasty, we'll have to regroup together and hit them one at a time. If they poke out any tendrils, avoid them, and whatever you do, don't let any of them bite into anyone's head."

"Very well. Now let us kill Banes!" Storm-Eye growled a ferocious call to battle, and the group sprinted across the chamber and into the nest.

The nest was made of the same fleshy material as the previous chamber. As the Garou burst through the sphincter, the flying Bane screeched in shock and anger. Its fellows immediately launched off from their conversation on the wall and took to the air, up near the ceiling. Cries Havoc charged into the center of the chamber, yipping taunts and distracting the creatures while the others ran in quickly behind him and spread out. Julia found herself teamed up with Carlita in the left side of the room. The Bone Gnawer hefted her fang dagger and grinned evilly as they approached the nearest Bane. "I'll carve, Lady Di."

One of the Banes screeched a phrase in some tortured, phlegmy language, and the door-sphincter contracted closed with a wet slapping noise. Julia shivered, chilled by the sudden premonition that something was badly wrong. "Heads up, everyone," she said loudly. "I think something's…"

A new Lore Bane popped out of a hole in the roof that she hadn't noticed before, and joined the others. Then another. Suddenly, it seemed like there was a stream of the vile monstrosities pouring into the room, cackling to each other with evil amusement. Julia tried to keep track of how many there were, but they were bobbing and weaving around, filling the space near the ceiling and obscuring the hole from time to time. They were moving too fast to count. A dozen, perhaps? Far too many.

"Oh fuck," said Carlita softly.

Julia glanced desperately back at the entrance to the chamber, but it was sealed tight.

"We fight together," growled Storm-Eye, moving toward the center of the room. Like the others, Julia darted to join her, keeping a nervous eye on the Banes. The Garou exchanged glances and formed into a loose circle, facing outward.

With a deafening collective screech, the Lore Banes plummeted down from the roof toward the gathered werewolves. It was like being caught up in a whirlwind of teeth, claws and wingtips. A Bane dove straight down at the back of her head, mouth open for a bite, and Julia desperately ducked aside. She wanted to punch out at it as it sailed over her, but her hands were fending a second Bane away from her leg. She couldn't spare them without getting mauled. Banes nipped and harried continually from every side.

She felt a sharp pain in her abdomen and saw a Bane clinging to her, digging its claws in. It was getting ready to take a bite out of her. She punched down, knocking it away, but felt another one latching on to her shoulder as she did so. Behind her, a howl of pain told her that someone was in trouble—Rochelle, perhaps—but there wasn't time to even call out. Julia grabbed at the new assailant, twisting and writhing to try to avoid further entanglement, and kicked away another Bane coming in to attack, buying herself a moment of quiet. She was bleeding quite heavily from her shoulder, and she hadn't even made a dent in one of them.

"This is no use," yelled Cries Havoc, behind her, then grunted in pain. "Anyone remember any tales?"

A Bane dove at Julia's face, and she punched at it, forcing it off course. It screeched at her, and a bundle of long, flailing tendrils dropped down from its abdomen. They were tipped with wicked hooks, and as the Bane veered away from her hand, two of them tore into her fingers. It felt as if they were trying to rip part of her very essence away, stealing a part of her. She heard someone scream and realized it was her own voice. She gritted her teeth, snarled and pulled the hooks out with her good hand, dodging out of their path as the Bane jerked them away. The vile piece of shit wasn't going to get her stories just yet.

A wild idea hit her and, a moment later, her leg erupted in agony as a Bane sank its needle-sharp teeth deep into her already rickety knee. Julia slashed down at it, forcing it to let go to avoid being hit. She was starting to weaken, and she hadn't even done any damage. She decided to try her last-ditch gamble.

"Cover for me," she said. Ignoring Carlita's wild-eyed glance from beside her—the Bone Gnawer's face was covered in blood—she ducked into the center of the ring, sat down and quickly retrieved her PDA. She shut down the Net-Spider program with a brief pang of illogical regret and triggered her invocation routine. Behind her, someone fell to the ground howling. She couldn't make out who, but she could feel the body writhing around against her back. Fighting off a Bane, she hoped. There wasn't much time—five could not hope to hold against that many enemies for long.

The PDA screen started pulsing, and Julia closed her eyes, forcing her mind into calm. She had to work hard to push the fear and the guilt away, and harder still to banish the hope, but after a few seconds, she felt her thoughts turn crystal, and calm descended. She closed her ears to the battle, and the sound of her friends' pain, and touched the screen. Her finger sank into it, pushing out a burst of force.

"This is Julia Spencer, Glass Walker of the Old City Sept." She was shouting, pushing both her voice and her mind as hard as she could to add to the waves of power beating out of her fetish. Without the Gauntlet to cross, the ripples of energy were almost visible. "I call to those who dwell around the campsite hearth." Massive pain burst in the center of her back, a thousand miles away. She ignored it. "I call to those who share in the pleasure of a jug of ale. I call to those who delight in the thrall of an audience. I call to the spirits of tales lost. Arise! Fight to be heard once more!" She poured all of her soul into the call. There was nothing to lose. "Awake! Awake! AWAKE!"

There was a staggering burst of force as the invocation program crashed under the pressure of the energy she was pouring through it. Trance broken, Julia opened her eyes. The PDA had shut down or burnt out. She looked up. Incredibly, the air was free of Banes, and the others were turning round to look at her with expressions varying from surprise to delight.

"Quick, princess." Carlita helped haul Julia to her feet. "That witchy whammy of yours might not last for long."

Julia looked around the room quickly. Pete was getting up slowly, his ear almost ripped from his head. All the Garou were drenched in blood. North Wind's Son was swaying where he stood, and Cries Havoc was limping a little. Stunned Banes lay all over the floor, flapping feebly. Two of them were still airborne, but neither looked particularly steady. They all seemed to sparkle, as if they were twinkling with tiny motes of inner light. Under different circumstances, it could have looked quite pretty, but she could see the effect fading moment by moment.

"C'mon," said Carlita, "let's get them while they're down."

Julia nodded and leapt on the nearest Bane. She stabbed her hands and feet through its wings, crouching over it, and pulled them taught. It yowled and snapped at her, and the barbed tail flicked up to score deep, painful lashes in her back, but she held on. Carlita dropped to one knee in front of it, using her momentum to hammer her fang dagger up to the hilt between its eyes. It screamed in agony. She then shifted grip and pulled the dagger down toward the mouth, cutting the Bane open. Suddenly it disintegrated, dissolving into a foul slime. Julia immediately braced herself for a confusing burst of excited tale spirits, but nothing happened. She shared a concerned look with Carlita.

A flutter of movement drew her eyes upward. Up near the top of the ceiling, a dancing cloud of silver motes told her where the tale spirits were. She smiled and pointed it out to Carlita. "I think they're giving us a chance to do some more damage," she said.

"Then let's oblige them," replied the Bone Gnawer.

As they dashed to the next nearest Bane, Julia risked a quick glance around. Cries Havoc had one of the Banes by the tail and was actually whirling it around him like a mace to fend off the two that were airborne. Storm-Eye and North Wind's Son were ripping chunks out of another limply wriggling monstrosity. Rochelle was wrestling with a lively one that had managed to wrap itself round her chest, while Pete slashed at its back and tail.

Julia tried the same maneuver she had before on their next target. This time, though, the creature managed to snatch one of its wings out of the way at the last moment. It wrapped its tail around the leg that was pinioning it and used the leverage to pull its mouth to Julia's calf. It sank its teeth in, ripping at her skin. The teeth were as sharp as needles, and the pain was immense. Julia stabbed down with her claws into the thing's back as Carlita moved into position, and was glad to feel it squirming in pain. Then Carlita stabbed her dagger through the Bane's side and twisted it in the wound. The Bane screamed, releasing Julia's leg in the process, and exploded into a gust of foul air.

"C'mon," said Carlita urgently. "Cries Havoc could do with some help." She reached out a hand and pulled Julia to her feet. The Bone Gnawer was right. Cries Havoc had lost his grip on the Bane he'd been swinging around and was ducking and weaving as three lashing tails sought to entangle him. Julia leapt at the nearest creature, grabbing its tail as high up as she could, and pulled it down as she landed. The Bane, taken by surprise, smacked into the floor. As it lay there dazed, she dropped onto it and bit into the back of its rancid head, slashing at its sides with her claws. It writhed and screamed but couldn't get clear. She ground her jaws together hard, and the thing burst, leaving a truly foul residue in her mouth.

Carlita had another one pinned to the wall, her fang dagger through its shoulder. It could only writhe there and spit hatred at her as she tore it to ribbons. Free to concentrate on the third Bane, Cries Havoc had severed most of its tail, and it was having difficulty flying. As Julia looked, he leapt up and slashed its wing into tatters. It tried to stay aloft but couldn't maintain height. He spitted it on his claws, then hammered it into the wall repeatedly.

Across the room, Rochelle was helping Storm-Eye and North Wind's Son finish off another Bane that had got into the air, while Pete licked a nasty forearm wound clean. Looking about, Julia realized that the battle was all but over. Cries Havoc's Bane sludged out of existence. She looked up and saw that the tale spirits were now a bright ring of silver light. It seemed to be dancing and spinning, bobbling a little as it whirled. Rochelle bit through the last Bane's back, almost snapping it in half, and it perished. Julia just had time to notice the whirling ring of tale spirits start spinning down like a silver vortex before her mind exploded in a riot of color, and everything went white.

Chapter Nine

The cloud of newly freed tale spirits dispersed, blissfully happy to be free after untold years of vile bondage. They rippled off through the Umbra in all directions, singing their stories. Many people, both Garou and otherwise, had strange dreams and visions that morning. A young Kentish girl had a fleeting vision of huge worms of corruption gnawing at the ground beneath her, and collapsed into hysterics from which she could not be raised. On the shores of Loch Fyne, an old Ragabash woke to find that he knew where the Ratkin laired in the sewers beneath Manchester, and which passwords would gain him an audience. In Boston, a Silent Strider suddenly recalled a legend about the castle at Knossos, in Crete, and knew what had happened to a Black Fury pack there in 1712.

Lurking in its Umbral prison, tied to a caern deep in the Serbian hills, the beast Jo'cllath'mattric felt its servants die, and thrashed in anger and trepidation. This was a delicate time, with the Spiral Dancers trying to free it coming under attack. Further distraction could be disastrous. It immediately dispatched one of its fastest servitors to the Lore Banes' keeper to gather information. The messenger flew swiftly, following the pull of the target's essence. This liberation came at a price, as some of the minor Spiral Dancer Theurges working at the caern suddenly collapsed as their eyes burst from the strain of having Jo'cllath'mattric momentarily redirect their ritual. This concerned the Wyrm-beast not at all.

Mick was still locked down to his secure operating table in the D-wing of Megadon's Long Island lab when the messenger popped into existence above his head.

He was dimly aware of it but paid it no attention. Every thought he had was concentrated on his search for the name.

If the messenger was put off by Mick's inattention, it showed no sign of it. It started talking immediately, speaking in the snarling, phlegmy language that the Lore Banes used. "The great master is displeased. Prepare to answer to his satisfaction, or feel the full wrath of the mighty Jo'cllath'mattric."

The name seared through Mick's entire being. It was like a bolt of lightning. His whole body had a spasm as the name bridged the gap between self and ego, between will and volition, between mind and body. It was a white fire of purest agony, melting him down and casting him anew. In the holy clarity of the pain, he found what he had been missing.

The messenger was still speaking. Something about his Banes being killed. That meant they'd found the club. Whoever *they* were, he would find them and kill them. He said as much to the messenger and then, aware that his words might go back to the great lord, added some groveled apologies and explained that he had been brain-dead for a while. The messenger told him to make sure he did so by whatever means were necessary, and winked out.

Mick focused his strength and his rising anger and shifted into Crinos. Then he slowly pulled up his right arm. The metal shackle, although stretched by his change in form, somehow resisted. Furious at being defied by a mere band of steel, Mick redoubled his efforts. He concentrated all his rage on moving his arm and screamed an incoherent yell of effort. The shackle burst, freeing his arm. From there, it was only a few minutes' work to break the other shackles and rip the various experiments and mechanisms from his body.

He heard rapid footsteps approaching and waited by the door. A young woman in a white coat opened the room and came in, stopping just inside the room when she saw the mess. Mick kicked the door closed behind her, then stooped down quickly and bit through the top of her head before she had time to scream. He watched her collapse in a silent fountain of blood. She was pretty, too, and he regretted not having time to stop and play—or feed—properly.

Mick promised himself that he would take the time to enjoy a decent meal once he was away from the facility. In the meantime, though, there was a little errand he had to run before he left. The human doctor, Galland, had often spoken as he had inflicted his pathetic torments. It was high time Mick paid another visit to the doctor's office—unbound, this time—and showed him that he had in fact been listening after all.

It only took a few minutes to track his way back through the building to Galland's office. As Mick padded down the corridor toward it, he saw a tired-looking woman approaching the door, her back to him. Galland's secretary, by the look of her. Mick raced the last fifty feet, and as the woman turned in the doorway to look incuriously down the hall, he lunged forward and stabbed his claws straight through her neck, picking her up off the floor and carrying her into her office. She gurgled desperately, clutching at his arm in frantic terror. Holding her up by the hair with his other hand, he turned his claws around slowly in her neck, enjoying the sight of her writhing in agony as she died. Then he flexed his claws sharply, and her head came away with a wet rip. The corpse fell bonelessly to the floor.

Galland's main office was in the next room. Mick charged at the door for the hell of it, bursting through it in a cloud of splinters. The doctor was in there, all right, writing away on some piece of paper, the stupid bastard. By the dumb look of amazement on his face, security hadn't warned him—or they'd tried, and he'd been too arrogant to answer his own phone.

Mick casually tossed the severed head into Galland's waste-paper bin, looked at the doctor and said, "My name is Mick, you fucker. Not 113. *Mick.* And that word, by the way, was Jo'cllath'mattric."

Galland blinked in surprise, and Mick leapt straight over his desk. He landed on the doctor in a crouch, sinking his claws into Galland's shoulders and thighs. The man had time for one pointless gasp of terror before Mick bit his lips and tongue out with one broad snap, and then carefully chewed the eyes from his head, first the right and then the left.

By the time security found Galland's shredded remains, Mick was out of the window, through the park and away into the night.

***

"It was Tiny here who came and woke us all up in the end," said Julia. The whole group was back in Nicola's office, briefing the elders on events at the club. "We were back in the physical world, unconscious, in breed form. I have no idea how long we were out for."

For two-thirds of an hour, growled Storm-Eye, back in Lupus. *If you were more in touch with nature, you would always know when you were.*

"Probably. Anyway, he roused us. All those tale spirits at once—it must have been way too much. It's a good thing they held off. We were lucky, anyway. They totally suckered us. Me. I led us into a near-perfect ambush, and it was total luck that invoking the tale spirits dazed the Banes. We'd have all been slaughtered otherwise."

"I'll let you in on a secret. We make our own luck," said Blake, smiling.

"It was a quick bit of thinking," said Rochelle. "You must have got a lot of power behind that invocation, too."

"Thank you," said Julia. "I'm just glad no one was permanently hurt. I feel irresponsible enough as it is."

"We lucked out," said Carlita. "Again."

"Still, we've got all sorts of information," Julia said. "My head is still buzzing with it. I also ripped the hard drives out of the computers in the club before we left. I expect all the important stuff is warded, but there may be some useful data on them—addresses of some of the minions in London, perhaps, or something."

"I'll get Rob and Jared on it straight away," said Nicola.

"Did you say that you left the place burning?" asked Karen curiously.

"Yes, we set fire to it," said North Wind's Son. "It seemed the best thing to do."

It would have provided a lair for other Wyrm-beasts, said Storm-Eye.

"Oh, I wasn't being critical," said Karen. "I was just checking. There was no sign of that Gerbovic character, was there?"

Carlita smiled viciously. "We already killed him a couple of months ago."

He attacked us several times shortly after we were first here, said Storm-Eye. *We did not see his human face then and did not connect his name to the Dancer that beset us*.

"Until one of the tale spirits cleared up his identity for me," said Carlita.

Storm-Eye ignored the interruption. *We fought and vanquished him and left him on the riverbed. That he has not been seen since confirms that he is dead.*

"That's a good thing. Did anyone see you leaving the club afterwards?" asked Blake.

"Not as far as I could see," said Julia.

"Yeah, the streets were still pretty empty," said Carlita.

"You've done well," said Nicola. "It could have been a horrendous cock-up, and I want you to remember that, but the bottom line is that it wasn't. You've cleared up an infestation and recovered all sorts of knowledge and lore that may prove very useful— we'll have to see what you recall as your memories sort out all the new material and integrate it properly."

"There's more," said Julia. "One of the reasons we targeted this nest in the first place was to try to recover some information about Jo'cllath'mattric. Well, one of the spirits that shared itself with me held the tale of how the beast was originally born. It used to be a benevolent spirit, one whose job was to eat dangerous and obsolete ideas. The Wyrm turned it in on itself and forced it to eat part of its own mind, driving it mad. The resulting Bane was rechristened Jo'cllath'mattric. Before it was turned, it was known as Macheriel. Its old name still has power over it— although the story is pretty vague on what form that power takes."

"That could be extremely important," said Nicola. "We've received word that King Albrecht and the Russian Silver Fangs have joined Margrave Konietzko and others in an attack on the beast's lair. Apparently, the Spirals have been trying to free it from an ancient prison. Sergiy Dawntreader has led warriors from the Sept of the Dawn there as well."

"Is there any news?" asked Cries Havoc. Julia winced. The Sept of the Dawn in Ukraine was Cries Havoc's home as much as Old City was hers, and to hear that his elders and septmates were in a battle without him couldn't sit well.

"The battle continues, as far as we can tell," said Nicola. "We have no other news."

A small howl of discontent escaped Cries Havoc's lips before he caught it. Of all of them, he knew best the dangers even such elders faced in such a battle.

"We go to Night Sky to bring word of the name to the elders, then," said Storm-Eye. "From there to battle with the Dawntreader if we can." Cries Havoc perked up at that.

"I'll let you get on with it, then," said Nicola. "I think we're more or less done. Blake? Karen?"

"I'd like a quiet word with Julia, if she doesn't mind," Karen said.

"Of course," said Julia with a twinge of nervousness.

"Unless anyone objects," said Pete, looking at Nicola, "Rochelle and I are going to knock up a little commemorative number. There's a Galliard in California who's set up a nice little site on GWnet to trade digital versions of tale-songs and I've been meaning to get something to him. What's his name again?"

"Chris MacEnryght," said Rochelle. "Not a bad musician in his own right, actually."

"I'm not convinced," said Nicola gravely. "Who would be doing the music?"

"I would," said Rochelle, grinning. "Don't worry."

"Ah, okay. That's fine by me then. So long as everyone who was there is okay with it. Yes? Okay, great. Knock yourselves out. I'll expect to hear it, along with some of the stories you learnt, on Saturday night. Don't go posting it before then. Right, meeting adjourned."

"Hey, princess, we'll be in the garden when you've finished your chat." Carlita's voice was light, but she looked a bit concerned.

"I'll see you there soon," said Julia. "John, do you want to call Evan again?" He nodded, and she passed him her mobile. "Here you go. Try to be quick, eh? International calls cost a fortune on that thing."

The others filed out, and Karen moved to a seat opposite Julia.

Julia smiled at her wryly. "Looks like I'm charging off again, boss."

"It does, doesn't it," said Karen. "We'll keep your room for you. We've got plenty of space. If you need a job again, we'll always be able to find something for you. I'll explain to your father. Be careful in the East. Drop me an email from time to time and let me know how it's going. Oh, and when you feel up to a promotion challenge, just let me know."

Julia looked at her, speechless with gratitude.

Karen grinned. "Feel free to say thanks."

"I'm sorry. Thank you, Karen. For everything. You're being extremely generous. You may see me back here in a couple of days time anyway—we still haven't spoken about long-term plans."

"Well, I suppose it's possible," Karen said, smiling. "But somehow I think you'll find that something else keeps cropping up."

"There was something that an old Uktena said to me, actually. About the Weaver…"

Karen arched an eyebrow. "They're an odd bunch. Worth paying attention to, though—when they're talking about the mysteries, anyway. Still, your travel plans aren't actually what I wanted to talk to you about."

Julia shuffled her feet uncomfortably. "Look, Karen, I know I underestimated the strength of the nest on this operation and risked three members of the sept, and I'm sorry. I'm not much of a planner. I'd normally leave that side of things to Storm-Eye or John North Wind's Son, but we were hunting that Spiral through rumor and data trails, not through a forest."

"I'm not cross, Julia. As a matter of fact, I think you did well. Being able to think on your feet is one of the most vital survival traits there is. You gave it your best call based on the evidence you had, and it turned out well enough. Blake was right; in many ways, good luck is a skill that comes from intuition, reflex, wits and understanding. That's not what I want to talk to you about either."

"Oh," Julia said, feeling a bit foolish. "Okay then. What's up?"

"Is the Net-Spider routine purged?"

"Yes, it's gone," Julia said, a touch wistfully. "Once we were clear of the club, I managed to reboot the PDA, and it had been purged."

"Were you tempted to stay in there?"

The question caught Julia by surprise. "Yes. Almost more than I could resist. I've never known anything like it. It was beautiful... While I was in there, my body was just one tiny node in the network, and I could feel the whole thing. In the same way that I can feel my left foot right now. I could make it do things... the power was incredible. Dizzying. The freedom, too. It was really hard to wrench myself away from it both times. I'm not sure I could have done it a third time. I might have ended up staying in there for good, becoming part of it."

"Any regrets?"

"Not really. There's too much important to do out here. Still… I guess learning the routine properly is something to aim for."

Karen nodded. "There's a lot of Garou who would not have come out the first time, let alone a second. You showed a lot of wisdom and self-discipline there. You've done well this week, Julia. I'm proud of you. The news is spreading—I bet you have scores of emails waiting for you. I'm very interested in this recovered knowledge of yours, too. How conscious is it?"

"They're like memories that you haven't thought of for a very long time. They're there, waiting, but out of the way until you go looking for them."

"So you have no idea what you've learnt?"

Julia racked her mind, looking for answers. "Partly. I can feel all sorts of stuff up there, and I don't really have much idea about a lot of it. There are some lessons in there that I can feel near the top, if that makes any sort of sense. How Ilenya taught her human lover to withstand the Curse, and the price they both ended up paying. The sixteen ways to flatter Grandfather Thunder without angering him. Where to find a certain moss that, when a bear-spirit is bound into it, will nourish a body for up to three months. A simple rite that will attract the attention of a Curiosus, in time."

Karen was silent for a few moments. When she replied, her voice was thoughtful. "There's some intriguing ideas there. Don't be too cagey with what you've learnt, Julia. Some pieces of it will almost certainly have come to you to pass to someone else. Plus, you'll get a great reputation if you can go around producing useful bits of lore when needed. In fact, I may have to chain you in front of a keyboard and get you to type it all up for us some time."

"Sounds marvelous," said Julia. She smiled wryly. "Oh, and there's also a story about a young Garou who was reluctant to leave the home she knew and venture out into the world, but eventually took the plunge."

"How does that one end?"

"I'll let you know."

***

Back in the courtyard, Julia found the rest of the Silver River Pack looking subdued.

We have discussed the matter, said Storm-Eye, barking in lupine tongue. *We are going to travel to the Finger Lakes Caern as soon as the Gatekeeper has opened a bridge for us. He says that the way seems clear.*

"Fair enough," Julia said. "I'll just go grab my stuff." She realized that they were looking at her strangely. "What? No time? All right, I guess I can travel light."

"Are you sure?" asked Cries Havoc. "This is your home. If you leave in a hurry again, with no idea of when you're coming back…"

"Oh, for Gaia's sake," interrupted Julia. "Not you, too. What kind of packmate would I be if I ran out on you?"

"You tried it once before, your highness," said Carlita.

"That was that bloody Lore Bane nibbling away at us all." A traitorous voice in the back of her mind suggested that maybe it wasn't the Lore Bane. It reminded her about Rob Thompson's smile, and her father and Uncle Bill, and her work at the sept. Then she looked at the Garou in front of her and thought about everything they had achieved and shared, and she smiled brilliantly. What was it Blake had said? Head in the way of heart? "I care about you lot. I'm coming, and that's that. You'll have to tie me up to get me to stay behind."

That is good to hear, said Storm-Eye, the others chiming in their agreement.

"So, do I have time to pack a small bag or not?"

So long as it is small, said Storm-Eye, with a quick wag of her tail.

"It will be, I promise," said Julia. "Why are we going to Finger Lakes, anyway? I thought we were headed for Night Sky near the battle site. Is Albrecht expected back in New York?"

John North Wind's Son shook his head slowly. "I've spoken to Evan, but I didn't get a chance to explain to him about Jo'cllath'mattric. It's Mari. She's dying."

Chapter Ten

Megadon's nearest neighbor on Long Island was a large power plant. A foolishly arrogant executive of about the right size surprised Mick with his versatility. He provided a half-decent suit (quickly attuned), some cash, a cell phone, a bit of light entertainment, a hearty breakfast and, afterward, transportation.

Mick started heading toward New York City, and he tried the club's private line just in case. He wasn't too surprised when no one answered. They would have had to get through the fomori before they could have reached the Banes. He dialed another London number.

A woman answered the phone guardedly. "Hello?"

"Delia, it's Mick." Delia was an art dealer and heroin smuggler who longed to become a fomor, for some insane reason. Perhaps she thought she would become more powerful or live longer or something. Mick had promised her that he would arrange it for her when she was worthy. She was more useful as a human agent, though—even though she was tiresome, she could deal with more subtle problems than the fomori could manage—so he kept her dangling.

"How may I serve, master?"

"On the door of the house opposite the entrance to Club Release—the green-painted one—you'll find a small white opal set into the wood, with a tiny glyph scratched into it. The stone is by the top hinge, and it's not obvious, so you'll have to look closely. Get a hammer and a screwdriver or chisel or something, and go and smash the opal."

"At once, master."

Mick sighed, irritated by her passivity. "Aren't you even curious, woman?"

"I live to serve and prove my worth, master."

"Yeah, well, go break that stone. Did this number come up on your phone?"

"It did, master."

"Right, then call me back as soon as you've done it."

"Yes, master. Is there anything else?"

"Just fucking get on with it." He hung up. The opal had a small spirit bound into it, which Mick had set to watch the club and memorize what it saw. When freed from the stone, the spirit was compelled to come to Mick so that he could dredge its memories for information. He'd questioned it a few times before, *in situ*, and used it to identify a gang of idiots who'd tried to raid the place one night.

A while later, the phone rang. It was a stupid bloody ring tone, too. Mick briefly regretted killing the idiot so quickly. Death was too good for some people. He sighed and answered the call.

"Master."

"Hi, Delia. You did it?"

"Yes, master."

"Good. How was the club looking?"

A hint of nervousness crept into her voice. "I'm afraid that the club has been burnt down, master."

Mick felt the rage surge within him. "The evil bastards. There was no need to do that to my club. I'm going to tear their fucking hearts out."

"Yes, master."

"You can fuck off, too, you stupid bitch." His anger made him petty. "Go back to your home and stay inside it, without eating or drinking, until I next call you." *Let's see how dedicated you really are.*

"Yes, master." If she was dismayed, Delia didn't show it. Fine. He might just let the bitch die of thirst. There were others.

Mick hung up, slammed the phone down in the passenger seat and fought down the urge to punch out a window or run a passing cyclist off the road. No sense attracting too much attention for no gain.

He was just starting to come into the Minneola suburbs when his watcher-spirit announced its presence. He pulled over, ignoring the idiot in the car behind, and closed his eyes. "Show me a clear image of anyone who entered the club in the last twenty-four hours."

A picture immediately formed behind his eyelids, a cluster of firemen in breathing masks dragging a hose into the smoking ruins of the lobby area. He winced at the state it was in, and then ordered the spirit to go earlier. This time, the image was of an oddly mixed group of men and women. Mick blinked in astonishment, breaking the image, and had to settle his mind again before it returned. It was the little bastards who had put him in the lab in the first place. Not content with somehow forcing his own servitor to betray him—at least he'd had the presence of mind to gut that faithless piece of crap, even through the brain-burn—they'd had the temerity to burn his damn club down. They were going to pay for this.

Mick got out of the car and walked in front of a car coming up the road. The driver, shouting angrily, had no choice but to stop. Mick shifted into Crinos, punched through the windshield and dragged the now-hysterical woman out of her seat. He punched her in the side of the head to knock her out, and then bundled her into the back of his car before taking off back down the road to somewhere a bit quieter. Done properly with the right promises and the aid of Jo'cllath'mattric's holy name, a lingering death would call his tribal patron, Whippoorwill, or one of its spirits, at least. They loved to snatch the souls of the dying, and they saw all sorts of things. They might be able to tell him where the little bastards were.

As soon as he knew where they were going to be for the next day or so, he was going to make the proper arrangements to take care of them once and for all. By *any means necessary*, the messenger had said. Those filthy tree-huggers may have trashed his club, his charges and his servitor, but he still had the authority to round up enough help to be sure of evening the score.

***

The journey across the moon bridge was eerily quiet. The Silver River packmates had made quick arrangements with Nicola to send a message to Night Sky about the history of Jo'cllath'mattric, but they didn't say a word after that. Julia had expected more debate, surely Cries Havoc wanted to go to Night Sky and help the Dawntreader, but the news from there implied that the elders were cut off. If they could get vital information to Albrecht it would be through his packmates Evan and Mari. Cries also seemed to understand John's need to help them in their time of need, much as he had helped Cries in his. A testament to how far the once-cantankerous pack had come.

They could all hear the threatening rumble of the Umbral storm in the background during the crossing, but otherwise there was no sign of any activity, either near or far. It seemed as if the spirit world itself was ⸻ eath nervously. It made everyone feel ⸻ y crossed the bridge in silence. Julia ⸻ admitted it to anyone for the world, but

"Yes, master." If she was dismayed, Delia didn't show it. Fine. He might just let the bitch die of thirst. There were others.

Mick hung up, slammed the phone down in the passenger seat and fought down the urge to punch out a window or run a passing cyclist off the road. No sense attracting too much attention for no gain.

He was just starting to come into the Minneola suburbs when his watcher-spirit announced its presence. He pulled over, ignoring the idiot in the car behind, and closed his eyes. "Show me a clear image of anyone who entered the club in the last twenty-four hours."

A picture immediately formed behind his eyelids, a cluster of firemen in breathing masks dragging a hose into the smoking ruins of the lobby area. He winced at the state it was in, and then ordered the spirit to go earlier. This time, the image was of an oddly mixed group of men and women. Mick blinked in astonishment, breaking the image, and had to settle his mind again before it returned. It was the little bastards who had put him in the lab in the first place. Not content with somehow forcing his own servitor to betray him—at least he'd had the presence of mind to gut that faithless piece of crap, even through the brain-burn—they'd had the temerity to burn his damn club down. They were going to pay for this.

Mick got out of the car and walked in front of a car coming up the road. The driver, shouting angrily, had no choice but to stop. Mick shifted into Crinos, punched through the windshield and dragged the now-hysterical woman out of her seat. He punched her in the side of the head to knock her out, and then bundled her into the back of his car before taking off back down the road to somewhere a bit quieter. Done properly, with the right promises and the aid of Jo'cllath'mattric's holy name, a lingering death would call his tribal patron, Whippoorwill, or one of its spirits, at least. They loved to snatch the souls of the dying, and they saw all sorts of things. They might be able to tell him where the little bastards were.

As soon as he knew where they were going to be for the next day or so, he was going to make the proper arrangements to take care of them once and for all. *By any means necessary*, the messenger had said. Those filthy tree-huggers may have trashed his club, his charges and his servitor, but he still had the authority to round up enough help to be sure of evening the score.

* * *

The journey across the moon bridge was eerily quiet. The Silver River packmates had made quick arrangements with Nicola to send a message to Night Sky about the history of Jo'cllath'mattric, but they didn't say a word after that. Julia had expected more debate, surely Cries Havoc wanted to go to Night Sky and help the Dawntreader, but the news from there implied that the elders were cut off. If they could get vital information to Albrecht it would be through his packmates Evan and Mari. Cries also seemed to understand John's need to help them in their time of need, much as he had helped Cries in his. A testament to how far the once-cantankerous pack had come.

They could all hear the threatening rumble of the Umbral storm in the background during the crossing, but otherwise there was no sign of any activity, either near or far. It seemed as if the spirit world itself was holding its breath nervously. It made everyone feel edgy, and they crossed the bridge in silence. Julia wouldn't have admitted it to anyone for the world, but she felt almost reluctant to talk, in case the noise made somethingbad happen. By the time they got to Finger Lakes that evening, she felt totally frazzled.

Evan Heals-the-Past was there to greet them. He looked dreadful—thin, dark eyed and pale. He smiled when he saw them, though, and went straight to John North Wind's Son. The two Wendigo shook hands warmly, and then Evan slapped North Wind's Son on the back and smiled at the whole pack. "Welcome back to Finger Lakes. Thanks for coming so quickly. Mari is fading rapidly. I don't think she's got long. I've been just sitting here for weeks, watching her get weaker and weaker…" his voice trailed off.

"We'll do everything we can," said North Wind's Son. "Between us, we may be able to find a way to help her. Did you warn the sept's elders we were on our way?"

"Yeah," said Evan. "I did. Nadya Zenobia—she's the Black Fury Theurge who's looking after Mari—was kinda doubtful, but I think she'll try anything at this stage. She said you're free to do what you can; she's in council with Alani, the Grand Elder, tonight. Either way, you're welcome here. At least there's plenty of room for you to stay. It's quieter here than when you last came through after the Tisza River thing. A lot quieter, actually. A whole load of people are off at all sorts of moots and meetings. Albrecht's stirred the whole northeast up. Europe, too, from what I understand." Evan grinned fondly. "I hope he hasn't let his mouth get him into too much trouble."

"Julia's Glass Walker pals in London said he got the Russian Fangs to work with the others, so that's better than you might expect." North Wind's Son pointed out Julia and quickly identified the rest of the pack for Evan, who smiled in greeting.

Julia nodded. "He's impressed a lot of people. One of the Walkers in our Ingoldstadt Sept in Germany even said that he had managed to forget Albrecht was an American, because he had such a German heart."

Evan snorted, amused. "I'll be sure to tell him that when I get a chance."

"Do you know how to get hold of him?" asked North Wind's Son.

Evan shook his head. "Not offhand. I dare say I could track him down. Why?"

"We have information about Jo'cllath'mattric."

"Its original name," said Julia. "From before it was turned to the Wyrm. It's said to give power over the spirit. We sent a messenger to Night Sky, but if you have a more direct route, that might be good."

"Okay, I'll start trying to track him down in the field if I can. Before I do, though, would you mind coming to have a look at Mari? I'd love to have some good news about her to give him, rather than bad. He's going out of his mind."

Of course, said Storm-Eye. *That is why we are here.*

"Great," said Evan. He started leading them away from the heart of the sept and up toward the lake.

"Evan, have you found anything out about Mari's condition?"

"From what they said at Anvil-Klaiven, it seemed to be a Bane similar to the ones you have been fighting, except that rather than try to eat her memory, it was intertwined in with her spirit. Since then, it's vanished inside her somewhere, and it seems that it's taken Mari with it. Nadya also said that Mari's Chimare has vanished."

"Has it? Losing your dream realm seems to ring a bell somewhere..." Julia tried to remember the thought.

Evan let them toward a familiar-looking wooden cabin beside the lake. "Maybe seeing her will jog your memory." He opened the door, turned on a dim light and led them into the cabin's one room. The cabin was dimly lit by a single candle, shutters tightly closed. The room smelt strongly of an unfamiliar incense. Mari Cabrah was lying on the bed, barely breathing. If Evan was looking worn, Mari seemed paper thin—frail and wasted and as white as a sheet. There was hardly anything to her, just skin and bones and a shock of black hair. The pack filed in, squeezing into the room, and looked at Mari in stunned silence.

Cries Havoc was the first to speak, a minute or so later, and when he did, he sounded distant, half-lost in memory. "Funny you mentioned Chimare, Evan. She looks like Elya Touched-by-Gaia."

Julia kept silent, not wanting to interrupt his train of thought. She glanced around at the others quickly, in case anyone was going to ask the obvious question, but they looked like they were going to stay quiet, too.

Cries Havoc didn't appear to notice. He didn't even try to tell the story properly. "She was a Fang, the daughter of a powerful lord. She… well, the short version is that she fell under a Wyrm curse, and her mind had to run into her own dreams, fleeing from the curse which sought to turn her to the Wyrm's side. I think the curse must have been some kind of Lore Bane, thinking about the way it's written, which is probably why the tale was eaten. Anyway, she slipped into a trance and could not be roused. She got thinner and thinner and paler and paler, and eventually her body passed into dream altogether, to be with her soul. She's still in the dream realms somewhere, if you know how to search for her. I can see the way she looked, in my mind's eye." He pointed at Mari. "She looked like that."

Storm-Eye nodded. *I too find that I have memory of a Wyrm-beast attempting to force a brave warrior to turn by attacking him through dreams.*

Evan looked horrified. "You're saying that the Bane is trying to turn her into a Spiral?"

"She looks like Elya in the story, and the Wyrm was trying to convert Elya," replied Cries Havoc.

"There was a Welsh Ragabash who got lost in someone else's dream." Julia was amazed to hear herself speaking. It felt like she was learning the information as she spoke it. "His friend had to do a ritual to show him the path home, before he was able to find his way back to his own mind."

"What did it take?" asked Evan.

"Time, mostly," said Julia. "The actual process mainly involved attuning to the victim and... um... it was like surfing through the Umbra on the victim's personal wavelength, if that makes any sense."

"Not much," said Carlita, grinning.

"Would you be able to try it?" The mingled hope and sadness in Evan's voice was heartbreaking.

"I don't know if it will help," said Julia. "I don't even know if I'm up to it. But I'll do the best I can."

"What do you need?"

"Some lemon grass, or verbena, or some other lemony incense. Fresh lemons, in a pinch. Even a citrus air freshener would do, actually." She thought about the sept she was in. "Although I guess the Gaians here are more likely to have the incense. I have my own lighter. Your presence, to help connect Mari and I. A bottle of water, for if we get thirsty. A thermos of coffee would be better, actually. I might just doze off, otherwise. Um, just a bit of something to eat first, perhaps, because I'm pretty hungry. Oh, and somewhere between six and twelve hours without anyone else entering the cabin. I can be roused if it's urgent, but if I am, it'll break any connection we're making to show Mari the path."

"I'll fetch your stuff and warn everyone to make sure no one comes in," said Evan. He made his way out of the cabin.

When he was clear, Julia turned to her packmates. "There's something I didn't tell Evan."

"Let me guess," said Carlita, somewhere between disgusted and worried. "This is insanely dangerous, right?"

Julia couldn't stop a smile. "Not insanely. But there is a risk that instead of showing Mari the way out, I'll just be trapped as well. Evan will be safe, though. If I do get caught up, you're going to have to find someone else that the tale spirit has spoken to, or some way to call the spirit itself. That means you may need details of the story. The Ragabash in the story was a Fianna named Caradoc Sleeps-on-Idris, and he was seen as half-mad himself, or a poet, or both. He came from a sept called Dysynni. Wish me luck, okay?"

"Does disturbing you make it more dangerous?" asked Cries Havoc.

"No. If I'm already trapped, you won't be able to rouse me, and if I'm not trapped, then it will just bring me straight out. It'll just break any connection I have to Mari's spirit. Oh, and if the problem is something else, then I'll be fine, I just won't get anywhere. If I'm not out within thirteen hours, start worrying."

"Thank you, Julia," said John North Wind's Son. "This means a lot."

Carlita snorted. "So it's 'go in and hope it's quiet' again, huh? That the only plan your mighty brain can come up with, Lady Di?"

"Yep," said Julia, grinning broadly. "Never was much of a strategist. Or do you want to tell the Wendigo that we'll wait a while and think about it?"

"I'm not telling Evan anything," said Carlita.

"Not telling me what?" said Evan, coming through the door with a bundle of stuff.

"Oh, nothing," said Carlita. "That wacky Brit humor must be rubbing off on me."

Evan looked at her dubiously, so Julia crossed over to him. "What do we have?"

"Some lemon verbena incense and a burner, a fresh bottle of water, a couple of portions of chicken, and a pack of caffeine tablets. They didn't have any vacuum flasks, I'm afraid."

"It'll be fine. Did you explain what I was going to try to, uh, Nadya?"

"She's still in council. Michael, one of the sept's other Theurges, will explain when she comes out."

"Okay. Let's get on with it, then. Sooner I get this done, sooner I can actually get some sleep."

"Good luck, princess," said Carlita.

"Thanks. Now get gone, and close the door behind you."

Julia took her time with the food and chased it down with three of the tablets. There didn't seem to be any real point hurrying. Once she was feeling a little less hollow, she lit a stick of incense, settled Evan comfortably into the chair near the head of Mari's bed and sat down cross-legged on the floor between them.

"I'm going to serve as a bridge," said Julia. "Hopefully, I'll be able to find a way to the edge of wherever it is that Mari is trapped and open a channel between you and her. I'm going to need you to tell me about her during the process—memories you have, things that she's done, what sort of person she is, anything that might help bring her back to herself."

"That will be easy," said Evan sadly. "I haven't done much else for the last month."

Julia smiled. "That's probably why she's still alive, you know."

Evan blinked. "I'd love to think I'd been doing even a little good. I've never felt this helpless before."

"Well, you're vital now," Julia said. "I'm going to be in a trance for most of the time, so don't worry if I don't acknowledge what you're saying. Later on in the ritual, you might slip into trance, too, but that's perfectly safe. First, we need to be connected. I want you to place your right hand on Mari's forehead."

Evan did as instructed, and Julia stretched an arm out, resting the elbow on the edge of the bed, and placed her hand over his.

"Good. Whatever happens, don't move your hand until I tell you to, Mari wakes up or we go past twelve hours. Even if I move my hand away. You're not in any danger, I promise."

"You keep saying that." Evan shot her a shrewd glance. "Are you in any danger?"

"I'll be fine," said Julia breezily.

"If you're sure," said Evan doubtfully.

"Oh, I'm sure," said Julia, hoping she sounded a bit more convincing than she felt.

Evan shrugged. "Okay then…"

"Okay, here goes. First, I'm going to get into trance. When I squeeze your hand, start talking about Mari to me. Naturally, though, not on fast-forward. Have a drink when you want one. When I squeeze your hand a second time—when we've made some sort of contact with wherever Mari is—stop talking, close your eyes and try to relax, and I'll guide you into trance. Then you'll be like a sort of homing beacon, and hopefully your ties will be able to guide her back. Any questions?"

"I guess not," said Evan.

"Great. Good luck." Julia opened her PDA screen, looked into it and started calming her mind. *I am not my thoughts, but that which thinks them. I am not my emotions...*

Within moments, she was grounded, centered and relaxed. Mari's presence beside her did not feel like a Garou would, not even like a wolf or human would, in fact. To say that there was something missing was a colossal understatement. Mari's spiritual presence was on a par with a goldfish in a bowl—a tiny spark of life force, a few automatic processes, nothing more. Evan, by comparison, was a raging storm of churning turmoil.

Julia made her hand squeeze Evan's, and then, as he started talking, let the words wash into her and over her. Taking the process step by step from the story of Sleeps-on-Idris, Julia allowed herself to slowly build a sense of Mari Cabrah from Evan's words and the fragments of soul that remained. Hours passed as she allowed her consciousness to gradually acclimatize to the woman, seeking to gather an ever-stronger impression of the feeling of her. It was nothing as concrete as an awareness of memories or traits; more a feel for the pattern of her spirit—a core of inner fire, fierce and proud.

Once she had the shape of the Black Fury's soul clear and strong in her mind, she pushed the sense of it back out, into the awareness she had of both Mari and Evan. Julia held the shape on the pair of them, allowing it to infuse with their natural energies, using the common bond of the soul image to bring the two of them together.

Was that a spark of resonance? Julia would have held her breath, if her body hadn't been on autopilot. She waited, anxiously. Suddenly it flared again, a small, crystalline sensation in a place that defied location. Evan's words fed the spark, and it grew stronger and harder. She could hear him talking but had no conscious awareness of what he was saying. Suddenly it felt as if she were rushing forward at an incredible pace. She was getting closer and closer to something. Something big. It turned out to be a smooth wall of energy, dark and featureless. Just as she was about to smash into it, she stopped dead, just touching it.

She could feel the spark there still, the node linking Evan and Mari. She seized it, hard, and sent her body the message to tell her hand to squeeze Evan's for the second time. A moment or two later, she felt his consciousness change. She soothed it down further and directed it into the spark that she was holding. She felt him slip into a trance, and then his sense of Mari poured through the spark, through Julia herself and through the dark wall.

Now all that remained was to hold the call open for as long as possible, and to hope Mari could find it. She should, with luck. If the creature attacking her didn't beat her to it, that is. Julia was strongly aware that she wouldn't be able to feel either of them approaching, and she could put no wards or barriers in place. If the creature found her, it would probably eat her mind.

Squashing her uncertainty, Julia held onto the spark and waited.

***

Slowly, Evan became aware of an impression of trees in his mind's eye. It was an ancient forest, the trees gnarled beyond reason. The place felt horrible, oppressive and unpleasant. His viewpoint flitted along above the treetops, seemingly weightless and insubstantial. The silence was absolute, but he couldn't tell if that was because everything was quiet or because his hearing wasn't working here. He looked around more closely but couldn't spot any sign of even a single living creature.

It was impossible to tell which direction was which, so he decided to go as high as he could and see if there was anything that distinguished itself from the rest of the region. Within moments, Evan was dizzyingly high up, and he had to fight down a sudden burst of vertigo and remind himself that his body was sitting in a chair.

From up high, he could see that the forest was shot through with a network of twisting paths and ravines. They seemed to meander back and forth, forming a wrinkled labyrinth that… It was just like a brain. A large, dark, twisted brain. There was a larger break in the canopy down off to Evan's left, with an ugly-looking blotch in the middle. Uninviting as it was, it was the only real feature, so he decided to head toward it, trying his best not to think of it as a blood clot.

***

Storm-Eye was out at bawn's edge, listening to the sounds of the forest night. The time she had spent in the city had left her hungry for the peace that only nature's touch could bring. Her companions understood and did not seek to join her. She roamed around the caern's perimeter idly, not hunting, not pushing herself, just letting the clean air wash the Weaver-stench out of her bones.

When the forest became *too* silent, it was several moments before she noticed. She froze instantly, and slowly, carefully scented the air. There. The vile reek of corruption curled on the air, subtle with distance but growing stronger. It was approaching. She turned tail and ran for the caern at full speed, howling out a mournful warning as she did so.

As she approached the caern's heart, she was met by a group of the sept's guards, in Crinos, coming out toward her quickly. *Wyrm-taint*, she growled at them. She sniffed deeply again and realized with dismay that she could still smell the foulness. *Coming. Can you not smell it?*

"Yes," growled the group's leader. "Come, fall back to the main area. Our numbers are depleted. We are too few to defend the outer woods."

We will fight with you, said Storm-Eye.

"Gather your people then. The enemy are through the bawn, in force."

She nodded and ran toward the lake, where she had left her pack waiting outside the hut, in vigil for Mari. She found them already under attack. A mixed group of fomori shock-troops and warrior Banes had engaged the pack. The Wyrm's forces had the benefit of numbers and were trying to enclose the Garou.

Storm-Eye bulked up into Hispo and darted round the back of the encircling creatures. John North Wind's Son noted her approach and howled a loud, defiant cry. It drew attention and allowed her to get close to the enemy. She neatly hamstrung three of them before the others realized she was there. Once they understood that their companions were collapsing in pain, the others turned to react, so as she approached the fourth, she boiled up out of Hispo and into Crinos, using the momentum to slash a Scrag Bane nearly in half from top to bottom. With a big hole torn in the enemy line, the pack was quick to regroup. North Wind's Son leapt howling at the center of the line, seizing another Scrag and ripping it to pieces, while Carlita and Cries Havoc moved to the middle of the hole, took stance back to back and started carving into the fomori at either end.

Storm-Eye glanced at the cabin, and was horrified to see that the door was open. She darted toward it.

***

The woman found herself running along a path toward a sickly looking glade. For a moment, she questioned why, tried to work out how she came to be here, but the thoughts were meaningless. She left them aside. She felt tired and was glad to stop running when she reached the clearing.

There was a dark pool in the center of the glade. The water glinted in a myriad of dark colors. It made it look like oil. Reeds and rushes whispered around the water's edge. She glanced at them incuriously, too tired to really pay much attention. It felt like she had been running for years.

There is no need to run, child. The voice was familiar from somewhere, as oily and sinister as the pool in front of her. A voice to disbelieve on principle, if only she could remember why. *You can have peace. It is yours for the asking. Would it be so bad, to have to run no more?*

Exhaustion seemed to bubble up inside her out of nowhere. Her limbs felt like lead. Perhaps it wouldn't be such a bad thing to give in. *You fought as hard as anyone could, girl. There is no more to prove. There is nothing more to earn. Only this. You can have peace. Just ask.*

She knew it was wrong, and her mind cast around desperately for a reason to resist, but there was nothing to take strength from. She could feel her resolve weakening, and she looked around the glade desperately. Everything was dull, muted, corrupt. The vile lake, the hungry reeds around it, the warped trees. She looked up at the sky, and a tiny glint of brightness caught her eye. A speck of silver, flickering through a myriad of different abstract shapes, dancing in the wind over the oily pool. After the oppression of the glade, it was a beautiful sight. She watched, entranced, as it flickered through a score of forms. For a brief moment, it even looked like a sharp, pointed silver tooth.

It would be a strange creature that had teeth of silver. The idea seemed somehow familiar. She raged against the lethargy overwhelming her, fought again and again to gain access to her memories or, failing that, even to clear thoughts. Silver teeth. She pictured a set of silver dentures and suddenly realized she hadn't felt amused in... how long? Far too long. She'd forgotten amusement existed. Not dentures. The silver teeth had to be sharper. Silver fangs. A shiver ran through her. That felt almost like something she remembered... But not quite, not a whole mouthful. A single one. A silver fang.

The voice was saying something, but she blocked it out and dug as deep as she could, focusing on the concept of the silver fang. The voice howled at her, tried to get her attention. It failed. Suddenly she was aware that a stupid, savage-looking cop was looming in front of her. She shrank back instinctively, aware of the voice gloating in her mind.

The mote danced between the cop and the woman, but only she seemed to be aware of it. The purity of its silver sheen gave her strength. It looked like the light glinting off... suddenly, at last, a clear image came into her head, of a huge silver blade, curved and engraved, with an ornate handle. While the voice howled furiously at her, the cop swung a heavy punch, catching her hard in the face. She shook it off, unconcerned now. There had been a corrupt cop, once, who had come up against the silver blade. He hadn't lasted a second. She could remember his expression as the sword sliced through his chest. Albrecht hadn't even broken stride.

Albrecht. The Silver Fang. The familiar face crashed into her mind and grinned infuriatingly. She could put words to that expression... as if he was saying, "C'mon, Mari. Snap out of it! You've been through worse than this."

Finally, finally, Mari Cabrah realized that she knew *exactly* what was going on. She grabbed hold of her name and her gifts and finally turned the full pent-up force of her white-hot fury on the hapless Bane that had dared to chew its way into her spirit.

**

Julia felt Mari explode back into her own consciousness. The force of her spirit burst the contact and flung Julia straight out of her trance before she had a chance to brace herself. Mari was still under attack, but she was back in herself. There was nothing more Julia could do. Evan's spiritual presence could still help Mari, though, so Julia left him in his trance and just sat there for a moment, dazed yet exultant, and listened to the racket coming from outside the hut.

She returned to proper awareness and suddenly understood that there was a fight going on by the lake. Then she was hit by an overpowering sense of corruption, and she looked up. A tall, oily black Crinos-form werewolf was standing just inside the doorway.

She recognized him at once, her eyes now used to the dim half-light, and sprang up, placing herself in front of Mari and Evan and shifting to her own, light-brown Crinos.

"Oh, did I wake you? Shame." Mick sounded amused. "Hey, I know you! You're one of the bitches I'm looking for. One of the ones that have been causing me so much trouble. You're going to wish you'd never been born, slut." He flexed his claws menacingly.

"Talk is cheap, asshole." If she could make him frenzy, Julia decided that she might just have a chance.

"So is your miserable life." He advanced slowly, confident in his superiority. "I'm going to enjoy killing you slowly."

"Burning down your shitty club was the best thing I ever did," said Julia, sneering. "That decor was screaming to be put out of its misery. Talk about tasteless. Once a turnip-grubbing peasant, I guess, always a turnip-grubbing peasant."

Mick screamed in rage.

Julia mustered all the scorn she could. "Oh yeah, and *nice* number plate, you sad, dickless little twat."

Howling in fury, Mick leapt for her. Julia ducked under the swing and raked across his stomach with both sets of claws. He twisted back faster than she could have imagined, though, turning what should have been a deep slash into a pathetic nick. He back-handed her casually across the face as he avoided her blow, knocking her sideways, and spat, casually, at her feet. Julia retreated a couple of steps to regain her balance. Several of her teeth were loose. The Spiral was as strong as he was fast.

As Mick closed on her again, Julia feinted a punch and kicked out hard and low, cutting deeply into his lower leg. Mick had already taken the opening her feint had left, though, and raked his claws down her side and stomach. It was a heavy blow, and the pain distracted her. She slashed out at him ferociously, all teeth and claws, to try to drive him back for a moment, but he simply swayed aside, favoring his left leg slightly, and buried his talons into her already-damaged side. He was just too fast for her. Julia suddenly understood that she was totally outclassed and let out a quiet, mournful howl. Mick grinned savagely at her and jerked forward, smashing his forehead hard into her face. She stumbled back into the wall, dazed.

"No need to worry, pet," said Mick, pausing momentarily. "You've still got a few minutes left. Of pain."

Julia hissed at him furiously and advanced a few steps. As she did so, she saw Storm-Eye creeping into the cabin in Hispo and felt a wild surge of hope. Mick kicked out, hard, and knocked Julia sideways. She stumbled slightly as she went, crouching a bit to keep her balance despite the blood running down her stomach. His teeth snapped just over her head. Thinking back to the Bane in the club, she jumped straight up and sank her claws into one of the ceiling beams. As Mick reached up to swipe at her legs, Storm-Eye darted in behind him and bit deep into the back of his knee. He screamed in pain and rage, and Julia focused all her fury on the worthless piece of shit, swung once, hard, and lashed out, kicking him viciously in the head with both feet.

Off-balance, dazed, half-blinded by the blood in his eyes, and with both legs damaged, Mick fell back over Storm-Eye. She was out from under him in a flash and buried her teeth deep in his throat. As Julia jumped down to join her, Storm-Eye snapped her jaws together around his neck and twisted. With a wet ripping sound, his head came clean off.

Storm-Eye joined in Julia's delighted victory howl, and then the two of them shot out of the cabin to help the rest of the Silver River Pack in their battle.

Evan was in the cabin, continuing the process of filling Mari in on the events that she had missed while she'd been ill. Julia knocked on the open door and went in, smiling back at them.

"Did they ever find out what was behind that attack?" Evan sounded curious.

"Alani Astarte thinks that it was a last-ditch attempt to stop King Albrecht from getting the information about Jo'cllath'mattric."

Evan whistled. "I bet she's delighted you brought the Wyrm down on her."

"I think she'll forgive us in the end," said Julia. "She did mutter something about Uktena under her breath, though. Still, we did help out as much as we could, and we've been doing patrols on the roster. It's not as if she doesn't realize the importance of the information, either. Did you get hold of King Albrecht in the end?"

Evan nodded. "I finally managed to find a number for Night Sky, and I caught him there. I told him about Mari. He's on his way here right now."

"Did you spill the beans about Jo'cllath'mattric's real name?"

Evan shook his head, grinning. "Nope. Your message made it there, but the details of the story aren't clear yet. Looks like there was quite a battle, but no one's sure if Jo'cllath'mattric is done with or not. And no one's seen hide nor hair of Arkady. Anyway, I figured you could fill him in far better than I could."

Mari laughed. "I can't wait to see his face when you tell him, Julia."

"I bet," said Julia, grinning. "How are you feeling, Mari?"

"Weak, but okay. I'm getting stronger quickly. I owe you one."

"*We* owe you one," said Evan. "Collectively and individually—and that includes Albrecht. Feel free to collect some time. Big Sis clued me in on the risk you were taking."

"It wasn't much," said Julia. "All I did was show Evan how to light a beacon for you to home in on, Mari. You two did all the hard work."

"I think I'm going to puke if I have to listen to any more of this pious modesty crap from the princess here." Carlita was standing in the doorway, face pulled into what was supposed to be an expression of disgust.

"Stow it, Big Sis," Julia said with a wide grin. "You're spoiling my image here."

"You're doing that yourself," replied the Bone Gnawer rudely. "Anyway, you've got the chance to really screw up now. Albrecht's coming. The Gatekeeper says he'll be at the caern in just a few minutes." She cackled at Julia's expression. "Thought you'd want to know, so you could double-check your makeup or whatever." She grinned and was gone.

***

Elsewhere, in the Umbral realm that had been its prison for time immemorial, the Forgotten Son Jo'cllath'mattric raged. And in that rage, it thrashed, and in that thrashing it felt the weakness of the remaining bonds.

It would be free soon...

About the Author

Tim Dedopulos has been writing for over ten years and intends to continue for as long as they'll let him. He currently has over seventy published works under his belt, most written under one or other of his many odd pen names. He has contributed to several books in the **Hunter: The Reckoning** game line and is the author of **Hunter: Apocrypha**.

His other works include material for a number of other RPG lines—particularly the futuristic urban horror game *SLA Industries*—as well as a wide range of nonfiction books for a variety of publishers. Notable highlights (and lowlights) include *Conspiracy Theories*, *The Ultimate Insults Book*, *Baking Soda Secrets*, and *The Complete Guide to a Good Abdomen (In Just Five Minutes a Day)*. The latter three always remind him uncomfortably of Troy McClure and help to make sure that he never takes himself too seriously.

Tim likes to think of himself as a cynical dreamer and fallen romantic and firmly believes that most people are far too quick to give up on the magic in the world. When he isn't chained to a desk, he can often be found at pubs, gigs, stormy beaches, ancient hill forts and stone circles all across southern England.

His web address is www.midnight.demon.co.uk/gw.html, for what it's worth.

Acknowledgments

Dropping out of third person for a moment, I want to acknowledge several people who really helped me during the writing of this book. I owe extra-special thanks to Philippe Boulle for taking the time to help me to do the best job I could, as well as giving me loads of support and advice and trusting me in the first place; to Xanthe Holford for her invaluable feedback; to Dave Allsop and Jared Earle for having faith in me; to Paul Addicoat and Dr. Jest for a heap of expert advice; and, not least, to Megan Leggo for support beyond the call of duty in the face of extreme provocation. Thanks, guys.

THE FINAL BATTLE

Tribe Novels 7:
Black Spiral Dancers & Wendigo

by Eric Griffin
& Bill Bridges

ISBN 1-58846-822-4
WW11156

In the climax of the Tribe Novel series, the Garou's backs are against the wall, and they must fight or die.

In Tribe Novel: Black Spiral Dancer, the mad Lord Arkady comes face to face with the Wyrm itself.

In Tribe Novel: Wendigo, John North Wind's Son and his Silver River Pack find their destiny revealed at last when they face the monster Jo'cllath'mattric.

December 2002

WHITE WOLF PUBLISHING

WEREWOLF
THE APOCALYPSE

EXALTED

Trilogy of the Second Age™

by Richard Dansky

Journey to the Second Age of Man,
a time before the World of Darkness,
in this first fiction release for Exalted.
Meet Eliezer Wren, a simple priest
who makes the mistake of stealing
the Prince of Shadows' plunder
and ends up on the run from the
Prince's unliving hunters. With him
comes Yushuv, a boy who comes
face-to-face with his own destiny,
and with the Unconquered Sun.

BOOK ONE
**Chosen of
the Sun™**
ISBN 1-58846-800-3
WW10080

BOOK TWO
**Beloved of
the Dead™**
ISBN 1-58846-801-1
WW10081

BOOK THREE
**Children of
the Dragon™**
ISBN 1-58846-802-X
WW10082